Coming Close

COMING CLOSE

A Novella and Three Stories
as Alternative Autobiographies

by B.H. Friedman

FICTION COLLECTIVE

First Edition
Copyright © 1982 by B.H. Friedman
All rights reserved.
LCCN: 81-71643
ISBN: 0-914590-71-5 (paperback)
ISBN: 0-914590-70-7 (hardcover)

The author wishes to thank the editors of *New American Review* and *The Hudson Review,* where, in somewhat different form, "Drinking Smoke" and "Moving in Place" originally appeared.

Published by Fiction Collective with assistance from the National Endowment for the Arts and New York State Council on the Arts.

Typeset by Open Studio in Rhinebeck, N.Y., a non-profit facility for writers, artists and independent literary publishers, supported in part by grants from the New York State Council on the Arts and the National Endowment for the Arts.

Jacket design: Ray Witlin
Front cover image: based on drawing by Myron Stout
Photograph of author: Charles Schaefer

To Jeanne and Fritz Bultman, with love.

FICTION. An assumption or supposition of law that something which is or may be false is true, or that a state of facts exists which has never really taken place.

Black's Law Dictionary

Tell all the Truth but tell it slant—
Success in Circuit lies

Emily Dickinson

Only half the story is true. The rest
is necessary, like clouds on a cloudy day.

John Yau

Anything processed by memory is fiction.

Wright Morris

Coming Close

Watching Father Die

has not yet begun. As a child I am watching him live, watching the large movements of his life in which I am a speck carried here and there by his mass and energy.

It is a Sunday in the fall of 1927, just over a year after my birth. Mother has dressed me in the pale blue cashmere suit and cap brought back from Paris by her older brother, she has placed me in the English carriage which is a gift from her parents, and she is now tucking me under the monogrammed blanket which is also a gift from them. I am warm. I kick at the blanket. Mother tells Father to be sure to keep me covered.

It is her day to read the *Times* and to study the slick brown pictures in the rotogravure, Father's day—he works the other six—to be with me until his afternoon bridge game. Mother, in silk nightgown, cut-velvet kimono and high-heeled slippers, walks us to the front door of the apartment. While we wait for the elevator, Father glances at his watch and impatiently rotates the gray felt hat in his hand; Mother kisses me good-by many times on the cheeks, the nose, the eyes, the ears. I will be gone for two hours.

"GOOD MORNING, CHARLIE," Father greets the elevator operator. "BEAUTIFUL DAY." His voice crowds the small cab. Everything about Father is large. His broad sholders block Charlie from my view. His freshly shaved face shines above me, still exuding the scent of witch hazel. His features are sharp as the razor he keeps in his medicine chest, far beyond my reach. The smooth angular planes of his face are emphasized by the dome of his head, a clean curve, prematurely bald.

I feel the elevator dropping. Above the door I watch the lights flash on and off in meaningless images — 5, 4, 3, 2, G. We reach the lobby. Charlie jiggles the leveling handle, we bounce to a stop, and the door opens.

"NICE LANDING." Father's voice booms off marble. He puts on his hat, wheels me to the entrance, greets the doorman, tips the carriage up gently as he lowers me two steps onto the sidewalk. We are on our way.

The west side of Broadway is bright. Storefronts shimmer in the morning sunlight. I squint, watching Father push me along. He rocks from side to side. (As he tells me often he was in the navy DURING THE WAR.) I see him best each time we reach a curb. There, with the lightest pressure of his fingertips, he lifts the front of the carriage. As he bends and I rise, our eyes meet. His are gray like mine. For a moment I feel I am being held up to a mirror and am entering it. Then his eyes shift left and right, and we cross the street.

"SUNDAY DRIVERS. CAN'T BE TOO CAREFUL."

Our destination is Bloom's, a haberdashery ten blocks up Broadway. On the way Father stops to look in the windows of other stores and to greet friends. These stops often coincide. He knows every storekeeper in the neighborhood and many of them stay open on Sundays, if not actually selling, then taking stock or working on their accounts. At shoe stores Father himself does business — his business — pricing items, asking how they are moving, selling the shoes he "makes." In a quieter, more confidential tone than usual he describes his spring line: mules, oxfords, sling-pumps, sandals, evening slippers, bedroom slippers; new numbers with fancy straps, ornamental buckles, pompoms.

Outside he tells me: "NICE LITTLE ORDER. FIVE CASES. WOMEN'S SHOES ARE WHERE THE MONEY IS. STYLE KEEPS THE WHEELS TURNING. CHILDREN'S AREN'T BAD EITHER. THEY GET WORN OUT OR OUTGROWN. MEN'S JUST LAST TOO LONG."

To me, his words are abstract. They have no more specific meaning than those of *Blue Skies* or *I Found a Million-Dollar Baby*. But, as in these songs so often on the radio, I recognize happy music. Besides, Father is smiling. He pulls out a cigar to reward himself for the sale, bites off the end, spits it from the middle of the sidewalk to the gutter, lights up, puffs along now. He is the engine of my carriage.

But Bloom's is his real reward, not only for this morning's quick sale but for the week's work. At Bloom's there is seemingly as wide a selection of white-on-white shirts as there are patterns of snowflakes—wonderful stars, diamonds, circles, stripes; combinations and variations of these, all offered to Father.

"HAVE THAT...HAVE THAT...THAT'S NEW...PRETTY..."

From the 16-35 pile he selects two shirts, then moves on to the racks of boldly colored ties, looping them around his index finger to simulate a knot, shifting them to his thumb, holding them against the subtle whiteness of the shirts, and playing the geometry of one against the other.

"Underwear? Socks?"

"NOT TODAY. I'M ALL SET."

"Two ties. Two shirts. Twenty-four fifty. Make it twenty even."

The discount must have been negotiated before my birth. Father is obviously a regular customer, very regular. He places the package at my feet and we are on our way again, now toward home.

I am about six. School is closed for the Christmas holidays, and Father takes me downtown to get shoes at his place, the three-story warehouse on Reade Street which I have visited half a dozen times since I was old enough to walk and be paraded in front the THE CREW. Above the noise of the subway, he shouts once again:

"THEY SAY A SHOEMAKER'S CHILD NEVER HAS SHOES. I DON'T WANT THEM TELLING ME THAT. YOU SHOULD ALWAYS HAVE TWO PAIR—EVERYDAY AND DRESS."

I look down at the pair I'm wearing, badly scuffed rubber-soled "moccasins" with torn stitching. They are very everyday. Father's highly-polished, pointed, black wing-tips make my shoes look even more shabby.

"One pair black, one brown?" I ask.

"I DON'T LIKE BLACK ON BOYS."

We get off at Chambers Street, a block from Reade, the heart of the shoe and hide wholesale district. At the top of the subway stair there is a shoeshine stand, three cracked-leather chairs, all empty, two steps high on a platform above brass footrests.

"OUR FIRST STOP."

Father takes the two steps in one, stands up there, reaches down, yanks me to his level. I climb into the chair next to his, sit as far forward as I can, stretch to reach the footrests.

"TWO SHINES. THEY'LL EVEN OUT. MINE'S FOR LUCK."

The elderly Italian bows his head and goes to work on my shoes.

"He needa a shoemaker."

"YOU SHINE THEM. I'M THE SHOEMAKER."

The man, spitting a lot, gets my shoes looking pretty good, then starts on Father's, dulls them, brushes them, spits on each tip, snaps the polishing cloth over them and around the heels, and finally restores the shine they had.

"POLISH PROTECTS LEATHER."

Father gives the man a dime a shine and a dime tip, and helps me off the stand.

"USED TO TIP A QUARTER. MAYBE WILL AGAIN WHEN ROOSEVELT TAKES OVER."

We walk to Reade Street. The scale of the buildings is low and comfortable; and Father knows even more men here than uptown on Broadway. MEET so-and-so, SHAKE HANDS WITH so-and-so. Large leathery hands squeeze hard, enveloping mine. The men tell me that I'm a chip off the old block, a future shoe man. My life is laid out as clearly as this grid of city blocks.

A hunchback with powerful arms protruding from a heavy leather vest stands in a doorway. There is another introduction, another crushing handshake. Father pats him on the hump as we depart.

"LUCKY."

"Lucky?"

"TOUCHING THE HUMP. HIS BAD FORTUNE IS OUR GOOD FORTUNE. POOR GUY. BENT LIKE THAT. AND HE'S IN A DYING BUSINESS TOO. RAZOR STRAPS. PRETTY SOON NOBODY BUT BARBERS WILL BE BUYING THEM."

We are at Father's building. My name, the name of his father, dead long before I was born, is in large gold flourishing letters over the entrance and is stencilled in smaller gold letters on the glass panel of the door and on the display windows to either side. Beneath the name, in each place: *Established 1883*.

"FIFTY YEARS NEXT YEAR. I STARTED WHEN I WAS SEVENTEEN. JUST BEFORE THE WAR. TWENTY YEARS NOW. IN ANOTHER TWENTY YOU'LL BE IN CHARGE. BUT I WANT YOU TO START WITH THE EDUCATION WE DIDN'T HAVE,

MY FATHER AND ME—AND MY BROTHER. I WANT YOU TO
GO TO COLLEGE. THEN MAYBE GET A LAW DEGREE. ONE
THING ABOUT AN EDUCATION, THEY CAN NEVER TAKE IT
AWAY."

Through the glass Father's world is visible: the shadow of his
father's name (mine now) and the date when he founded the business,
all lengthened and askew, stretching across the scarred brown
linoleum floor toward the heavy oak table where his younger brother
sits smoking a cigarette and reading the *News* while another man,
THE VETERAN, gray-haired but Father's age, smokes a pipe as he
goes through the morning mail.

As soon as we enter, my uncle puts down the newspaper, crushes his
cigarette in a glass ashtray surrounded by a miniature tire (the advertisement of a company that also makes rubber heels and soles), and
strides toward me. He is tall and handsome as Father but not, I've been
told many times, as serious and responsible—a thirty-one-year-old
CONFIRMED BACHELOR WHO DRINKS, FOOLS AROUND,
HAS TO BE GOTTEN OUT OF TROUBLE.

"Starting early," he says, smiling.

As he lifts me to his height, hugs me, and twirls me around, I feel that
he will welcome me just as warmly when I arrive for keeps, that he
looks forward to the day when I spring his trap and replace him in it.

The gray-haired man gets up, still puffing on his pipe, although
GASSED DURING THE WAR. He is ON COMMISION, earns more
than my uncle, almost as much as Father. He's BLEEDING THE
BUSINESS but must remain because of his CONNECTIONS. Buyers
for the chain and department stores trust him.

I do too, because he shakes hands so gently.

"GIVE ME YOUR COAT OR YOU'LL CATCH COLD WHEN
YOU GO OUT."

Father hangs it and his own and his jacket on the clothes rack
between the sample shelves and the table. He leaves his vest on and
rolls up his sleeves. He is at work, going through the orders that have
arrived in the mail.

The doors of the freight elevator creak open. Two more men
appear, standing in front of a load of stacked shoe cartons. They take
off their work gloves, greasy from the cables of the old-fashioned
elevator, and shake hands with me.

"We'll take you for a ride later. Now we gotta get these cartons on the street. Another shipment's coming when this one's picked up."

A full case weighs over fifty pounds. Each of the men tosses one lightly onto his shoulder and goes out the front door.

By now Father's secretary/bookkeeper—mostly the latter but still one woman filling the job of two—emerges from her office in the back.

"CAN YOU KEEP HIM BUSY FOR A WHILE?"

"You can be certain of that," she replies with a slight brogue, taking me by the hand and leading me to her office.

It is crowded with so many delights I don't know where to begin. I glance from the old safe to the adding machine to the typewriter to the stacks of ledgers and stationery supplies, all things to play with, toys. I go first to the safe, decorated with gold letters and numbers like those on the exterior of the building and on every shoe carton in it. The door of the safe, at least half a foot thick, is open. Inside there are many compartments filled with record books, folders, binders, a petty cash box, and a corporate seal, standing alone, the erect proud shining central icon of this miniature temple. I remove it from its cubicle, place it on a corner of the desk, and for several minutes press its image onto scraps of paper fed to me by Father's bookkeeper. Then I close my eyes and read once again, but with my fingers now, the name, the date—this tiny bulge of history, the seal of an ancient kingdom to which I am heir.

"THE TRUCK'S HERE."

Father waits at the door with my coat. I put it on, go out, and watch his men receive the new shipment. The truckers have lowered the tailgate and tip the cartons so that Father's men can slip them easily onto their shoulders. As each carton is carried inside, Father glances at the label and calls out style numbers, sizes, and colors to his brother who checks them off on a sheet attached to a clipboard. When all these cartons are inside, Father's men help the truckers load the outgoing shipment.

Business looks like fun, all cooperation and team-play. It sounds like fun too. The grey-haired man is on the phone, already selling the shoes that have just come in:

"...not too early to buy for spring. Who knows what the price will be then? They're cheap now, a steal at thirty-nine a case. Besides, you'll sell most of them this winter. This is resort wear, quality merchandise, gorgeous styling..."

His voice fades as the overhead elevator door slams down and we begin our ascent to the third floor. It is open—about the length of my school basketball court and half the width, but without bright lights, just small bare bulbs, hanging from sections of the ceiling. Each of them has to be turned on separately. In the gloom I see cartons everywhere and smell the dry acidic odor of cardboard and leather.

Father's men arrange the shipment in a new row, stacked like the others, according to style and size. The men explain that the factory— it is outside Boston—packs the shoes this way, in plain boxes, except for the size stamped on each, and that when an order comes in, their own job is to make up new cartons according to what styles and sizes the customer has ordered.

"But doesn't Father make the shoes?"

"Make them? No, he buys them and sells them."

At lunch, at the neighborhood restaurant Father and my uncle go to, I ask Father, "Don't you make your shoes?"

"NOT EXACTLY. I DON'T SIT AT A BENCH AND MOLD THE LEATHER TO A LAST AND CUT AND STITCH IT." He winks at his brother and they laugh. "NO, WHAT WE DO IS MAKE MAKING POSSIBLE FOR MANUFACTURERS. WHEN WE ORDER A LINE, THEY KNOW IT'S SOLD. MONEY IN THE BANK. IN BUSINESS FIFTY YEARS—ALMOST FIFTY—OUR CREDIT MAKES THE SHOES."

My uncle, drinking a double scotch while Father and I finish our tomato juice, says, "Lofty economics. Awfully lofty. Awfully, awfully lofty."

"WHAT DOES THAT MEAN?"

"Oh, you know. Why don't you just tell him we're jobbers, middlemen?"

"THAT'S WHAT I'VE BEEN TELLING HIM. WHY DON'T YOU EAT LUNCH AND STOP DRINKING?"

Like an obedient child, my uncle cuts a piece of beef tongue and piles some spinach on it—the day's special. With his mouth full, he says, "Sorry," turns to me, "Your father's a great salesman," then back to Father, "Tell him about the woman who came in yesterday."

Father smiles, accepting the apology and compliment. "WE DON'T USUALLY SELL TO PEOPLE WHO COME IN OFF THE STREET, BUT BUSINESS BEING WHAT IT IS—WELL, THIS IS A NICE-

LOOKING WOMAN WHO EXPLAINS THAT HER HUSBAND HAS JUST DIED AND THAT SHE WANTS TO BURY HIM RIGHT. SHE ASKS IF I CAN GIVE HER SOMETHING REALLY NICE IN A BLACK SHOE, STRAIGHT TIP, 11A, FOR MAYBE TWO DOLLARS. OF COURSE, THAT'S EASY, BUT I TELL HER I'LL SEE WHAT I'VE GOT AND GO TO THE SECOND FLOOR WHERE THE STAPLES ARE." I look puzzled. "MEN'S SHOES, NURSE'S OXFORDS, THINGS LIKE THAT. AMONG THE DUSTY CARTONS IN THE BACK THERE'S A DISCONTINUED LINE OF HIGH-BUTTON BLACK SHOES FROM BEFORE THE WAR, STUFF WE SHOULD HAVE THROWN OUT LONG AGO. I FIND A PAIR OF 12B AND SHOW THEM TO HER. 'THESE ARE WHAT YOUR HUSBAND WILL BE HAPPY IN. THEY'RE BUILT FOR ETERNITY. HE'S GOING TO WANT A LITTLE ANKLE SUPPORT ON THAT LONG LONESOME ROAD AND HE'S GOING TO WANT SHOES THAT AREN'T TOO TIGHT, SO I CHOSE A PAIR JUST A LITTLE LARGER THAN WHAT HE'S BEEN WEARING. PUT A PAIR OF WOOLEN SOCKS ON HIM AND HE'LL BE THANKING YOU FOREVER.' WHEN I SEE THAT SHE'S SOLD—NOT UNTIL THEN—I BRING UP PRICE. 'I SHOULDN'T LET THESE GO FOR LESS THAN TEN DOLLARS, BUT, BECAUSE OF THE CIRCUMSTANCES, BECAUSE I WANT YOUR HUSBAND TO BE COMFORTABLE, BECAUSE I WANT YOU TO BE COMFORTABLE ABOUT YOUR HUSBAND BEING COMFORTABLE, I'LL SPLIT THE DIFFERENCE. SIX DOLLARS AND THEY'RE YOURS.' THE WOMAN HAS TEARS IN HER EYES. OVERCOME WITH GRATITUDE. SHE ADMITS THAT SHE HADN'T GIVEN ENOUGH THOUGHT TO HER HUSBAND'S COMFORT, HADN'T THOUGHT AT ALL OF *HIGH* SHOES. SHE COUNTS OUT SIX DOLLARS AND THEN—D'YOU KNOW WHAT?—SHE KISSES ME. BY GOD, SHE KISSES ME."

Father's laughter explodes, and by this time my uncle, too, is laughing so hard that he spits the last of his tongue and spinach across the table, almost hitting Father. But that doesn't matter—they're friends again, brothers as always. Although I don't really understand the story or find it funny, although, in fact, I find it sad, I laugh with them, thinking once again that business looks like fun, sounds like fun, even now tastes like fun. My lamb chops were delicious and pie à la mode is on the way. Lunch at school is nothing like this.

When we leave the restaurant, Father takes me down the block to a wholesaler of boys' shoes, a tiny thin man, not much taller than I am, who Father has known since they CAME DOWNTOWN in their teens. He wears steel-rimmed glasses and looks almost as if he could be one of the more eager students in my class at school.

"WHAT DO YOU HAVE IN 7½A? THE BEST YOU'VE GOT."

He shows us a pair of sharkskin-tipped dress shoes with a pierced shark's tooth dangling from one of the laces.

"Comes with," he says, taking it off and showing it to me.

I can see the tooth already on my key ring. I like it so much I hardly look at the shoes as the little man, using a shoe horn, slips them on my feet.

"Walk around. See how they feel. Those tips won't scuff like what you've been wearing. Sharkskin's like iron."

It feels like iron, but I don't say anything. I want that tooth. When I've walked the length of the showroom and back, Father bends down and squeezes the sides of the shoes and then the tips.

"WHAT SIZE DID YOU GIVE HIM?"

"7B, the closest I had."

"NOT CLOSE ENOUGH. THE BOY HAS A YANKEE FOOT. LIKE HIS FATHER. WALKS LIKE ME TOO, DID YOU NOTICE? HE COULD'VE BEEN IN THE NAVY. WHAT OTHER SHOES DO YOU HAVE?"

He shows us crepe-soled moccasins, the right size. I try them on. They fit perfectly.

"Like walking on air, aren't they, young man?" I nod, still wanting the sharkskin, the tooth. "Fact is you *are* walking on air. A lot of little bubbles trapped in those soles."

A lot of little bubbles—and me. I remember Father's story at lunch. "I usually wear heavier socks. Maybe I should try size 8 in the sharkshin."

"The wall-last on these moccasins will give you plenty of room for heavy socks."

"YOU DON'T NEED TO SELL HIM. WE'LL GET THESE. LET'S SEE A PAIR OF 8A'S IN THE OTHER."

I try them on, walk to the end of the showroom and back. Again Father squeezes the shoes.

"MUCH BETTER. A LITTLE EXTRA LENGTH BUT JUST ENOUGH TO GROW IN. THE BOY'S GOT A HEAD ON HIS SHOULDERS."

And, a moment later, I've got a shark's tooth on my key ring.

"WHAT'S THE TARIFF?"

"For you, seven-fifty."

"SEVEN-FIFTY! FIVE'S FAIR. LET'S FLIP FOR IT."

"You mean for the difference—five or ten?"

"COME ON, WE'VE KNOWN EACH OTHER TOO LONG FOR THAT. FIVE OR SEVEN-FIFTY."

Father reaches into his pocket, takes out his LUCKY COIN with the image of a pig's head on one side and its tail on the other, one of the few things in the world for which I would trade my new shark's tooth. He flips the coin high, catches it with his right hand, slaps it onto the back of his left, says, "CALL IT."

The little man hesitates, seeming not quite able to understand how he got into this position. He adjusts his glasses as if hoping to see through Father's hand. "Heads," he says finally.

Father lifts his right hand, smiles immediately, extends his left hand for the little man to squint at. There's the rump of the pig with its cute little curled tail. "PRETTY AS A PICTURE." He hands his friend a five-dollar bill, then a cigar, "FOR LUCK." As we leave he squeezes the little man's cheek between thumb and index finger, the way sometimes he squeezes mine. The gesture is confusing, both affectionate and condescending, slightly painful and slightly sensuous, a small embrace for a smaller world than his.

"YOU KNOW," he says as we walk back to his place, "LUCK IS IMPORTANT. BUT YOU'VE GOT TO PROTECT YOUR LUCK. AS IT TURNS OUT, I GOT THE SHOES FOR FIVE DOLLARS. ALL I DID WAS MAKE SURE THEY WOULDN'T COST TEN. YOU'LL BE LUCKY TOO, IF YOU PLAY LIFE RIGHT. YOU'RE STARTING OFF LUCKY. WHEN I WAS YOUR AGE, I WASN'T GIVEN TWO PAIR OF SHOES AT A TIME. AND I'LL TELL YOU SOMETHING ELSE. AS MUCH AS I WANT YOU TO GET AN EDUCATION, I WANT YOU TO MAKE A LOT OF FRIENDS TOO. IT'S

NOT WHAT YOU KNOW, IT'S WHO YOU KNOW. REMEMBER THAT."

At public school I have many friends—mostly poor Jewish, Irish, and Italian kids whom I play with after school and invite to our apartment on rainy weekday afternoons and sometimes on Saturdays for lunch before going to a movie. They are tougher than the children I knew when I went to private kindergarten. They play harder; hit harder; and talk faster, with heavier New York accents. They are, I suppose, the kind of kids Father wanted me to meet when, long ago, Mother argued that I should continue at private school. Behind the closed bedroom door the argument goes on for years.

"I don't like the boys he associates with. All our friends send their children to private school."

"IF I'VE TOLD YOU ONCE I'VE TOLD YOU A THOUSAND TIMES, I DON'T WANT HIM TO GET SPOILED. I DON'T WANT HIM TO GROW UP TO BE A SISSY."

Mother names several of their friends' sons who aren't sissies. Father names several who are. "BESIDES, THERE'S A DEPRESSION ON."

"You know Pop would gladly pay the tuition. I'd gladly pay it—I'd sell some jewelry."

"STOP RUBBING YOUR FATHER'S MONEY AND YOUR GODDAMN JEWELRY IN MY FACE. IF THERE'S ANY TUITION TO PAY, I'LL PAY IT."

I'm doing well at school. The work is easy and I get good marks. At ten, having skipped twice, I'm in the sixth grade. Mother tries a new tack:

"The school isn't challenging enough. He'd have more competition at one of the good private schools."

Father doesn't answer right away. Competition is something he believes in, though he thinks of it usually in physical rather than intellectual terms. "HE'S DOING FINE."

"It's too easy. You say you don't want him to be spoiled, but he's being spoiled."

"LET ME THINK ABOUT IT. BY HIGH SCHOOL WE'LL CON-

SIDER A CHANGE. MAYBE ONE OF THOSE FANCY
SCHOOLS'LL HELP HIM GET INTO THE RIGHT COLLEGE."

"A lot of the good schools begin at the seventh grade."

"YOU'RE NAGGING."

During the past six years Father's other arguments have been
destroyed. Under Roosevelt, the economy is recovering. Shoes are
selling. Father is talking about expanding, maybe getting into the
retail business, maybe even into manufacturing. With dreams like
these, he begins to join Mother in her criticism of my friends. They just
aren't the kind of kids who'll be bankers, lawyers, and top executives,
the kind of CONTACTS I'll need in business, bigger business.

Unwittingly, my sixth grade teacher becomes Mother's ally.
Through the fall term he has been using flash cards on which are
printed larger and larger numbers for the class to add and subtract. He
flashes one at me:

$$\begin{array}{r} 84 \\ -87 \\ \hline \end{array}$$

"Minus three," I reply.

Almost everyone in the class laughs. They know you can't subtract a
larger number from a smaller one. They know that much.

The teacher raps his ruler on the desk. "He's right. I wasn't going to
get into minus numbers until next term. For now, I would have been
satisfied with the answer 'It can't be done.' But his answer is right."
Using the analogy of a thermometer, he talks a little more about minus
quantities, then asks me to see him after class.

What he wants is a meeting with my parents. Later, he tells them
that if I weren't so young he would advance me another class, that I
probably won't get very much out of the next two years of grade
school, and that he hopes, at least, I will go eventually to one of the
more demanding public high schools, maybe the Bronx High School
of Science.

After a few nights, Father, sitting in his favorite chair, deep and
heavily upholstered, repeats the entire conversation to Mother's
brother who listens, pacing our living room with his before-dinner
drink in hand. He is almost a head shorter than Father, not as conven-
tionally handsome, but better proportioned, more athletic, more

graceful. His energy fills the room, a physical energy expressing intellectual impatience.

"...I SAID THE BOY HAD A HEAD ON HIS SHOULDERS. FOR ALL I KNOW HE MAY BE A *GENIUS*."

My uncle stops short, questioning with his body as well as his mind the loose use of this word. "I wouldn't know about that. I've never met a genius, if you mean a *real* genius—a Leonardo, a Shakespeare, a Newton, a Mozart, an Einstein. In my dealings with people, I'm satisfied with *competence*."

Father flushes, sinks deeper into his chair, intimidated by the names of these artists and scientists he knows little about, little compared with my uncle who has gone to college and earned a Phi Beta Kappa key, never worn but given to Mother. She wears it on her charm bracelet among clusters of old watch keys, fob pendants, and gold coins. It is there now, on her wrist, hidden among the other charms.

My uncle goes back to an earlier part of Father's recitation: "Of course you should have him transfer to another school if he can't make further progress at this one. You should be looking at schools—" he names several—"so that you can get an application in now and have him enrolled in the fall. Tell me if I can help—I know men on the boards of some of these schools. But I guess that won't be necessary if he's a genius."

Father is silent through most of dinner, digesting my uncle's remarks along with the food. When he tries once, in rather vague terms, to discuss Roosevelt's economic policies, my uncle smothers him with specific figures concerning gross national product, balance of trade, unemployment, short- and long-term interest rates; then, realizing that all of this can only lead, as it has in the past, to his attacking Roosevelt, Father's great hero, he shifts gracefully to a joke he has recently heard.

"Speaking of interest rates, there's this fellow who's been trying for a long time to get a loan from his bank. He's been kicked from one officer to the next until finally he begs for a meeting with the president. The meeting is arranged. Sitting behind his big desk with the would-be borrower's loan application before him, the bank president recites the terrible risks that he and the other officers see in the proposed financing. The borrower answers his points one by one. Though the arguments are strong, the banker, whose face is as cold and expressionless as a chip off Mt. Rushmore, says nothing until the man is through. Then, after glancing once more at the application, he says, 'I don't really like the loan—your projections look optimistic—but you've maintained decent balances with us, so here's what I'll do: One of my eyes is glass. If you can guess which, I'll approve the loan.' The borrower studies the banker's eyes. 'The right one,' he says without hesitation. The banker is surprised. 'All right,' he says, 'you've got the loan, but tell me how you knew.' 'It looks more human.' "

My uncle laughs as if hearing the joke for the first time. Father joins him, laughing even louder. Mother titters—she never really laughs out loud, considers it unladylike. "That's marvelous," she says, "marvelous." I try to laugh as loud as Father, wanting to show everyone that I understand these funny adult stories, but I can't do it, and end up coughing.

Soon after my uncle leaves, I hear my parents' voices once again from behind their bedroom door, that door behind which I was conceived and behind which even now my life is still being arranged and manipulated.

"THAT BROTHER OF YOURS IS ARROGANT, SARCASTIC."

"Sometimes he's impatient."

"IMPATIENT! YOU THINK HE CAN DO NO WRONG."

"He was right about the school."

"YOU MEAN HE AGREES WITH YOU. YOU THINK HE'S RIGHT ABOUT EVERYTHING. YOU EVEN THOUGHT THAT STORY WAS SO *MARVELOUS.*

"You laughed hard enough."

"I WAS BEING POLITE. THAT'S MORE THAN YOUR BROTHER IS."

"He was polite. He was trying to be entertaining while you were brooding."

"STILL AM. BUT THE DAMN THING IS HE DOES TAKE AN INTEREST IN OUR SON, MIGHT DO HIM A LOT OF GOOD SOMEDAY. AND HE IS SMART. I RESPECT HIM EVEN IF I DON'T LIKE HIS STYLE."

"Well?"

"WELL WHAT?"

"Private school."

"ALL RIGHT. LET'S START LOOKING."

What my parents find, since both think I'm too young to leave home and therefore don't consider preparatory schools outside New York, is a school in the Riverdale section of the Bronx to which I, like the sons of several of their friends, can commute by subway. Except for its location, it is in every sense a prep school. From the first form on, the entire curriculum is designed to prepare boys for college, preferably an Ivy League college.

Besides learning what I need to know to get into college, I learn to wear a shirt, tie, and jacket at all times; I learn to address my teachers as "Sir"; and I learn that there are many boys much smarter than I am. My parents like the way I dress, they like my improved respectful manners, and they are satisfied with my marks, always in the high eighties but never, like the best students, in the mid-nineties. As Father now says, "I DON'T WANT A GENIUS. JUST GIVE ME A NORMAL BOY."

In the fall of 1942, during my senior year, Mother's brother invites me to lunch. Though I have visited the Stock Exchange on a school tour, his world in the financial area at the southern tip of Manhattan, much farther downtown than Father's place, is still mysterious. My uncle's address—on Wall Street, in an office building he *owns*—is, for me, as exotic as Sherlock Holmes's 221B Baker Street.

I wear what has become a uniform: tweed jacket, white button-down-collar shirt, striped tie, gray flannels, white wool athletic socks, plain brown rubber-soled shoes—except for the shoes, everything loose and baggy the way my classmates and I imagine boys dress at college. In this outfit, it seems odd to enter the subway on the downtown side of the street where I usually exit when I return from school; odd, also, to see a few soldiers and sailors in their *real* uniforms sprawling at midday in the almost empty cars; and odd, finally, to roar out of the Chambers Street station where, when I go downtown, below Times Square, I usually get off.

Wall Street is crowded with men and women rushing to and from lunch among the gray shadows of gray buildings. The people themselves look gray, anonymous. Just as I am certain sometimes when I go to a movie or sports event that I will run into someone I know, I am just as certain now that I know no one. I wonder if these people can be known, if the color of their personalities can be separated out from all the grayness. I wonder if I can be separated out, if I look like a foreigner from uptown. And yet there is something I like about the impersonality of Wall Street, something protective. I feel as if, under this gray blanket, I am part of the street's dense mass and nervous energy. More than ever before I feel like a New Yorker.

My uncle's building, designated only by a number, is wedged between two much larger ones, named for banks. I enter the richly marbled lobby; find his name on the directory, following that of my maternal grandfather; and take the elevator to the top floor. There I face a pair of glass-paneled doors on which, in small black letters are his name and, again above it, that of my grandfather. Though the tower floor is comparatively small, I am surprised that they occupy all of it—my uncle really, since Grandfather is retired and comes in only occasionally.

The receptionist/switchboard operator announces my name ("Mr. _____ to see Mr. _____"). After a moment my uncle's secretary appears and leads me down a corridor flanked by private offices and an open engineering space. My uncle has a yellow pad in front of him on an almost bare desk. He puts down a short pencil that suggests bridge and golf scores, numbers rather than words.

"You're looking very collegiate," he says, standing to shake hands, then motioning me to a chair opposite his desk. "I guess you're thinking about that."

I name the colleges to which I've applied.

"It doesn't really matter which you go to. They're all good; they can all teach you much more than you can learn. It's different at the graduate level. Then you might want specialized instruction from a particular teacher or a strong department. But for now it's enough if you get a reasonably broad education and learn how to think, how to make connections between the things you learn."

While he speaks I study the low bookcase to his right. On the top shelf, most prominent, is a framed photograph of his wife, my new aunt, a stunning brunette, formerly a model and still as beautiful as any motion picture actress. I know from Mother, "He kept her for years because pop objected to his marrying a Catholic. Even when she agreed to convert, Pop continued objecting to the inequalities of the match—intellectual, educational, economic—until I interceded." In the photograph of her wearing a loose blouse and short golf skirt, exposing a figure as gorgeous as her face, I can see nothing objectionable. She is surely as much a prize as the two small loving cups which stand beside her on the same shelf—one, I learn later, given to him by friends at a card club for having been dealt, in defiance of huge odds, two yarboroughs in one week, and the other by a golf club for having made a hole-in-one.

"Father thinks I should prepare for law school, that that would be a good background for anything."

"Let's talk about it at lunch. You must be hungry, you're a growing boy."

He laughs as he stands again and looks up at me. At sixteen I am as tall as Father.

In a lunch club at the top of a building across the street, the conversation continues: "Of course there's nothing wrong with law. Take an introductory course or two, see how you like it. There's a lawyer in one of those offices you passed on the corridor. He works full-time on leases. And I use outside counsel for more important matters. Lawyers are necessary. They'll always make a living. But the point is you can get all you want. You can buy them for a hundred or so a week. And accountants. And engineers. Any specialist. What you can't buy is really good executives, men willing to make decisions and capable of making the right ones. At least you can't buy them cheap."

After lunch we walk around the perimeter of the club looking down at the city. "That's the most valuable real estate in the world," he says. "Prices are depressed now, but after the war there's going to be the biggest building boom you've ever seen. All those returning servicemen are going to need homes, jobs. The skyline's going to change. There'll be hundreds of new apartment houses and office buildings. If I had more capital, I'd buy everything in sight. There are millions to be made, millions."

The word hums on his tongue. The buildings below us are no longer gray. They sparkle like so many diamonds and rubies and saphires displayed for our viewing, our pleasure and, ultimately, our possession.

Farther away, a convoy of supply ships is moving out into the harbor.

"I guess I'll be in the navy in a couple of years," I remark. "Father says it's much less strenous and dangerous than the army."

"It was for him. I don't think he was ever on a ship. He worked in some naval procurement office, not far from his business."

"Are you sure?"

"Pretty sure, but ask him."

That night there are a lot of questions to answer before I can ask mine.

"DID YOU WEAR THOSE SOCKS TO YOUR UNCLE'S?"

"Yes."

"YOU SHOULD KNOW BETTER. HIS PLACE ISN'T A GYM. DID HE TAKE YOU TO HIS CLUB FOR LUNCH?"

"Yes."

"AND YOU WORE THOSE SOCKS! DON'T YOU KNOW HE'S CONSERVATIVE, A REPUBLICAN? THAT CLUB IS FULL OF REPUBLICANS."

"He said I looked collegiate."

"WHAT DOES THAT MEAN? I BET HE WOULDN'T HIRE ANYONE WEARING WHITE SOCKS. DID HE TALK ABOUT THE FUTURE?"

"He thinks after the war there's going to be a real estate boom."

"HE DOESN'T NEED ANOTHER BOOM. HE WENT THROUGH ONE AND THEN LOST ALMOST EVERY BUILD-ING HE HAD. GOD KNOWS WHY HE'S SO OPTIMISTIC." Father pauses, reconsiders. "MAYBE YOU'VE GOT TO BE OPTIMISTIC TO DO THE THINGS HE'S DONE. ANYWAY, I WAS ASKING ABOUT *YOUR* FUTURE."

"I think he was trying to interest me in the real estate business. There was nothing definite."

Father smiles and nods at Mother. They both seem pleased. I wait a moment before asking my question.

"I WASN'T EXACTLY *ON* A SHIP I WAS ATTACHED TO THE FLEET HERE. FIRST CLASS PETTY OFFICER, IN SUPPLY. THERE WERE A LOT OF WOMEN ATTRACTED TO ME THEN. ASK YOUR MOTHER."

"That's true. He was stunning in uniform, the best looking man I ever met."

I am too well prepared for college. The courses required during freshman year duplicate those taken in high school. Except for some reading for the advanced section in English to which I have been assigned, I am on my own, learning to drink beer, play bridge, and improve my wardrobe with a black knit tie and white buckskin shoes (immediately dirtied to neutral gray).

I don't have to work until the third term, the beginning of sophomore year, accelerated because of the war. Then I elect courses in subjects I've never taken before—philosophy, economics, Russian and French literature—and even these, I discover, are not really work in any difficult or unpleasant sense. They require mostly reading— listening to enduring, powerful, often passionate voices, typically from the past, but here now, on the printed page. I begin to think I would like to spend my life listening to such voices, carrying on my own dialogue with them, more leisurely than the present one, rushed by examinations and term papers. And I begin to seek out those students who respond as I do and dream not only of studying the world's great books but of someday writing books of their own.

Among my new friends is a boy from San Francisco, 4-F and therefore able to remain at college while most of our classmates leave for the army or navy. His dream is not as vague as mine. He writes poetry, publishes much of it in the literary magazine, and at the age of eighteen, only a year older than I am, actually calls himself a poet. As we walk across campus, his long blond hair blowing in the wind, his shirt collar open, how passionately he says, "Shelley, Keats, Byron, Rimbaud—they were all writing poetry at my age, they all knew they were poets."

I ask Mother if I can bring him home during spring recess, since it would be difficult and expensive for him to go to California.

"Of course, dear," she replies on the phone, "we love to meet your friends."

Although he and I have talked for hours about particular writers, painters, and composers, discussing their strengths and weaknesses, which we are surprised to discover are usually the same, we have barely mentioned our own families, what Father calls BACK-GROUND. Father gets to that the first night, before dinner.

"WHAT DOES YOUR FATHER DO?"

"He's dead."

"OH. SORRY. WHAT *DID* HE DO?"

"Ran the family business."

"WHAT WAS THAT?"

"He ran the family business."

"YES, I HEARD YOU. WHAT WAS THE BUSINESS?"

"Lumber."

"OUT OF MY LINE. KNOW SOME SHOE PEOPLE ON THE WEST COAST."

Father waits for my friend to name those his family knows. There's silence.

"MY BROTHER-IN-LAW IS IN REAL ESTATE AND CON-STRUCTION. HE MIGHT KNOW YOUR FAMILY."

Further silence. Father tries once more:

"DO YOU KNOW WHAT YOU'RE GOING TO DO?"

"Tonight?"

"WITH YOUR LIFE."

"Yes, I'm doing what I'm going to do."

"WHAT'S THAT?"

"I write poetry."

"THAT'S *REALLY* OUT OF MY LINE. YOU'RE LUCKY YOU CAN AFFORD TO."

The silence, the longest yet, is broken only when Mother excuses herself to speak to the cook. She returns to the living room after a moment—another moment, there, of silence. "Dinner," she says with a subtle sigh, brief as if she had whispered the words *Thank God*.

During the meal—all favorite foods of mine—she carries the conversation: "Do you get enough to eat at college?...There are shortages of everything here. The butcher put this steak away for me when I told him you were coming home...What's the weather been like? We've had nothing but rain..."

After dinner, on the way to Nick's to hear jazz, my friend asks, "Will there be an inquisition each night?"

"Probably. But you were being hard on Father. There's nothing so strange about his wanting to know what your father did or what you want to do. Those are the things everyone wants to know."

"Are they? How come *you* never asked? All of that's bullshit. That's why I love poetry, music, philosophy. They cut through those details and stay with the essentials."

"There's detail in great art. You've told me *Moby Dick* is your favorite novel. It's full of detail. And so's Proust. And Vermeer. And the great operas. Most of life is detail. The issue isn't eliminating it but refining it…"

The conversation goes on all the way to Nick's, a conversation that seems superficially about aesthetics but is really, on my part, a defense of Father. I can admit to myself but not to my friend that I would like Father to be less bullying, less crude, just as I can say to myself but not to my friend that I agree, at least partly, with Father's assertion that he is lucky he can afford to write poetry. At other times my friend and I have talked about the possibility of a perfect friendship, one in which there is no censorship. Now I realize that he too is censoring, that in attacking only the questions Father has asked, he is sparing Mother. If what our Fathers do and what we want to do are details, then surely the food we eat and the climate we live in are details too.

I am happy when we arrive at Nick's. Here it is harder to talk, harder to think. I feel refreshed by the raucous blast of Chicago jazz and calmed by the boilermakers we drink. Now my friend and I are riding the same waves of sound, bobbing our heads and tapping our feet to the same rhythm, sharing the same facts, the names of every man in the group and of every piece they play.

As the trombonist completes a powerful solo, I think for a moment, only a moment—the thought floats away on beer and whiskey—how much that brassy trombone voice sounds like Father's, how human it is, how sad and angry. Everyone applauds—tables full of servicemen, college and prep school kids, their dates—and the set is over.

"That's poetry," my friend says, high and happy as I am, "no-bullshit poetry: the way everything harmonizes—the brass, the reeds, the rhythm section."

"Life is poetry!"

"There you go again. Life is prose." He pauses and then, declaring a truce, adds: "Unless you listen very carefully."

A few days later my friend's girl arrives in New York from another college, and I have lunch with Father at his usual restaurant, but alone this time—his brother is ON A BINGE.

"I HARDLY SEE YOU. WHAT HAVE YOU AND THE POET BEEN UP TO?"

"Nick's, Kelly's Stable, The Famous Door, The Onyx Club—" I catalogue what Father will consider comparatively acceptable.

"I KNOW YOU LIKE JAZZ. I JUST HOPE YOU'RE NOT DRINKING TOO MUCH. YOU SEE WHAT HAPPENS TO MY BROTHER. HAVEN'T EVEN HEARD FROM HIM. HE'LL CALL ONE OF THESE DAYS. FROM ST. LOUIS. OR THE WEST COAST. NEEDING CARFARE HOME. YOU LOOKED HUNG-OVER YESTERDAY. DO YOU DRINK A LOT?"

"Mostly beer."

"GOOD. AND WHAT HAVE YOU TWO BEEN DOING DUR-ING THE DAY?"

"We went to some of the second-hand book stores on Fourth Avenue and got a few out-of-print things," I begin slowly, hoping that Father will interrupt me and unload whatever is on his mind. But he waits. "We went to the Metropolitan Museum." I pause again, and again he waits. "And the Modern." Another pause. "And a matinee at the Philharmonic—"

With each phrase more blood rushes to his face. It is almost purple. His eyes, so much like my own, bulge now as if wanting to seize me across the restaurant table. He can stand no more. He has all the evidence he needs that I am no longer the boy he sent to college. Under the table I brace myself, holding the chair very tight with both hands.

"CHRIST, YOU'RE BECOMING AS ARTY AS YOUR FRIEND. DO YOU WANT TO BE A POET TOO?"

"I don't know what I want to do."

"WELL, IT'S TIME YOU DID. YOU'VE GOT TO BE REALISTIC TO BE IDEALISTIC. MAYBE HIS FATHER WAS RICHER THAN I AM, BUT AT LEAST YOU KNOW ENOUGH AND CAN AFFORD ENOUGH TO GET A HAIRCUT. AND TO WEAR A TIE. NOT THAT I LIKE THE ONE YOU'RE WEARING. YOU LOOK LIKE YOU'RE IN MOURNING. MAYBE YOU WILL BE IF YOU HANG AROUND THAT POET. HE MAY THINK HE'S A PRINCE BUT HE LOOKS TO ME LIKE SOME KIND OF SCREAMING QUEEN."

"He's not. He has an idea about eliminating details."

"WHAT KIND OF DOUBLE-TALK IS THAT? SINCE WHEN ARE A HAIRCUT AND A TIE DETAILS? LOOK, YOU HAVE TWO CAREERS OPEN TO YOU—THAT'S TWO MORE THAN MOST PEOPLE—YOU CAN COME WITH ME OR, PROBABLY A

BETTER OPPORTUNITY, YOU CAN GO WITH YOUR UNCLE.
WE BOTH GET HAIRCUTS. WE BOTH WEAR TIES."

During Spring Term, my last before enlisting in the navy, I become
increasingly involved with a girl in my economics class. At first I am
aware only of a strong silhouette to my left: straight black hair falling
to her shoulders, dark sleek skin cut by the heavy line of unplucked
eyebrows that obscure the eyes themselves in shadow, nose sharply
defined from flat bridge to fine triangular nostrils over deep philtrum,
sensual mouth moistened slightly by her tongue which moves periodi-
cally between her lips as she concentrates on the lecture (concentrates
as I am unable to), cleft chin, large breasts visible even under her loose
sweater, long hands on which, when she's not taking notes, she supports her chin. She wears no make-up on her face, no polish on her
fingernails. She doesn't have to.

As she turns to ask the professor a question, her eyes appear so dark,
so intense it is almost impossible to detect the transition from pupil to
iris. Her teeth flash brilliantly white, making her skin appear even
darker than it is. Her voice is soft and Southern:

"What you say is based on accepting the concept of private property. Would you discuss the distribution of goods, assuming their
communality?"

"Hear, hear!" a student wearing heavy glasses calls out from the
back row.

"This isn't a political forum," the professor says quickly, restoring
order by dropping his voice. "I was, of course, describing the system as
it exists here, the Capitalist system. However, the mechanics of distribution would be remarkably similar under, *say*—" he smiles as he says
"say," knowing perfectly well that his next word is exactly the one
that both the beautiful girl who raised the question and the obstrepor-
ous boy who supported her have in mind—"*say*, Communism. What
would be different is the motivating principle. Under Capitalism
goods flow toward economic power, demand backed by cash or
credit. Under Communism, *ideal* Communism—" he smiles again—
"they would flow simply toward need."

"Then the distinction you're making is between greed and need," the girl says.

"I don't like slogans," the professor replies. "The distinction I'm *trying* to make is between a system that works, though in some areas it can certainly be reformed, and a system that hasn't yet proved itself..."

After class, as most of us walk toward the recreation building for lunch, I hear the boy in heavy glasses telling the girl, "The prof's performance was something, wasn't it? What a demonstration of bourgeois evasiveness."

They sit a few tables from the one at which I wait for my San Francisco friend, she in her sweater, skirt and saddle shoes, he in a flannel shirt, corduroys and work shoes, both gesticulating as they continue to talk, plotting, I suppose, the overthrow, or at least the radical reform, of our government. And yet I envy the bond they share. I envy any bond anyone shares with her.

When my friend arrives I point her out to him. He glances and says, "She's not your type. Probably has hair on her chest. And that guy she's with is a creep. He's the one who's always writing angry editorials in the paper—'Education in the Service of the Revolution,' stuff like that."

Two days later, after my next economics class, I ask her to have lunch with me.

"I'd love to," she replies, just like that, without coyness, without pretense.

Even then and as we cross the campus, it is apparent that she has been just as aware of me as I have of her; that my looks, clothes, style seem as exotic to her as hers do to me. There is between us, if not a bond, a tug, an attraction of opposites, a sexual urgency that transcends economics.

I suggest going to Pop's, a hamburger place just off-campus, not wanting yet to introduce her to my friend. We sit in a booth, talking for two hours. She tells me about growing up in Baltimore—her family's poverty, her father's involvement with labor organization, his present high-paying defense job, her mother's interest in Marxism, her own schooling and the tuition scholarship on which she has come to college. She bubbles with the details of life, and I find myself responding, speaking openly about my own family, describing my parents, the two businesses becknoning to me, my imminent enlistment in the navy.

"But you really don't know what you want to do?"

"No. I'd rather be rich than poor."

"That's sensible—*you* can't know how sensible—but isn't there some kind of work you really like, something you'd be happy doing *forever?*"

"That's a long time. I like philosophy and literature. I wouldn't mind reading the rest of my life, but I suppose there's a limit to how far one can stretch his education."

"You set the limit. Don't you like economics? I don't like this course because it's so conservative, but you should."

"I took it because I thought I should. I like it because you're in it."

The meeting between my friends is worse than I feared. When he suggests "formal purity" as a standard by which to judge literature, she suggests "social usefulness." When he mentions T.S. Eliot, she mentions Mayakovsky. When he accuses her of being more interested in propaganda than in literature, she says he lacks commitment. When he cites his favorite quotation from Shelley, "Poets are the unacknowledged legislators of the world," she somehow works in her favorite quotation from Proudon, "Property is theft," which she has previously quoted to me in response to my telling her about my uncle's real estate business and which she may be using now because I have also told her about my friend's family lumber business. However, she says these things to me at least partly in a spirit of teasing, affectionate teasing. With him the spirit is one of open confrontation, class war. He knows what he is doing; he has committed himself to elitist poetry—Eliot, Pound, Stevens, Cummings, and the rest. I don't really know what I'm doing or what I want to do; for me there's hope.

"Your dark lady is certainly angry," he says to me later.

"You hardly know her."

"I don't have to—I took a course once in which we read Marx."

"And she took one in which she read Eliot."

But it's not that simple. As I spend more and more time with her, so much that I begin to fall behind in my courses, I realize that there is an overlap between her passionate interest in politics and his in poetry, that both of them in their different ways are expressing intense idealism. I mention Father's "YOU'VE GOT TO BE REALISTIC TO BE IDEALISTIC."

"He's right," she says, "if he understands that idealism is simply a higher form of realism. In that sense, Communism is a religion."

"And Capitalism?"

"A false religion," she replies, kissing me to show once again that there is nothing personally aggressive in her words.

As spring grows warmer, we often take a picnic lunch and a blanket far off-campus into the woods. There we stretch out and explore each others' bodies as we have been exploring each others' minds, our mouths often now too busy for words, our hands too busy for gestures. Her body is as beautiful as her face—all smooth, soft curves which sometimes tremble beneath my fingers. I begin to know her body almost as well as my own. At first, as we play with each other, embrace each other, excite each other to orgasm, we avoid actual intercourse.

"No Capitalist infiltration of the Party cell?" I ask.

She smiles, showing her beautiful teeth, and bites me tenderly on the neck. "You know I'd like to as much as you. It's just—"

"I know, but you don't need to be afraid. I don't want a child any more than you do. I promise you won't get pregnant."

"And if I do, you'll pay for the abortion."

"That's nasty."

She apologizes by nibbling my neck again, as I grope for a condom in the pocket of my pants lying beside me.

"I think I was as much afraid of pain as pregnancy," she says afterwards, "but that didn't hurt much. With all the talk about Communist free love, my mother never really told me anything; got me through puberty—that's about all."

"Mine did. She told me nice girls don't. She made me feel as if I'd be robbing something precious. But it's about giving, isn't it?"

I have about three weeks between the end of the term and induction into the navy. I tell my parents that I want to spend a few days with them, two weeks in Baltimore, then the last few days with them again.

"Two weeks! Two weeks!" Mother repeats shrilly and incredulously. "We may not see you for months, years—we may never see you again."

"BITE YOUR TONGUE. WE'LL SEE HIM ALL RIGHT. EVERYONE SAYS THE GERMANS CAN'T LAST MUCH LONGER."

"And the Japanese—what about them?"

"WHEN OUR TROOPS ARE FREE TO MOVE FROM EUROPE TO THE PACIFIC, THEY'LL MAKE SHORT WORK OF THE JAPS." Father turns to me. "YOU MUST BE PRETTY SERIOUS ABOUT THIS GIRL. WHAT DOES SHE DO?"

"Economics major."

"I SEE!" Father looks pleased—pleased, generally, because I am involved with a girl; pleased specifically because she is no dreamy poet but sounds down-to-earth.

"WHAT DOES HER FATHER DO?"

I name the company he works for.

"THEY'RE HUGE. WHAT'S HIS POSITION?"

"Supervisor."

"IN A PLANT?"

"I think so."

Father looks less pleased. "I DON'T MIND IF YOU GO TO BALTIMORE FOR A FEW DAYS." He is negotiating. "PROBABLY A GOOD IDEA TO SEE HER FAMILY. BUT THEN YOU OUGHT TO HAVE HER HERE. THERE'S NOTHING LIKE SEEING SOMONE IN RELATION TO YOUR OWN FAMILY. THAT'S THE TEST."

We compromise. I will go to Baltimore for a week, then have her come to New York for a week.

The week in Baltimore goes quickly. So that she can tell her parents where she has been during the day, we race through several museums, Johns Hopkins University, the Enoch Pratt Free Library, and the Westminister Churchyard, looking for Poe's grave. But most of our time is actually spent in my hotel room. Evenings I meet her parents only briefly, at the door, as we are going off to a movie or restaurant or bar. They look exhausted, standing in the drab hallway, her father wearing an open denim shirt, her mother in an apron. They are busy with their own lives. They ask me no direct questions, remark once that they are sorry to hear I'm going into the navy, and otherwise express no interest in my existence. They seem pleased when we leave and are always asleep when we return.

"It's going to be different in New York. My parents want to get to know you."

"Yes, I've been thinking about that. I'm not sure I want to be inspected. I'm not sure I want to be put up at some hotel at your expense. Originally you were going to come down here for two weeks. I would have loved to spend every moment I could with you, but I didn't bargain on your parents. I'm not in love with them."

"You don't even know them."

"I know enough about them."

"You're a snob. You tease me about class distinctions, but you won't meet my parents, and your own didn't want to meet me."

"They were around. I didn't notice you trying to meet them, to know them. You hardly said a word."

"They didn't make it easy."

"No, they never have, but at least they've left me free to make my own decisions. I don't want to come to New York."

"Will you write?"

"Of course. As soon as you send me your address in the navy. I don't want your parents to count my letters."

"WHAT HAPPENED?"

"Nothing."

"SOMETHING MUST HAVE HAPPENED. YOU CAN TELL ME. AND YOUR MOTHER. WE'RE YOUR BEST FRIENDS. THERE'S NOTHING YOU'RE GOING THROUGH THAT WE HAVEN'T BEEN THROUGH. DID HER PARENTS OBJECT?"

"No."

"WELL, THAT'S IN THEIR FAVOR. JUST REMEMBER, YOU'RE AS GOOD AS ANYONE ELSE. I'D KILL ANYONE WHO HURT YOU."

The induction center is like returning to public school. There are the same faces, the same names, the same clothes, the same accents, the same pushing and shoving—the rediscovery of negative quantities.

And at boot camp, as at public school, not since then, I am again one of the brighter boys.

By now I have learned that there are advantages to being bright — privileges leading to advancement leading to further privileges. I have still to learn that there are disadvantages too, that though intelligence and education may "score well" on tests, they do not necessarily do so in life, especially not here, in the navy.

"Readin' again?" one of my mates asks as I lie on my bunk before lights out.

"I was trying," I say, smiling, as I put down the Armed Services Edition of *War and Peace*.

"That's a funny title. Do ya think there'll ever be peace again?"

"History tells us wars end."

"History's a crock of shit, ain't it? Christ, how I hated that stuff."

"It's hard to escape."

"School, ya mean? I managed."

"I meant history."

"Ya talk in riddles, doncha? History's a crock —"

When the lights go out, I begin to think maybe I've returned to a world even more primitive than public school, a dark world where everything *is* shit, a world of unfocused toilet training. From the polished tips of my shoes, protruding from laced leggings, to the croped hair on my head, barely visible under squared sailor hat, and beyond to the tightly made "sack" I lie on and the carefully arranged locker I stow my gear in — each piece of clothing stenciled, folded, rolled, and tied with square knots, so my name shows — everything is neat and clean, artificially disciplined, contained within the chaos out there in the larger theaters of Europe and Asia where, I suppose, we will soon be killing neatly and cleanly.

I fall asleep with an image in my mind of the top of Father's dresser, the way it has looked every night for as long as I can remember. There, precisely ordered, marching across its polished mahogany surface, are the small things he wears and carries during the day: wrist watch, tie clip, gold pencil and leatherbound diary, keys, wallet, cigars, matches, folded pocket handkerchief, pile of change and, off to one side of that, all by itself, the pig coin, a single concession to chance.

There are other links with home. Day after day at mail call, my parents' voices are delivered to me in short letters containing little news but leading always to the same closings. "Take care of yourself, dear," Mother ends her letters, as if she imagines that away from her, I am suddenly independent, caring for myself and free of the navy's grip, as tight as her own. And in script so large and agressive it seems to roar, Father scrawls, "TAKE IT EASY, YOU'LL LAST LONGER," intending no more irony than Mother but reminding me of his own uneasy example. Indeed, after a few weeks, Mother writes, "Your father's stomach has kicked up. The doctor thinks he has an ulcer, caused probably by aggravation—your being in the navy, his brother drinking too much, price controls and other business irritations." And in response to my response: "YES, THEY'VE GOT THE OLD MAN DRINKING MILK AND EATING POT CHEESE AND SOUR CREAM. NOTHING TO WORRY ABOUT. IN FACT, THE DOC-TORS SAY THAT WORRY CAUSES ULCERS."

I have only a vague idea of what an ulcer is—a sort of corrosion of the human plumbing, nothing very serious or painful if it can be cured with dairy products, certainly nothing that can endanger Father's vast vitality. I turn to other mail, the mail I prefer and save for the end. First, a letter postmarked from San Francisco:

"...My mother has introduced me to a man who has a private press. He publishes small editions of works that have lasting, if not immedi-ate commercial, value. And he prints his books to last, using the highest quality materials and hand-setting the type. Working with him this summer, I have a greater appreciation than ever of the weight of a word on the page. He has allowed me to print a few of my poems (enclosed), is impressed by them, and promises to print a collection in the fall. So you will be receiving that ere long. You can imagine how excited I am at the prospect of having a book published. Somehow, although the work already exists in manuscript, in college magazines, and now on a few pages of rag paper, it is not the same, does not have the same purchase on permanence. What a phrase! Is *purchase on posterity* better? Anyway, I hope that such matters as alliteration and language in general do not seem trivial to you within the context of what you are doing. You know I believe that poetry is worth fighting for..."

And, finally, from Baltimore:

"...Every time I see a battle photograph I am so glad that your training continues. Somehow I can't and don't want to imagine you overseas. No, I hope you stay right where you are, fighting to save the world for Capitalism. However, from what you describe of your training, I hope also that it's not too boring. You mustn't give in to total passivity. Can't you find time for reading? Aren't there some fellows you find interesting? If all else fails, why not organize the navy, set up a union. The worst that can happen is they'll kick you out...."

As I finish reading her letter, I feel someone looking over my shoulder.

"Christ, ya getta lotta mail. My girl says she don't have time to write. Probably already in the sack with another guy." He pauses. "Whatsa matta, doncha wanna talk?"

"Sure, I do. Very much."

August 25, just as my boot company is about to graduate, the Allies liberate Paris. It looks as if the war is almost over. Scuttlebutt swells to a torrent, carrying us in one moment to Europe as part of an occupation force and in the next to the Pacific. The facts emerge slowly: none of us who have qualified for petty officers' training will go on to those specialized schools; instead, everyone will be shipped south for amphibious training. The rumor now is that we are headed for the invasion of Japan.

Our first stop is Fort Pierce, a base on an island off the east coast of Florida. There boot companies from all parts of the country are scrambled and broken up into Landing Craft Vehicle Personnel crews, each consisting of a cockswain, a signalman, an engineer, and a bowman. No one has any idea why he has been assigned to his particular job. Initially, I am our signalman. I flatter myself by thinking that somewhere along the line, perhaps on some test, I showed a remarkable aptitude for recognizing signs and symbols and that someone up there, in Washington, noticed. But this is nonsense. It's all like a flip of Father's pig coin.

While we familiarize ourselves with the LCVP and the jobs aboard it—steering and speed control; communications, including semaphore, lights, and flags; the maintenance of the diesel engine and of the bow ramp mechanism which will permit a jeep and a squad of soldiers to land on that distant Japanese beach—it becomes clear that I'm an awkward signalman. There's a problem in coordination.

Although I have no difficulty receiving messages, I am slow sending them. My arms, hands, and fingers do not respond quickly enough to the words which flash and blink through my mind. At the end of a month, three of us switch jobs. I become engineer, the bowman takes over as signalman, and the engineer goes to the bow. Only the cockswain stays put. He handles the boat as easily as a tractor on his family farm.

Now, every day after morning classes and lunch, there are maneuvers. Miles offshore we join hundreds of other small boxlike craft. Out there we toss and bob like so much flotsam, our square bows battering the waves, our flat bottoms responding, even on a calm day, to each swell and ripple of the sea. Our stomachs churn and turn with the movement of the boats. Often we vomit. Always, at the end of the day, we are relieved as we hit the beach for the last time.

Ours is a good crew, one of the best. We are proud of ourselves as, among the first to land, we walk across the beach, carrying our salty life jackets to the recreation building.

Over beer, the cockswain tells me, "You've really got that engine tuned. I must have hit fifteen, sixteen knots."

"I was worried about that one big wave as we were coming in. You took it just right. For a second we were almost flying."

"How about me?" the signalman says. "Didn't I get you off to a good start? Half the other guys missed the signal, never turned until they saw us heading for shore."

"I got the ramp down fast, didn't I?" the bowman asks, waiting. Having enlisted with his parents' consent on his sixteenth birthday, he is the youngest member of our crew and his is the easiest job, just flipping a crank when we beach, handling the bow line when we dock or come alongside a larger craft.

"Yes, you did."

"You really did."

"You sure did."

We speak as a unit. We laugh as a unit. We stagger back to the barracks as a unit. Most nights we are too tired to do anything but collapse on our cots. I have stopped reading and almost stopped corresponding. Once a week I call home, collect.

I can hear Mother, who always answers the phone, telling the operator, "Yes, yes, we'll accept the charges," and then yelling breathlessly to Father, "Pick up the other phone, pick up, pick up, it's Fort Pierce."

I am Fort Pierce, Florida, U.S.A., their world, their universe. For a moment my own weight is crushing. I tell them what I've been doing. I tell them I'm tired.

"But surely," Mother replies, "You could drop a short note to Grandpa and one to my brother. That's not asking too much, is it? We tell them about your training, but it would be reassuring for them to hear from you directly."

"All right. I may be writing to you again too. We start night maneuvers next week. There won't be time to call."

"NIGHT MANEUVERS! ISN'T IT ENOUGH THEY SEND YOU OUT IN THOSE FLIMSY BOATS DURING THE DAY?"

"The invasion may be at night."

"STOP TALKING ABOUT THE INVASION. THERE ISN'T GOING TO BE ANY INVASION FOR YOU, IF I CAN HELP IT. I WASN'T GOING TO SAY ANYTHING ABOUT THIS—I HAVEN'T EVEN TOLD YOUR MOTHER—BUT A FRIEND OF MINE KNOWS AN ADMIRAL. HE'S GOING TO SPEAK TO HIM ABOUT HAVING YOU TRANSFERRED."

"Don't do that. I like the guys I'm with. We're—"

"YOU LIKE *THEM*. WHAT ABOUT *US*? WE DIDN'T RAISE YOU TO BE SHOT DOWN ON SOME JAP BEACH. I'M DOING WHAT I CAN TO PREVENT THAT. DO YOU WANT TO MAKE ME SICKER THAN I AM?...DO YOU?"

"No. Of course not."

"Listen to your father. He loves you. We both love you."

"AND THE NAVY DOESN'T. TO THEM YOU'RE ONLY THAT NUMBER WE WRITE ON YOUR MAIL."

Tired as I am, I can't sleep. Father's voice still roars, smothering my own. I've said only that I like my crew, and that makes him sick. What if I'd said that I'll resist transfer, that I consider myself part of a unit outside the family unit, that I'm looking forward to the invasion, that I'm already part of that too? What then? What murderous then?

Trying to remove all this from my mind, I begin, as I have on other nights soon after coming to Fort Pierce but seemingly long ago, mentally stripping the LCVP diesel engine: starter, fan, water pump, injection pump, fuel feed pump, oil pump, vacuum pump, camshaft, pistons, crankshaft, flywheel, oil sump, injection nozzle, glow plug, mixture controller, control linkage, ram manifold, exhaust manifold, exhaust.... The parts are real in my mind but they shrink, become miniature, and finally gravitate, as I do once again, to the top of Father's dresser. As I sink to sleep, the pig on Father's lucky coin snorts, "I WASN'T EXACTLY ON A SHIP."

As we go from Fort Pierce to Camp Bradford, Virginia, where our LCVP crews are assigned to LST's—four crews to each of the block-long Landing Ship Tanks—and from Camp Bradford to Great Lakes Gunnery School, and from there to a shipyard near Gary, Indiana, where we board a new LST and take it down the Mississippi to the Algiers Naval Base in New Orleans; as the weeks and months flow by, interrupted only by these stops on this mysterious itinerary planned by an omnipotent travel agency in Washington, we know that we are still moving, however circuitously, however many more months and miles ahead, to that Japanese beach, that Armageddon, which is at once our destiny and destination. In the face of this power, this inevitable movement and the swelling size of our armada, even Father is impotent. I can only guess how many other desperate fathers had friends who knew THE ADMIRAL, but mine never mentions him again. Instead, there are hints of proliferating ulcers, plural now, perhaps wounds caused by THE ADMIRAL's neglect.

From New Orleans I call home the day Roosevelt dies. He has been President since I was seven and was therefore the only President I've ever really known, the only one Father talked about, loved, depended on.

"...HE WAS A GREAT MAN, ANOTHER LINCOLN. I CAN'T BELIEVE HE'S DEAD, THAT HE COULD DIE WITH THIS WAR STILL GOING ON. ALL WE CAN DO NOW IS PRAY FOR TRUMAN. BUT HOW CAN A HABERDASHER RUN A COUNTRY THIS SIZE, FIGHT A WAR THIS SIZE? I THOUGHT IF THE GERMANS SURRENDERED—I DON'T KNOW WHAT KEEPS THEM HANGING ON—VETERAN TROOPS WOULD BE SHIPPED TO THE PACIFIC. IT MAKES ME SICK TO MY STOMACH TO THINK OF INEXPERIENCED KIDS GOING THERE."

"We've been very well trained, really we have."

"WELL TRAINED! DO YOU THINK TRAINING COMES OUT OF BOOKS AND LECTURES AND MANEUVERS? LIFE IS THE ONLY TEACHER. EXPERIENCE ITSELF. FIGHTING. TAKE IT FROM ME, YOU DON'T SEND A BOY TO DO A MAN'S JOB."

Mother cuts in: "Has there been any further word about where you're going next?"

"Just rumors. We'll go somewhere to pick up troops, or supplies, or both. When we get our orders we won't be able to make any more phone calls."

"You can write."

"Our mail will be censored. I'll tell you what I can, when I can."

"Take care of yourself, darling."

"TAKE IT EASY, YOU'LL LAST LONGER."

In Mobile, Alabama, trained civilians load our entire tank deck with ammunition—hundreds of wooden crates full of large shells, bombs, fuses—all chained to the deck and bulkheads, then braced with timbers.

"There won't be any troops on this ship," a knowing black tells us, laughing as he scoots down the bow ramp on a fork truck. "Why risk more lives?"

Carpenters hammer wedges in between cartons and chains, timbers and bulkheads. "Pillows for these babies, so they sleep well on their crossing," one of them says.

"Yeah," another adds, "and I don't recommend any of you sneaking down here for a smoke."

We laugh nervously. The cargo, a source of much dark humor, generates the jokes necessary to living on top of it. Soon, on our way to the Panama Canal, we too are joking.

On the main deck, next to a tank deck vent where, as in many areas of the ship, smoking is forbidden, someone asks, "How about a smoke?" With an exaggerated gesture, he offers his pack.

"No, thanks. Just finished one. Flipped it down the vent."

No matter how often such exchanges occur, they are followed by laughter, our only release from the weight of those crates, beneath us but on top of us too, always in our minds. However, later, as we steer a zigzag course toward Hawaii, while receiving daily bulletins of the terrible fighting on Okinawa, there seems to be a bright side to our situation: simply because of our cargo, we will remain behind the action.

Public scuttlebutt becomes private fantasy of weeks, even months in Hawaii. There I see myself being fed tropical delicacies by shapely women whose oiled bodies glow as they fan me with palm fronds, then join me in a perfumed bed strewn with exotic flowers. I hear the distant swish of leis and grass skirts. Before I sight Hawaii, the Pacific turns from blue to green, reflecting, over so many miles, not merely terrestrial vegetation but a jungle paradise creeping with soft pubic fern. How could Father want to deprive me of all this?

We anchor off Pearl Harbor. LCVP's are lowered—two to pick up fresh supplies, one to take the captain and the executive officer ashore for orders, ours to go to the naval post office. The cockswain guns out engine. No mail was delivered in Mobile or Panama. It's over a month since we've had any.

There are eleven sacks waiting. Mail call is announced over the ship's P.A. system when we return. As usual I receive more than my share: daily letters and a box of cookies from Mother, weekly letters from Father, a letter from Grandpa and another on the same business stationery from my uncle, a thin package from San Francisco which I know is my friend's book, a letter from Baltimore.

Quickly, while munching cookies, I read everything except the poems, which I save, wrapped, until later. Mother's concern mounts from letter to letter: "It is ten days since we've heard from you... fifteen...twenty.... Today a letter arrived that is so cut up we can't make anything out of it, but at least we know that you're alive." Father is consistently angry: "NOW THAT THE GERMANS HAVE SURRENDERED, WHY DON'T THEY FLY THOSE BOMBERS TO THE PACIFIC AND BLAST JAPAN OFF THE MAP? ROOSEVELT WOULD HAVE. WHAT'S TRUMAN WAITING FOR?" Grandpa is simply affectionate; my uncle, optimistic: "The war can't last much longer, not with the entire Allied military machine focused now on Japan. You should be back at college within months, and it's not too early to start thinking about what you want to do after that. There'll be splendid opportunities, golden in every sense." I imagine him, at his desk, thousands of miles away, his smile broadening until there's the flash of an inlay.

The letter from Baltimore begins rather mechanically. It is almost a rehash of the emotions expressed in my family's correspondence—concern for me, anger at the war's dragging pace, affection, questions about my future—all stated somewhat more cooly. Then she comes to the point, names the fellow with heavy glasses who was in our economics class, and continues: "I don't think you ever really got to know him. I'm not at all sure that if you had, you would have liked him. His values are very different from yours and, probably needless to say, much closer to my own. He is idealistic, dedicated to social reform, uninterested in money except for its more equitable distribution. He loves me as I am and accepts my family as it is. Recently, when he was here visiting us, he spent several days at the factory with my father. Later they talked for hours about labor problems. After the war, they both expect a tremendous growth in the power of the unions. He wants to do Labor work and so do I. Early in September, before the fall term begins, we plan to get married. None of this changes the way I felt about you when we were together. I will always think of you fondly and hope that you think of me in the same way. As ever,"

The last two words sting most. They are a lie. Nothing between us is as ever. In fact, nothing ever was—that is what made our relationship exciting. Again my mind travels across thousands of miles. I torture myself with the image of her loveliness being ogled by that fellow's eyes, too near-sighted to qualify for military service. With my all too perfect vision, I see them making love, not on a blanket in the sunlit woods or on the clean comfortable bed of a first-class hotel but in some shabby tenement room with knicked furniture, peeling wallpaper, worn carpet, dim lights. I squint, watching their bodies bounce in ecstasy. The image, in miniature, is reflected twice in the convex lenses of his glasses, rocking now on the rickety night table. I want to break the glasses. I want to seize the table and beat him with it. I want to tear her from his embrace. And yet behind these violent fantasies, there is a quiet reality more difficult to deal with: he asked her to marry him, he made that commitment; I never did, I never even asked her to wait for me. Soon I am composing the letter I will write, my own lie, saying how happy I am for them, as ever.

After a single liberty in Honolulu—one enormous drink, though still not large enough to wash her from my mind—we proceed westward on our slow zigzag course. Underway, we stand watch, four hours on, eight off. During the day, when not on watch we maintain surfaces not yet in need of maintenance—chipping and wire-brushing, then applying coats of red-lead and gray paint. Evenings we play cards and write letters. In port, after loading supplies and delivering and receiving mail, there is little to do but drink and shop for souvenirs, including prostitutes.

In all of these activities, Father is with me, a buddy from another war. His is the voice behind the voice which awakens me for watch: "Hit the deck! Get out of that fuckin sack!" On watch, he stands beside me, ticking off the seconds and minutes and hours for the larger clock which is the navy or perhaps life itself. In different rhythms, stated more noisily, he reminds me of wasted time as I wield chipping hammer and wire brush or toss cards onto the table and dollar bills into the hands of venders and whores. YOU HAVE ONE LIFE, ONE BODY, he remdinds me, PROTECT IT, PROTECT IT.

But sometimes now I go off entirely alone. Leaving Father with the rest of the crew, I find an isolated beach and spend the day there swimming, reading, dreaming about the future—a future dotted with islands like so many bases which must be touched before returning home.

Between Ulithi and Eniwetok a bulletin is announced over the P.A.: "Hear this, hear this. The Japanese generals on Okinawa have committed suicide. Only the mainland remains to be conquered." The news is received with cheers and the usual dark humor: "All it takes to commit harakiri is guts. Get it? Just guts."

…Guam…Manila…

"WHEREVER YOU ARE—WE GUESS PEARL HARBOR—IT WON'T BE LONG NOW. TRUMAN'S GOT TO SEND OUR BIG SHIPS AND PLANES TO JAPAN AND CRUSH IT, GRIND IT INTO THE SEA."

Along with hundreds of other LST's, each indentical except for numerical designation on bow and stern, we remain anchored off Manila, waiting, waiting for what may be final orders, absolutely final. We mark time by reviewing the number of American casualties on Okinawa—more than 12,500 killed, 36,000 wounded. The 110,000 Japanese don't count.

"Child's play compared with an amphibious invasion of Japan. The numbers will run ten, twenty times that."

"At least we won't have to worry about any wounded. If one kamikaze hits us, it's 142 *lives*. Period."

"Yeah, all scattered by the Divine Wind."

"What a day for the birds and fish."

But August 6 our itinerary is interrupted as if by accident: the dropping of two bombs.

A week after Japan's formal surrender, we're on our way, steering a straight course now to Yokohama. For the first time in almost half a year there's no censorship. I can tell my parents where we've been and what we've done, where we are and what we're doing, and I can seal the envelope. However, since I don't want to worry them by mentioning our cargo, the narrative must seem senseless.

"WHY ARE YOU GOING TO JAPAN *NOW?* ARE YOU CARRYING TROOPS? IF SO, WILL YOU BE BRINGING OTHERS HOME?"

In Yokohama small hungry-looking Japanese prisoners under heavy guard scurry around our tank deck, carrying loads that required trucks in Mobile. When the last crate is removed we are given liberty.

"Jap clap is the worst," the deck officer warns us as we go down the gangplank. "Your cock rots, drops off."

PROTECT IT, PROTECT IT.

There is hardly anything left of the city — chimneys and safes protruding from rubble, families clustered in shacks built from debris. It is impossible to imagine what Hiroshima and Nagasaki must look like. Have coke and beer stands been built there so quickly too? Are cafés there, as here, blasting American music into the street? Are brothers selling their sisters for a pack of cigarettes or a candy bar?

Mother writes, "It must be wonderful to be in Japan. You should be able to pick up prints, lacquered bowls, embroidered silk — all dirt cheap."

But we are already on our way back to Manila. With an empty tank deck, the ship rides higher than before, rolls more. I am sick for the first time since Florida.

In Manila we wait again for orders, wondering if we'll carry more ammunition to Japan, other supplies, troops — or if, finally, we'll be sent home. After weeks, all hands are called on deck. The captain waits for us to assemble. He is a rare sight. Except when we are going into port, he spends his time in officers' quarters, eating special food and drinking medicinal brandy intended for emergencies. Unlike the rest of us, during the past half year he has gained weight and lost color. I wonder if Father has changed as much.

"Men, I have disappointing news—" He pauses, we laugh, searching his face for the hint of a smile. The pale pudgy mask is expressionless, and yet we are sure that he means this introduction as some kind of drunken humor; we must be going home. "I know all of you are looking forward to returning to the States—" Another pause. More laughter, now slightly hesitant, slightly nervous. "However, there are still jobs to be done here. We've received orders to lift anchor at 1300 and proceed to Cagayan de Oro. A small town on the north coast of Mindanao. There, about four thousand natives fled the Japanese when they invaded the Philippines. They must be returned to Davao on the south coast. It took them months to get through miles of jungle and mountains. I estimate we can make the trip in about four days, eight for a round trip. If we can carry 250 passengers, we should be able to complete the job in four or five months." Once more the captain pauses. Now there are curses, moans, groans. "I don't want to hear any bitching. I'm older than you. I'm married. I have children. I want to return home too. And one other thing should go without saying: Our passengers are to be treated as such—with respect. They are our allies. They've been through a lot of misery. Our job is to get them home as comfortably as possible. There's to be no fraternization. That's an order—and it comes from Washington. Anyone who disobeys will be court-martialed."

They are waiting—hundreds of families on hemp mats, each with their few possessions beside them bundled in muted native fabrics. We drop our stern anchor. The winch spins as our blunt bow ploughs into the beach. The natives roll their mats and press forward, carrying their infants and bundles, as hundreds more come out from the shade behind a line of palm trees, to take their places, to wait there for eight days, until we return.

With a great crunching of gears and sand, our bow doors open and the ramp is dropped, exposing our empty tank deck. Bow lines are secured to trees. An officer with a megaphone shouts for a *senor* whose name appears on a sheaf of orders. A short dark man in a white shirt, khaki pants, and sandals steps forward and shakes hands. The officer speaks slowly, unsure of the man's grasp of English and of his role in this primitive-looking community.

"Please tell your people—your citizens—to stay back. No one will board until morning. Everyone's name will have to be checked." He points to a list. "Your people will be housed here." He turns and nods toward the tank deck. "We have provided portable toilets and wash buckets. We will feed your people. Otherwise, there will be no contact with the crew. The rest of the ship will be restricted, closed off. Tell them."

The man borrows the megaphone, repeats everything—in perfect English, for us; then in Spanish.

The next morning they file aboard. Family after family spread mats on the steel deck. It seems impossible that there is room for another person. Yet they still come, shifting positions until none of the deck shows.

Bow lines are taken in. The ramp lifts. The doors shut. The stern winch grinds noisily as it drags us off the beach. Natives on shore wave goodbye to us on deck. They can no longer see their compatriots, sealed below.

Even with our human cargo, the ship continues to ride high and roll constantly. Seasickness spreads through the tank deck like an epidemic. Everyone is vomiting. The vents don't supply enough fresh air. We open all the hatches. We lower swabs, pails of water, bottles of Dramamine. But still the retching continues. At noon, when we lower buckets of rice and tea, hardly anyone eats. By then the tank deck emits a steaming stench of vomit, perspiration, and excrement.

In Davao we scrub the tank deck, install two more portable toilets, take on supplies, including more Dramamine.

"I CAN'T EVEN FIND CAGAYAN ON THE MAP. I DON'T UNDERSTAND WHAT YOU'RE DOING THERE. IF THOSE FILIPINOS GOT ACROSS THE ISLAND ON FOOT, WHY CAN'T THEY RETURN THE SAME WAY? WHY DO YOU HAVE TO BABY THEM?"

Father is not alone in his feelings. To most of our crew, the "Gooks" are no longer our allies. They are vomiting, stinking enemies, detaining our return home now as the "Japs" did earlier. "Yeah, why did they run away from the Japs in the first place? Why didn't they stay and fight?"

I say nothing, I know nothing, but for the first time since joining the navy, perhaps for the first time in my life, I feel I am doing something useful.

The typhoon season begins. We are pounded by waves thirty, forty, sometimes fifty feet high, as high as our superstructure, and by winds of close to a hundred knots an hour. We no longer roll, we lurch, in corkscrew patterns, from side to side and up and down. As our bow smashes into wave after wave, the ship shudders, the steel squeaks and squeals as if in pain. The crew is as frightened and sick as our passengers, but at least we have air; they are confined to that reeking humid deck below us, with hatches sealed now against the driving rain.

"*I'll Be Home For Christmas* is always being played," Mother writes now, on new stationery from a new home, just moved into—a Fifth Avenue apartment house of her brother's. "I can't stand that song. I hate it. A few nights ago I threw a slipper at the radio. Your father thought I was going crazy. He started yelling at me. But it *is* bad luck, your being over there when everyone else is returning. You've been very philosophical and uncomplaining. We're proud of you."

The wind weakens, the sea calms, the ship steadies, Christmas comes and goes, and still the natives crowd the beach. It is March before we return the last of them to Davao. Then, having completed this circular detour within the larger circular voyage, we begin the long trip home.

"WE'VE RENTED A PLACE ON LONG ISLAND FOR THE SUMMER. YOU'RE ENTITLED TO A REST."

As we move slowly eastward from island to island, I *am* resting, as I have been during most of the past two years in the navy, and the year before that at college, and the years before that at home. I don't want more rest. I don't want more plans made for me. I want only to escape passivity, a passivity perhaps most intense during the past two years, but always there, during my entire life.

Like most of my shipmates, I want now to do something. Each of them talks abouts his particular dream—buying a gas station or small business, fixing up a farm or ranch—but mine is vague and negative.

After all these years I want only *not* to spend a summer with my parents. I want to see them. I want to see that they're well. But I don't want to stand a long watch over their well-being or have them continue to stand one over mine.

When we reach Pearl Harbor, I write to college, asking to be enrolled for the summer term and requesting a catalogue. Rather than a rest, that is what I feel entitled to: a catalogue, full of possibilities and of decision to be made—*by me.*

"WHAT'S THE HURRY? COLLEGE WON'T RUN AWAY. IT'LL BE THERE IN THE FALL. TAKE IT EASY, YOU'LL LAST LONGER."

Father sounds the same, but he doesn't look the same. The acid in his stomach has etched his face. There are deep lines across his forehead, under his eyes, and down from the corners of his nose past his mouth. The thin ring of close-cropped hair running around his head is now gray-white, hardly distinguishable from his skull.

Mother is less changed. There are only a few new, almost imperceptible wrinkles and gray hairs, subtle signs of worry and concern. Over and over, in one way or another, she tells me, "We want to look at you. We haven't seen you in two years. You mustn't rush off."

When she has her family for dinner, two nights after my return, once again she says approximately this.

Her brother looks annoyed. "He's wasted two years. Why shouldn't he make up for lost time? He ought to finish college and go out into the world. What do you think, Pop?"

"Is there anyplace else to go?" Grandpa replies.

As we all laugh, I feel an easing of pressure, similar to that aboard ship when jokes were made about our load of ammunition. Like then, I feel that once the words are spoken the disaster can't occur: an entire summer of being treated as a returning veteran—not an explosion but an impossibly long, slow-burning, nerve-racking fuse. However, I don't feel that the time in the navy was wasted or lost, and I don't feel the need to explain this to the family.

After dinner, my uncle says, "We could use a fourth for bridge. Do you play?"

"A little."

"Then you be my partner."

I am both flattered and nervous. This is the first time I have been invited to join them. Until now I have only stood behind my father, watching and, as he believes, bringing him luck. I look at him, wondering if he would prefer me to be his partner but knowing that my uncle is the only one who can carry me.

"Is half a cent all right?" my uncle asks. "I'll take his game, if we lose."

Father and Grandfather accept the stakes, light cigars, and the cards are dealt. The bidding is more refined, the conventions more complicated than at college or in the navy, where some still played auction bridge rather than contract. I underbid twice. I miss an easy double. I fail to make a setting lead. But still, because my uncle takes several bids in his hand which should properly have been played by me, we win four out of five rubbers, about ten dollars for each of us.

Grandpa pays me. "You've got card-sense," he says, beaming. "You played well. Just learn the conventions." Father pays my uncle. Everyone leaves.

"YOU'VE GOT NO RIGHT TO PLAY AT THOSE STAKES."

"I had nothing to lose."

"YOU DON'T NEED YOUR UNCLE'S CHARITY. WHAT YOU NEED IS MORE EXPERIENCE."

"That's what I was trying to get."

"DON'T BE FRESH. I'M STILL YOUR FATHER." He grabs his stomach, reaches into his pocket for antacid tablets, rips two from a plastic strip.

Mother rushes to him with a glass of water. "You mustn't aggravate your father," she says to me as he washes down the tablets. "I've never understood why men end up arguing when they play cards."

"MEN! MEN PLAY CARDS WITH THEIR OWN MONEY."

"Ohhh," Mother sighs, turning to me again, "it was nicer earlier in the evening, when my brother was urging you to join him."

"He didn't say that. He was talking about going out into the world."

"I know my brother. The world is *his* world."

"YOUR MOTHER'S RIGHT."

I follow them into their bedroom to say good night. Father is already placing his belongings on the bureau top—everything I remember, plus several of those plastically-sealed strips of medicine. "YOU DON'T KNOW WHAT I'VE BEEN GOING THROUGH. CHILDREN NEVER KNOW." He holds his stomach, sighs more deeply and painfully than Mother had. "MY BROTHER'S NO USE AT ALL. I'M THINKING OF SELLING THE BUSINESS. UNLESS...UNLESS..."

I shake my head, understanding what the business means to him but also understanding that, despite my name being on the door, I can't enter.

"ANYWAY, IF YOU'RE IN SUCH A HURRY TO RETURN TO COLLEGE, MAYBE YOU SHOULD. NOW. BEFORE YOU CHANGE YOUR MIND. THERE WAS A TIME..."

The unfinished sentence hangs heavy in my mind. I know the time he is speaking of: when I liked his business more and liked him more. I kiss him. I kiss Mother. I go to my room. I lie awake for a long time, thinking that I have not really said goodnight but good-by.

The next morning, long after Father has gone to work, a messenger arrives with a package for me from a book store. It is *Culbertson on Contract,* with my uncle's card enclosed and on it the single word "Compliments," scribbled by his secretary.

At college there is little time for bridge. I have too full a schedule of courses in literature and philosophy, and read for ten or twelve hours a day. Everything from Plato to Proust speaks to me. That words can last so long, sometimes thousands of years, seems a miracle in itself; that they remain alive is more miraculous still. I wonder if I have ever had a thought, ever even heard one expressed directly to me, that could live as long. Reading masterpieces, I feel as insignificant as I did at home or while standing watch in the navy, confronted by sea and sky. And yet my insignificance now is not so overwhelming—it has a human scale. Compared with Plato or Proust, I am still a child, but at last I see the possibility of growing up. I feel as if I am being given a second chance. I feel new.

Soon after the start of the fall semester, during one of our weekly telephone conversations, Mother mentions the name of a distant cousin. "She entered college while you were overseas. She was away

during the summer. I'd almost forgotten about her. Ran into her
mother this week and said you'd look her up. She's from the poor side
of my family, and I wouldn't want them to think—well, you know."

"DON'T NEGLECT YOUR STUDIES FOR HER. HOW'RE
THEY? ARE YOU TAKING ECONOMICS THIS TERM?"

"There's economic theory in some of my philosophy courses."

"THEORY'S NOT GOING TO HELP YOU READ A BALANCE
SHEET. I WISH I'D HAD YOUR OPPORTUNITIES. NOW THAT
I'M SELLING THE BUSINESS, I HAVE TO PAY MORE ATTEN-
TION TO INVESTMENTS. SOME COMPANIES' ANNUAL
REPORTS ARE GREEK TO ME. AND I DON'T MEAN GREEK
PHILOSOPHY. I'M DEPENDING ON YOU."

"Have you looked up your cousin?" Mother asks week after week.

"I have a lot of reading...several term papers..."

"You have to eat. Take her to dinner. I'll treat."

"It's not a matter of money."

"What then?"

"Time."

But that's not it either. By now the books are read, the papers
written. I want to call my cousin but feel trapped between Mother's
will to honor a promise made casually by her for me and my own will
to assert independence. Father comes to the rescue:

"FOR GOD'S SAKE MAKE THE CALL AND BE DONE WITH
IT. IT'S ONE NIGHT IN YOUR LIFE. I'VE HEARD ENOUGH OF
THIS NONSENSE. YOU'RE BOTH MAKING ME SICK."

My position is strong. Now I can call, knowing that I am protecting
not only Mother's honor but Father's health. And beyond these noble
gratifications, at the other end of the line, there'll be this waif I've
never met, the beneficiary of Mother's generosity, Father's, and my
own.

Almost as soon as I call for her at the dormitory, I know that she will
be more than one night in my life. She is stunning as she comes down
the stair, moving lightly and gracefully, her brown shoulder-length
hair bouncing on her blazer, her small well-shaped breasts bouncing
too beneath a white turtleneck sweater. Even when she arrives at the

desk to sign out, she seems still to be moving, bouncing. Her face opens in a broad smile. As we shake hands, she says only "Cousin," making it sound as if spoken in a play by Shakespeare.

Cousin!—the word and the idea behind it are there throughout dinner. The word, so innocuous. The idea—that our maternal grand-fathers (hers dead, mine ageing quickly and noticeably) were brothers, that we share the same blood—not so innocuous. Rather, titilating, romantic, potentially incestuous.

"Do you consider yourself engaged?" I ask, noticing that she wears a fraternity pin.

"Temporarily." She smiles seductively. "Dating gets to be tiresome and time-consuming. This way we both know we have dates for the big events—house parties, dances, football games—we don't have to think about that. It takes so long to get to know anyone, and it's usually not worth the trouble."

"Would he mind your going out with me?"

"No, I told him I had a date with a cousin. That was enough. *I* minded a little. My mother said you'd call. Months ago. Later she said you probably wouldn't, that your branch of the family thinks it's better than mine."

"Richer?"

"Yes, but she would never say that. She believes talking about money is profane, and yet that's her one prayer. That's why I'm here. She wants me to find a rich man and marry him."

"You seem to be on your way," I say, looking hard at the fraternity pin, a gold cluster of three Greek letters decorated with seed pearls.

"Oh, I suppose he'd marry me. The question has never come up."

"He must be blind. Or mute. Anyway, at least you won't have to waste time getting to know me, there won't be that trouble—our genes are old friends."

The theme continues until the end of the evening when, with several other couples, we stand in the shadow of her dormitory, saying good-night.

"Do you think it's all right for cousins to kiss?" I ask.

There's that seductive smile again—the flash of teeth now in the simi-darkness—as she raises her head. The kiss—one only—is long and warm. I feel the response of her moist mouth, the supple strength

of her slim small-boned body. For a moment we share a tugging
genetic energy.

With a slight pain in my groin, I carry the memory of all this back
with me to an empty bed.

At first there are dates—little events squeezed in between "the big
events" and the weekends still reserved for the fellow to whom she is
pinned—but, as Christmas vacation approaches, I am seeing her
almost every day, not just for an occasional dinner or movie but for
coffee between classes, snacks after classes, and the classes themselves.
She is enrolled in the Agriculture School, a tuition-free State College,
where she takes pomology, forestry, and other courses in which she
has little interest but which may, as her mother suggests, lead to a
career in landscaping, if not more directly to a suburban estate of her
own, lush with orchards and gardens. I begin to take her to classes of
mine that fall within her free hours, particularly one on Joyce and
Woolf given by a brilliant visiting professor from Scotland. For my
cousin, a course like this is a new experience, one which accrues to my
benefit. Not only does the lecturer's intelligence somehow rub off on
me but also the genius of the authors he is discussing. Having introduced her to them, I seem almost responsible for their creations. My
cousin and I are already talking about taking the same lecturer's spring
course on Yeats and Eliot.

Until now, her interests have existed mainly outside of class—in a
very busy social life and in an activity about which I know nothing, the
Dance Club. She introduces me now to that world of dance, much of it
done to radically modern music, as unfamiliar to me as the angular,
sometimes tortured movements it provokes. The instructor, a former
student of Martha Graham, is a powerful, tireless woman in her mid-
forties who makes enormous demands on the twenty or so girls and
half a dozen boys in the group. "Dance is not a recreation," she says.
"It is a life. You must live Dance, eat Dance, sleep Dance." I concentrate on my cousin, watching her strain to express, in a single gesture
or contortion, emotions that would require pages of Virginia Woolf's
prose.

Afterward, flushed and tired and happy, she says, "I love dancing,
but I would never want to be a dancer."

I mention ballets and musical comedies I would like to take her to over the holidays.

"I guess I should return this," she says, smiling as she touches the fraternity pin on the heavy sweater she has put on over her leotard.

"YOU'RE SPENDING AN AWFUL LOT OF TIME WITH THAT COUSIN OF YOURS."

"Yes, we hardly see you. I'm beginning to wish I hadn't asked you to look her up."

"I'm glad you did. I love her."

"LOVE! WHAT DO YOU KNOW ABOUT LOVE? FIRST IT WAS THAT GIRL FROM BALTIMORE WHO JILTED YOU. AND NOW THIS—THIS *COUSIN* YOUR MOTHER DUG UP. AND THERE'LL BE PLENTY MORE. THEY'RE LIKE TAXIS—YOU MISS ONE AND ANOTHER COMES ALONG."

"It's not like that. I want to see her all the time. I want to marry her."

"YOU WHAT? HAVE YOU THOUGHT ABOUT HOW YOU'LL LIVE? YOU HAVEN'T EVEN GRADUATED."

Father reaches for the antacid. Mother gets the water. They both look pale.

"I've been taking eighteen hours a term. With credit for military service, I'll graduate this spring."

"THAT AND A NICKEL WILL GET YOU A RIDE ON THE SUBWAY. IF YOU LIKE THIS GIRL SO MUCH, WHY HAVEN'T YOU BROUGHT HER AROUND?"

This is a question I can't answer honestly without hurting Father. I watch him holding his stomach, waiting.

"WELL?"

"I've been busy."

"TOO BUSY TO INTRODUCE HER TO YOUR PARENTS? THE GIRL YOU WANT TO MARRY! I WANT TO MEET HER." He turns to Mother. "*YOU* KNOW HER. WHAT'S SHE LIKE? WHY IS HE ASHAMED OF HER?"

"I haven't seen her in years. She was pretty. Of course she didn't have the advantages—God knows how she got to college."

"HOW DID SHE GET THERE?"

"She's in the Ag School. It's free," I reply.

"WHAT DOES SHE WANT TO BE, A FARMER?"

Mother paces. "There's no point in getting upset," she says. "It's not good for you. It's not good for any of us. You're right. We should meet her. We should see for ourselves."

Later, Mother goes over her date book with me. New Year's Eve is the only remaining night of my vacation when we can all get together.

"That'll work out. We're going on to my brother's, and you two can go to your parties. The four of us will just have a quiet dinner."

"Promise?" I ask, smiling nervously.

"I'll do my best. Your father's angry at me too."

Father pulls a thin platinum watch from the vest pocket of his tuxedo and looks at it intently. "WHERE IS SHE?"

"I invited her for between seven and seven-thirty."

"THAT'S EXACTLY WHAT IT IS. SEVEN FIFTEEN. I DON'T KNOW ABOUT YOU TWO, BUT I'M GOING TO HAVE SOME CHAMPAGNE." He lifts the bottle out of the bucket and begins to remove the wire from the cork.

"Why don't you wait, dear? You know it's not good for you anyway."

"I KNOW WHAT'S GOOD FOR ME. I'M ENTITLED TO SOME PLEASURE. I'M NOT GOING TO GET IT FROM EITHER OF YOU."

"Please," Mother says, walking across the room in her shimmering silver and white evening gown accented by a diamond necklace and bracelet. "Please."

She kisses him on the cheek. For a split second, when their heads come together, they make an elegant black and white compositon, as if posing for the advertisement of some mature luxury—a Napoleon brandy, a vintage Rolls, a mellow Steinway. I feel raw and sloppy in my gray flannel suit.

The instant passes. Their heads part. The compostion crumbles.

"ALL RIGHT. THEN I'LL HAVE A LITTLE OF THIS." He pours a shot glass of scotch and gulps it down.

"That's worse."

"STOP TELLING ME WHAT TO DO." He pours another. "I'M ALLOWED TO ENJOY NEW YEAR'S EVE. JUST LIKE ANYBODY ELSE."

The doorbell rings. As if by conditioned reflex, the angry expression on Father's face vanishes. He beams as he is introduced.

"I'VE HEARD SO MANY NICE THINGS ABOUT YOU."

"While I hang her plain navy-blue coat in the hall closet, I have the feeling that he has already priced it and is now pricing her blazer, silk blouse (maybe rayon), pleated gray jersey skirt, nylon stockings, blue pumps. His eyes linger longest there, at the shoes, probably not only pricing them but determining their size and source. And yet, as he examines her, he continues to smile benevolently. I'm sure Mother has asked him to "behave."

"Would you like to wash up, dear?" Mother asks, leading her to the guest bathroom.

As soon as they are gone Father drinks the second scotch.

"WHAT DO YOU THINK OF THAT OUTFIT?"

"Except for the high heels, it's about what she always wears."

"THAT'S WHAT I MEAN. SHE HAS NO SENSE OF AN OCCA-SION."

"We're going to a party in the Village. I'm probably overdressed."

"OVERDRESSED! YOU'RE NOT MUCH MORE PRESENTA-BLE THAN SHE IS. DON'T YOU KNOW YOUR MOTHER AND I WOULD'VE LIKED IT IF YOU'D BEEN ABLE TO STOP BY FOR A NIGHTCAP AT YOUR UNCLE'S."

While he is speaking, Mother returns to the living room. "You promised," she says, putting a finger to her lips just a moment before my cousin reapppears.

"WELL! TIME FOR THE PIPER-HEIDSIECK." Father pours and serves the champagne, lifts his glass, smiles. "AND ONLY A FEW HOURS EARLY TO WISH YOU ALL A HAPPY NEW YEAR." Still smiling, he faces my cousin. "TELL ME ABOUT YOURSELF," he says almost quietly. And the inquisition begins.

"I'M DYING. WHAT'D I DO TO DESERVE THIS?"

"You'll be all right."

"I KNOW WHEN I'M DYING."

Father lies in bed holding his stomach. The deep lines in his face go to the skull. On the night table there's an unfinished bowl of crushed graham crackers and milk. The newspaper is on the floor, unread. Mother sits by the phone, waiting for the doctor to return her call.

"Well, here's the prodigal," she says as I enter their room. "When did you get in?"

"After six."

"It must have been long after. I was up then, getting medicine for your father. I was worried about you. And I'm surprised my cousin lets her daughter stay out all night." Mother speaks softly, afraid of disturbing Father.

"She *is* twenty," I whisper, following her example, but now Father comes back to life.

"SHE DOESN'T ACT IT. SHE DOESN'T DRESS LIKE A GIRL OF TWENTY. SHE DOESN'T HAVE THE TABLE MANNERS OF A GIRL OF TWENTY. DID YOU NOTICE SHE USED THE SALAD FORK FOR THE BEEF?" I shake my head. "WELL, I DID. AND YOUR MOTHER DID.... TELL HIM WHAT YOU TOLD ME.... THIS IS YOUR MOTHER SPEAKING ABOUT A MEMBER OF HER OWN FAMILY."

"I said I didn't think she had the kind of background that would appeal to you—in any lasting way, I mean. She's cute and all that, but she lacks breeding."

"BACKGROUND! I DON'T NOTICE MUCH FOREGROUND EITHER. WHAT YOUR MOTHER AND I WANT IS FOR YOU TO STOP SEEING HER."

"I can't do that."

"WHAT DO YOU MEAN, YOU CAN'T? YOU WON'T?"

"I've told you, I love her, I want to marry her."

"OVER MY DEAD BODY."

We spend almost all our time together now—every hour except when we have separate classes; every meal except breakfast; every night except from twelve (one on Saturdays), when she must be back at her dormitory, until mid-morning coffee. Most days she comes to my room in the late afternoon. We do our homework. We make love. We have dinner. We read. We listen to music. Often we make love again. And then there's the walk to her dormitory.

"I hate this," she says one night while we are dressing to return. "We should be able to stay here in bed. We've never had a relaxed night."

I speak to a teacher and his wife who live off-campus and arrange for my cousin to sign out to their house over weekends. "We'll be together more than most married couples."

"Yes. And with none of the risks of marriage."

"I can't think of that."

"I can't think of anything else. I hate to think about graduation."

"I may stay on for a year. There are lots of possibilities."

"I know—you told me about your father and those taxis always coming along."

"I didn't mean it that way."

She knows I didn't, but her mother has said so often that she's wasting her time with me, that I'm not serious, that my parents would never approve, that she should never have returned that pin....

Like me, on Sundays she calls home. I listen to her end of the conversation while she paces in a semi-circle as if leashed to the phone. "Fine.... Yes, I'm sure.... It must be a bad connection.... Yes.... Fairly frequently.... Oh, more than that.... No.... No.... I know what I'm doing.... I'm not your baby.... I remember.... Yes, in the spring.... Hugs and kisses.... Goodbye." She hangs up. "Same conversation. How often have I been seeing you? Are we engaged? When are *they* going to see you? Mother's proud. She can't get over my having been to your home and your not having been to ours. She wants to even the score. I told her again that you'd come in the spring."

"Doesn't your father say anything?"

"Not much when she's around. Besides, the calls are expensive. They don't mention that, but it's understood."

I wish that my calls were as short. Since the beginning of the year Father's ulcers have bothered him more and more. Like my cousin's father, though for different reasons, he is on the phone only briefly now—just long enough to suggest a causal relationship between the pain in his stomach and what he calls my RECENT BEHAVIOR and NEW INSENSITIVE ATTITUDE. Then Mother brings me up-to-date on symptoms, medical procedures, dietary changes—his black tarry stool, indicative of internal bleeding; the awful bismuth compound he must swallow before x-rays; the duodenal perforations beginning to show on the plates; the belladonna which leaves his mouth parched— all of this within the context of shrilly spoken prayers that I will do nothing to further aggravate Father's condition.

Guilt begins to settle heavily in my stomach. I feel tension there. "Maybe ulcers are catching," I say jokingly to my cousin.

"You should talk to a doctor," she replies with complete seriousness. "I have a hunch your father's not as sick as they say."

We walk to the clinic. I reconstruct Father's case history, repeat Mother's recent descriptions. The doctor assures me that, based on what I've told him, Father's ulcers are peptic, not gastric; painful, not fatal. "And remember," he finishes, "you didn't cause them." I am relieved. My cousin is relieved.

"Sensitive doctor," she says as we leave the clinic.

"Sensitive cousin," I reply, taking her hand. "Sensitive, intuitive, intelligent, beautiful cousin."

We swing our clasped hands all the way to my room. The possibility of marriage seems more real.

It seems more real still, a few weeks later, when Mother tells me about an operation Father is going to have: "It's called a vagotomy. They cut the nerves that stimulate the flow of acid to the stomach. If all goes well, he should be able to eat and drink what he likes.... He'll tell you himself."

"YOUR MOTHER'S TOLD YOU AS MUCH AS I CAN. I JUST WANTED TO HEAR YOU WISH ME LUCK."

"I do. I'm sure everything will go smoothly."

"GOOD. ARE YOU STILL SEEING YOUR COUSIN?"

"Sometimes."

"DON'T GET TOO INVOLVED. YOU CAN DO A LOT BETTER. WHEN I GET OUT OF THE HOSPITAL, IF I'M FEELING THE WAY I USED TO, I'LL HELP YOU LOOK AROUND." He laughs emphatically so Mother and I will understand he's only kidding.

Once again my cousin and I go to the clinic. This time I ask about the vagotomy. The doctor explains the procedure in much more detail than Mother has. "As to risk, there's some—always a chance of infection, embolism, complications—but as operations go, this one's comparatively routine."

When we reach the front desk in the waiting room, I ask my cousin, "How about getting blood tests?"

She looks surprised, blushes, leads me to a couch.

"That's the strangest proposal I've ever had. And the only one."

We laugh.

"I'm too tired."

"Cards are relaxing. You look tense. A few rubbers may be just what you need."

Mother listens, smiling. "You won't go to sleep without saying goodnight, will you? Your father and I want to hear all about school."

There's no chance of my going to sleep. Not as Mother means *sleep.* I sleep standing, stumbling about my room, unpacking, undressing, putting on pajamas, opening windows, lowering blinds, smoking, always smoking. I turn the radio on, turn it off; open a book, shut it; pace; wait.

It's almost midnight before they leave. Father turns the double-lock, hooks the chain, and is loosening his tie as I join him.

"THAT UNCLE OF YOURS IS ONE SMART GUY. SAYS HE CAN TURN THE FIVE MILLION INTO FIFTY. I BELIEVE HIM. TOO BAD YOU DIDN'T STAY. HE SEEMED READY TO TALK ABOUT YOUR FUTURE—A JOB. HAVE YOU THOUGHT ABOUT THAT?"

"Not much. I like the courses I've been taking. I'm thinking of going on, getting a Master's."

"BELIEVE ME, YOU'LL LEARN A HELLUVA LOT MORE FROM YOUR UNCLE. WHO'S BEEN PUTTING THESE IDEAS IN YOUR HEAD? YOUR COUSIN?"

Mother, who has been tidying up the living room, seeming to pay no attention to our conversation, comes toward us now, looking worried.

"No, but I want to talk to you about her." My voice trembles. "I've been wanting to tell you—we're married."

Father's face becomes rigid, expressionless, gray. His body stiffens, arms dropped straight against his thighs. He clenches his fists as if simultaneously grabbing some invisible support and preparing to hit me. I don't know whether to step forward to catch him or backward to defend myself. I hesitate. He hesitates. Mother hesitates. Time itself hesitates, misses a beat. We are caught, frozen in this paralyzed moment which may decide the future of our lives.

His mouth opens. "YOU'RE NOT MY SON." The words explode as he rushes past me. "YOU'RE NO LONGER MY SON."

The bedroom door slams shut with the shattering finality of a last-act curtain. But there's this difference: I'm still in the play. And he knows his part. And I'm not sure of mine.

For another long moment, Mother remains motionless, staring, not seeming to recognize me. Only her expression moves—from terror to pity to accusation. "I told you," she says, before hurrying down the hall.

I hear them for hours—Father shouting, Mother pleading and crying. My bed rocks. I am back in the navy, riding out a typhoon, feeling the howling lash of Father's words, the salt spray of Mother's tears. And still, during this mid-watch, the storm rages; not until past four does it exhaust itself and become calm.

After ten the next morning their bedroom door is still closed. In front of it, on the floor, are some large chips of paint. Otherwise there are no reminders of the previous night. The apartment is quiet.

Not that I need reminders. I know I am fatherless. I wonder if I am allowed to have breakfast here or if I should go to one of the lunchonettes on Madison Avenue. I start toward the kitchen.

"I WANT TO SPEAK TO YOU."

Though Mother is resting, Father is in the living room. He has shaved, had breakfast, and read the paper which lies piled in neatly refolded sections, on the floor beside his chair. He sits, tapping his foot, waiting for me.

"ARE YOU IN TROUBLE? IS SHE?" I must look puzzled. "I MEAN, DID YOU WANT TO GET MARRIED, OR DID YOU THINK YOU HAD TO?"

"We wanted to."

Father watches me closely. "ARE YOU SURE? IF YOU NEED A DOCTOR, I'LL PAY. THEN WE CAN SEE ABOUT AN ANNULMENT. THESE THINGS CAN BE HANDLED."

"No. She's not pregnant. We're happy. I'm only sorry I upset you and Mother so much."

"THAT WAS LAST NIGHT. YOUR MOTHER'S RIGHT: WHAT'S DONE IS DONE. WE DON'T BREAK UP A FAMILY OVER A MARRIAGE. MAYBE THAT HAPPENS IN SOME OF YOUR BOOKS, BUT NOT IN THIS HOUSE. WHAT WE'VE GOT

TO THINK ABOUT NOW IS THE FUTURE. YOU'RE MARRIED.
YOU'RE ALMOST TWENTY-TWO. YOU SHOULD BE ABLE TO
SUPPORT YOURSELF."

"I still have a year of college coming on the G.I. Bill."

"AND THEN WHAT? ANOTHER DEGREE AND YOU'LL
HAVE A FEVER." He laughs scornfully and stamps his foot as if the
idea hurts him and must be crushed. "TALK TO YOUR UNCLE. IF
YOU PLAY YOUR CARDS RIGHT, YOU'LL OWN ALL THE
BOOKS YOU CAN EVER READ. AND NOW, WHAT ABOUT
YOUR BRIDE? HAVE YOU SPOKEN TO HER?"

"I told her I'd call. It was too late last night."

"YOU *SHOULD* CALL. TELL HER TO BRING HER PARENTS
OVER."

"... Yes, everything's all right," I say on the phone as Father takes
two bottles of champagne from the liquor closet. "Yes, *really.*" I hang
up. "They'll be here in half an hour."

"THAT'S QUICK. I'LL BET THEY WERE PLENTY WORRIED."

He goes into the bedroom to get his smoking jacket, in which he is
no longer allowed to smoke. Mother asks the cook to chill the champagne and fix a tray of canapés, then changes from her bathrobe into a
dressing gown. I put on a sportsjacket. We wait—Father tapping his
foot and looking frequently at his watch, Mother fussing with sprigs
of parsley.

"IT'S ALMOST AN HOUR."

"Forty minutes, dear."

"I KNOW WHAT TIME IT IS. AND I KNOW WHOSE FAMILY
IT IS. YOU DEAL WITH THEM."

Finally they arrive, my cousin in a rather matronly tailored silk suit
I've never seen before, her mother in a beaded dress that might be
suitable for an afternoon wedding, her father in a shiny navy-blue suit.
They look like they have come to a much more formal event than the
one my parents and I are attending. Perhaps their outfits are more
honest than ours—my mother-in-law is particularly involved with
formalities:

"... We're sorry the children didn't do things in the proper way. It's
not too late for a wedding." We, the children, shake our heads. "Well,
the least we can do is send out announcements. We owe that to our
family and friends."

"Yes," Mother says, "we don't want to hurt anyone. Everyone should be permitted to share our joy." Her tone is icy and sarcastic as with me last night.

My mother-in-law looks surprised and frightened. She rushes on: "And of course we'll want to help them furnish an apartment."

"That's easy. It's finding one that's hard. I'll speak to my brother. There may even be one in this building."

My cousin and I exchange one quick look of horror, but say nothing. Her mother is speaking again:

"Oh, yes, I haven't seen him in years—he was such a bright young man—do give him my love."

She waits for Mother's acknowledgement. There is none.

"THEY DON'T COME ANY SMARTER. EVERYTHING HE TOUCHES TURNS TO GOLD. BUT I'LL LET YOU IN ON A SECRET—I WOULDN'T EXCHANGE WHAT I'VE GOT HERE FOR ALL HIS MONEY." His hand gestures toward Mother and me, lingering in my direction. "GOOD HE DOESN'T HAVE A SON. OURS MAY GO WITH HIM."

"Is that what you want?" my father-in-law asks me.

"I'm not sure."

"Then take your time. I married young. When my father died. I rushed into his business. I'm still there."

"YOU'RE NOT COMPARING *THAT* WITH REAL ESTATE! ANYWAY, UNTIL THE KIDS FIND A PLACE, THEY CAN STAY HERE. NEXT WEEK WE'RE GOING ON A CRUISE."

"Or they can stay with us," my mother-in-law says.

"But you don't have a maid," Mother replies. "Wouldn't their staying here be easier, more comfortable?"

"I thought something was wrong that night," my uncle says, "and I still think your marriage was—well, rather precipitous. You know, there's something to be said for a traditional engagement period and wedding ceremony—the gathering of relatives and friends, the approval of society. One shouldn't be too quick to discard values one hasn't really tested. But you're married. What next?"

"I don't know. I've thought about teaching and writing—some form of scholarship."

"I suppose you can make a living teaching. But barely. As to writing, the odds must be a thousand to one against being successful. Starving helps, but that's a condition not likely to affect you. Not with your parents." He laughs. "Now consider the odds in business. Given your intelligence, education, connections, attractiveness—given *you,* and I've watched you grow up—I'd say the odds are at least ten to one in your favor. It's this simple—" He picks up one of those small pencils and scribbles on a legal pad: *"1/1000 or 10/1."*

"But you're only talking about economic success."

"Is there some other kind? Don't be romantic. In a capitalist society, success is rewarded with money. And when you have that, everything else is possible, including the leisure in which to read and write. You can do those things on the side. Look, I'm not talking about business as a nine-to-five job until retirement. How many hours a day do you think I work? Really work? How long do you think it takes to conceive a deal?" He rushes on, not waiting for the answers to his questions. "That's about how long." He points at the scribbles on his pad, pauses. "I'll tell you something I've never told anyone. When I first went to work for my father I felt guilty about nepotism. There I was, just out of college, being pushed ahead of men who had worked for him for years. But like weddings, there's something to be said for nepotism. There's the built-in insurance of familiarity, loyalty, pride—all sealed in blood. You can't always buy those things from strangers. Don't misunderstand. If you work for me, you'll have to prove your ability. But if you do that, you'll be sitting at this desk someday instead of in some dusty library." He draws a circle around the *10/1*, tears the page from the pad, and hands it to me. "Think it over."

I think it over. And over. And over. While my cousin looks for an apartment, while my parents cruise the Mediterranean, while my uncle waits for an answer—balancing his life, as usual, between business, bridge, and golf—I think it over. Every day, at the same pencil-marked and ink-stained desk I've had since grade school, I write for a few hours and then read the works of poets, philosophers, novelists, playwrights, essayists, historians, biographers, autobiographers, probing their minds, the minds of those they write about, and my own for an understanding of—*compromise.* It is that word, that concept which leads me from one book to another, underlining here, marking there, writing in margins and in my own notebook, until all life seems compromised, claustrophobic, contained—in books, in this bedroom, which has been "mine" since discharge from the navy.

Com-pro-mise—the word tortures me and I torture it, analyze it, syllable by syllable, nuance by nuance, ambiguity by ambiguity, tracing its meaning from mutual promise to settlement by concession and from these to subtle areas of risk and abandonment of principle. I make lists of those who never compromised (Buddha, Socrates, Jesus, Gandhi...) and of those who did (Svevo, Ives, Stevens, Eliot... lesser names surely, but more than large enough for me). I see this second group working in their banks and insurance companies as I imagine me in my uncle's office, living the possibility, however schizoid, of serving Mammon by day, my muse by night. Such an existence appeals more than dying in desireless meditation or, worse, by poison, crucifixion, assassination. To compromise begins to seem mature.

And yet, as I make my decision, even as I finally call my uncle to say I will work for him, my mind is still filled with reservations. Entering business is in some ways like entering the navy. I don't know where I'm going or for how long. I know only that this enlistment, unlike the other, will make my parents happy, happier than anything I've ever done.

I telegraph the news. The next day their reply screams all the way from Capri:

CONGRATULATIONS STOP MADE RIGHT DECISION STOP
MUCH LOVE
MOTHER FATHER

Life is all compromise now as I begin to learn about contracts, leases, building loans, long-term mortgages... a whole new literature, all in fine print, where nothing really lasts beyond a stipulated term (perhaps with a renewal option) and everything is subject to negotiation. However, in business, I am negotiating with others rather than with myself, and that is less painful. Besides, I have an encouraging teacher, more so than any I ever had at college. Again and again my uncle tells me, "No deal makes sense in which there isn't room for compromise. You can't figure everything down to the last penny. You can't always buy at the bottom and sell at the top. Ask high, offer low, then you have room in which to move."

Though he watches details and expects contracts and other legal documents to be tight and specific, his basic style, business and extracurricular, is expressed in rounded numbers like those he writes on his desk pad. Soon after I've joined him he says, "I made a bet on Truman—$500 against $7500."

"I thought you were for Dewey."

"I am, but he's no fifteen-to-one favorite, not in my book. Anyway, don't you see, with this bet, I win either way. And if the odds drop, as I think they will, I can hedge my bet. You've got to learn to measure the odds. They're what's important, no matter where you're playing or what stakes you're playing for. Do you want a piece of my bet? I'll let you have ten percent."

"Okay."

By election day the odds have dropped to ten-to-one.

"We can make $2,500," my uncle says, "but I'm inclined to let the bet ride. That whistle-stop campaign of Truman's is going to bring in a lot more votes than the pollsters think. If you want your $250, I'll hedge your part of the bet."

I hesitate. My uncle has never asked me who I'm for. He has taken it for granted that, like him, I'll vote for Dewey, because "he'll be good for business," and, thus I too will "win either way." That's his intellectual analysis, but my emotional commitment is to Truman. I like him and don't want to abandon him for the sure $250. If I win, I win. If I lose, I lose. For me, there is no winning "either way."

"No, I'll go along with you," I say finally.

"You made the wrong decision. You're just gambling on a long shot. My position is different from yours—economically, I mean. For you $250 is $250."

"$750 is more."

"We'll see," my uncle says, smiling. "Anyway, it's a nice round swing from minus $250 to plus $750. But whatever happens, don't go through life playing long shots, save some money to play the favorites."

After Truman's election, my wife and I are at my parents for dinner. She is wearing a new wrist watch.

"Oh, that's pretty," Mother says, noticing it almost immediately.

"Where'd you get it?"

"Cartier."

"CARTIER! PUT A BEGGAR ON HORSEBACK...."

Father's pained voice trails off. He has, as usual, been sitting in his deep chair, drinking scotch and tapping his foot. Now, for a moment, with an expression of intense hatred, he stares at the watch as if this small gold disc on its leather band symbolizes all waste, a waste of time itself. His eyes shift to me.

"HOW MUCH DID IT COST?"

"$500."

"F*I*V*E H*U*N*D*R*E*D D*O*L*L*A*R*S." In time, in volume, he stretches the amount until seemingly measureable only in light years. "SINCE WHEN HAVE YOU HAD FIVE HUNDRED DOL-LARS TO SPEND ON A WATCH?"

"I used part of what I won on the election."

"YOU BET ON TRUMAN! THE NEXT THING YOU'LL BE TELLING ME IS YOU VOTED FOR HIM." He waits. "WELL, DID YOU?"

"Yes."

He looks wildly around the room. "I DON'T KNOW ABOUT THE REST OF YOU, BUT I NEED ANOTHER DRINK."

Limping slightly, he walks to the bar and pours himself a large scotch. Mother uses the pause to excuse herself and my wife, to whom she wants to show some new dresses.

"DOES YOUR UNCLE KNOW?"

"What?" My wife is over two months pregnant, but I don't think she has yet said anything to my mother or even to her own.

"WHAT DO YOU THINK? THAT YOU VOTED FOR TRUMAN AND BET ON HIM."

"Voting never came up. I took part of *his* bet."

"LOOK, I DON'T CARE HOW MUCH YOU WON, THAT WAS A LOUSY BET. AND SO WAS VOTING FOR TRUMAN. YOU'RE SUPPOSED TO BE LEARNING REAL ESTATE, NOT BOOKMAK-ING. WHAT *ARE* YOU LEARNING?"

I am just starting to tell him when Mother announces dinner. Father gulps the rest of his drink, pushes himself out of the chair, and steadies himself on my shoulder as we walk to the dining room. "YOU UNDERSTAND, DON'T YOU, I DON'T MIND YOUR BUYING

THAT WATCH, IT'S JUST—IT'S THAT THINGS LIKE THAT SHOULD COME LATER. WHEN I WAS YOUR AGE I HAD TO REALLY WORK FOR $500. YOUR UNCLE'S A GENIUS, I KNOW THAT, BUT EVERYTHING COMES TOO EASY TO HIM. YOU OUGHT TO PICK UP HIS GOOD HABITS, NOT THE BAD ONES."

During the meal, with the help of a good Bordeaux, Father's mood remains comparatively calm. He talks about a grand slam he made earlier this evening at his club. "YOUR UNCLE'S GAME IS WITH 'THE EAGLES,' MINE'S WITH 'THE PIGEONS,' BUT ONCE IN A WHILE I GET A HAND I CAN REALLY PLAY." He lists several stocks he has ordered from his broker—"TELEPHONE...STANDARD OF JERSEY...IBM...GM"—mentioning each as affectionately as the names of "The Pigeons" with whom he plays bridge every afternoon, and putting a price on each stock always at least an eighth of a point below the previous day's closing. The more he talks, the more I feel how close his values are to those of my uncle and, within this context, how much less efficiently he performs. And finally I realize that these stocks he orders, most of which can't be delivered at his prices anyway, are a fraction of his portfolio; that his real investment, now as in the past, is in Mother's family real estate business; and that as much as for my uncle, I am working for Father.

The image of his Reade Street building, long since sold, suddenly fills my mind. I see its facade. I see my name there and, inside, on cartons, order pads, stationery, the safe, the seal.... I can smell the cardboard and leather.... I can taste the food at the restaurant down the block.... And yet now none of this seems real, hardly as real as the buildings just being planned for our Park Avenue sites. I wonder if Reade Street was real; if the shoe business was real; if, for me, any business but real estate was ever real. I try to remember Father's brother and the rest of the CREW, so different from my uncle's "staff." I ask about this *other* uncle.

"I DON'T SPEAK TO HIM OFTEN. ON HIS BIRTHDAY AND ONCE OR TWICE MORE A YEAR. SINCE HE SETTLED ON THE WEST COAST AND JOINED AA, THAT'S HIS LIFE, THOSE SUPPOSEDLY REFORMED DRUNKS. THEY'RE WHO HE SEES. HE'S MET A WOMAN WHO'S LOADED—WITH MONEY, I MEAN—BUT PROBABLY ANOTHER EX-LUSH. THEY TALK ABOUT GOD, THEIR DRY GOD. NOT JUST ON HOLIDAYS.

ALL THE TIME. I SUPPOSE BROTHER'S IN BETTER SHAPE BUT
HE WAS MORE FUN BEFORE HE GOT RELIGION."

"You don't remember," Mother says. "You've forgotten how sick
he used to make you."

"SICK?" Father looks puzzled. "I'M HEALTHY NOW."

"Cab or bus? Are you tired?" I ask my wife.

"I'm tired all right, but the bus will do fine. Don't put a beggar on
horseback." While we wait for the Fifth Avenue bus, she continues. "I
don't want to go there anymore. Your father's insulting."

"He didn't mean that. He's not angry at you or me or the watch. He
told me he wasn't. He just doesn't understand his own rage at that clot
in his leg."

"His leg! His head, you mean. He's irrational. I feel as if I'm watching an amateur production of *Lear*. Your father's a bore—all he talks
about is money."

"That's about all he has left. He sold his business. I got married. His
brother moved to L.A."

"And your mother?"

"She's more than money but..."

The bus arrives, almost empty. We go to the back where we can look
out both windows at the Christmas displays in the department stores
and Rockefeller Center. The city's wealth, shimmering silver and gold,
spills out onto the sidewalks.

"I wanted to give Father a present tonight. I wanted to tell him he
was going to be a grandfather. Would you tell him? It would make him
so happy, give him something to look forward to."

"I don't want to give him a present. Not now, anyway. Can't you
imagine what those phone calls would be like? From now until the
baby is born. Not only from your parents but mine. Every day for six
months. Of course, you'll be at the office—I'll get them. And afterwards, the visits—they'll be a worse nightmare. Your father will be
stopping by to see the baby, instead of playing that last rubber of
bridge."

"You certainly are the happy expectant parent."

"And you? I hardly told you the news before you were complaining
that we couldn't any longer live in four rooms, that you need that extra
room."

"I do. It's half my life."

"Business being the other half? Where do I fit in?"

"I'm not sure yet that business is the other half. It's interesting, the stakes are high…"

"Well, while you're making up your mind, you find the next apartment, and fix it up, and be sure it's down here. I don't want to be any closer to your family."

We get off at Washington Square, walk the two blocks to our building without saying a word and, as soon as we are in our apartment, I go to the second bedroom and shut the door. There is my old desk and chair (sent down by Mother when she converted my former bedroom to a "den"), a table on which I have spread the books I am presently studying, an old deep leather chair and ottoman where I do my reading, bookcases, floor and desk lamps, a worn Persian rug, wastebasket, several ashtrays, not much else. It is the homeliest, least decorated room in the apartment—the only one on the court, without a view—but I like it best. Here I have been doing the writing "on the side" that my uncle spoke of when he persuaded me that the odds on becoming a successful businessman would be more favorable. He was right about the odds. Evenings and weekends, using the energy left over from business, I've been able to squeeze out two articles and have already received about twenty rejections, each of them pasted inside the closet door—a disappointing collage which whispers, even through the door, *Shoemaker, stick to your last.*

The baby is born—a boy, named for a living painter and not (to Mother's consternation) for Grandpa who has recently died. The apartment is abandoned, including the rejections and a few recent acceptances. I have found a brownstone in the East Forties, a compromise between the Village and uptown where my parents and my wife's live. Besides seeing Father about once a week for dinner, he comes now to the house on Saturday mornings to visit his grandson. He loves the boy and is certain that he, like me, will eventually be head of the real estate company. Pinching his cheek, Father asks:

"DON'T YOU WANT TO SEE THE NEW BUILDINGS? THEY'LL BE YOURS SOMEDAY. TELL MOMMY TO PUT ON YOUR COAT AND WE'LL TAKE A LOOK."

While waiting Father peers up the stairwell. "I STILL DON'T

KNOW WHY YOU NEEDED THIS HOUSE. SOONER OR LATER
SOMEONE'S BOUND TO FALL DOWN THE STAIRS OR HAVE
A HEART ATTACK. WHAT DO YOU DO WITH ALL THIS
SPACE?"

He asks the question as he might ask about the empty space in some
of the abstact paintings hanging on the walls. It's just as difficult to
answer. Once again I try to explain: "We're on the third floor. Our
son's on the fourth, where there are two more bedrooms—for another
child and maybe eventually a sleep-in maid. I use the top floor."

"THAT'S WHAT I DON'T UNDERSTAND. WHAT DO YOU
DO UP THERE?"

Mother has been through the entire house and doesn't understand
that either. She has said, "The top floor, with its skylight, would make
such a bright cheerful nursery and, later on, a perfect playroom. Surely
one of the bedrooms on the fourth floor would be enough space for
you."

"It's quieter on the fifth, and I like to spread out my books and
papers and find them where I leave them."

"You know, you can't be sure you're going to have a second
child—your father and I never did."

"If we don't, we'll adopt one."

"You feel *that* strongly." Mother looks pained at the thought of
strange, probably inferior blood coming into the family. "Were you so
terribly lonely?"

"Not terribly but enough."

"Then why do you want to be up there all by yourself?"

I had no satisfactory answer to her question, any more than I do
now to Father's.

He is still peering up the stairwell. "IF I WERE YOU, I'D INSTALL
AN ELEVATOR. CAN YOU CHARGE IT TO BUSINESS?"

We have many prospective tenants for our new office buildings—
large corporations and service businesses which have become
crowded during the war. They can't expand in the older buildings,
can't even modernize there, over their own heads. There isn't room.
They come to us.

At first I negotiate only the less important leases, those covering the small tower floors which result from packing as much building as possible into the allowable zoning envelope. However, with experience, I am soon working on larger leases, soliciting larger companies, and making carefully prepared written proposals to them.

"You write well," my uncle tells me. "Your proposals are clear and well organized. As a matter of fact, you've sold me. We ought to take a floor on Park."

Our new offices are intended not only to serve the needs of our own business, growing as fast as that of our tenants, but to be used as showrooms, demonstrating the advantages of central air conditioning, flourescent lighting, acoustic ceilings, vinyl floors moveable partitions, modular electric outlets: the advantages of a controlled and efficient environment in which temperature, relative humidity, illumination (in foot candles), sound level (in decibels) are all constant and yet flexible — with provision for human change, movement, expansion and contraction built into these very ceilings, walls, and floors. All of this is by now standard, as specified in *Landlord's Work* clauses. There is also a *Substitution* clause under which Tenant may take a credit (as per an attached schedule) for standard work and apply that against special work to be done by Landlord at ten percent profit on ten percent overhead. In my uncle's office, in mine, in those of a few other executives, and in a large conference room, we show what we can do for our ten on ten. Wood paneling is perfectly matched. Built-in adjustable bookshelves are absolutely sturdy. Recessed plan drawers and tables coast smoothly into view on solid brass hardware. Rheostatically controlled lighting brightens and dims at the touch of a switch. Raw linen curtains hide aluminum blinds and soften the skyline. Heavy wool carpeting, extending from wall to wall and out into the executive corridor (protected by secretaries), hugs our feet. Here almost all materials are natural, beyond standard.

The first time Father visits, he gasps. "THEY'RE NOT LIKE ANY OFFICES I'VE SEEN. THEY'RE LIKE A WORK OF ART. LIKE A CHURCH OR A BANK. THIS IS REALLY LIVING. IT MUST BE HARD TO GO HOME."

"No, sometimes I want to feel a draft, or see a shadow, or hear the floor squeak."

Father stares, taps his foot, repeats, "HEAR THE FLOOR SQUEAK! I GREW UP WITH THAT—IN A BROWNSTONE—THOUGHT I TOOK YOU AWAY. YOU'RE NOT EASY TO UNDERSTAND."

I, too, find myself increasingly difficult to understand. The offices are comfortable, the working conditions "ideal," the compensation generous. I appreciate my GOOD LUCK. Yet, often with a tightly knotted stomach, I go home quickly after work and welcome the walk up the drafty, shadowy, squeaky stair to my study, cluttered now with books on art, architecture, city planning, utopian states and economies. Here, gulping whiskey before dinner and brandy after, I write about esthetic and economic questions it would be inefficient even to think about during the day in that cool, functional, shadowless environment. I write, "At home there's always the possibility that the decision may be important. At business the important thing is to decide." I improvise on the insights of great poets and architects—e.g., "Getting and spending we lay waste our money." and "A building is a machine to make money." I "find" poetry in such standard lease clauses as *Quiet Enjoyment, Recognition, Condemnation,* and *Subordination.* I present my own confusion about "the businessman as artist/the artist as businessman," citing, as I have for years, Svevo, Ives, Stevens, Eliot, and going back now to such heroic Nineteenth Century figures as Rimbaud the Gun-Runner and Melville the Customs House Clerk.

My tone is almost always ironic, feeding as it does on the tension in my stomach, in my life. Yet, somehow, I have willed such improvisational fragments into essays coherent enough to have been published more and more frequently in art, architecutre, and literary magazines and, recently, in publications of more general interest. An editor has even told me he would like to publish a collection of this work.

My parents' interest in my writing is negative. For them, it is something I do during what should be leisure hours spent more often with them and my immediate family, especially now their granddaughter, even cuter, they say, than their grandson and so much more interesting than anything I could write or read "up there, alone." Mother tells me politely that my work is "too specialized," and Father, saying the same thing in different words, that it's "ALL GREEK." However, there's no question in their minds as to where the fault lies. After all, if my writing was more popular and understandable, the magazines would pay more for it. Surely nothing I've written has the substance of the paneling in my office.

My uncle is more ambivalent about my writing. He feels some pride in my having beeen able to accomplish it "on the side," as he said I could, and he acknowledges that the magazines I publish in have some professional standing, even if they don't pay well. However, being a careful reader, he recognizes the connection between my literary irony and my life itself and fears that I may be drifting toward business—rather than toward writing—"on the side."

Holding my latest article in his hand, he enters my office and points to a brief passage he has marked with one of those little pencils of his.

…air rushing through sheet-metal ducts, hissing its seasonless snake song: 72° Fahrenheit, 50% relative humidity.

"I don't get this, but I'm sure it's not much of an advertisement for our buildings. It makes them sound noisy."

"I didn't intend it to describe *our* buildings specifically, or to be an ad. I was just playing with—alliteration."

"But you know that when you publish something, you do so at least partly *ex officio*, as a representative of this firm, and you do seem to be writing a lot lately. It's surprising you have energy left for business."

"Have I neglected anything? I never have my own work typed until everything here is completed."

"I know that. You've been doing a good job. Maybe you should consider doing this other stuff under a pseudonym. It won't help you in business. Whether rightly or wrongly, people will begin to think you're some kind of eccentric. It does seem a little loose, a little poetic. What I'd like to see, printed and signed, is that bank lease. When that's completed we'll get the biggest mortgage you've ever seen."

These particular negotiations, ultimately covering an entire building of 600,000 square feet, drag on for another four months, months of meetings with bankers, lawyers, architects and engineers. My uncle has said I'm writing a lot, but I'm not. My life is a blur of fine print—lease clauses, specifications, exhibits. I return home tired and tense. I buy more books than I can read, more paintings than I can hang in the house, more recordings than I can listen to. It is easier to buy art than to make it—easier to buy anything.

When the lease is signed, I decide for the first time in my life to have shoes made—really made, to order. I go to the best British boot-maker in New York, am measured for my last, select a supple brown piano calf, resolve every detail of styling—and I wait. In three weeks I return for a fitting. The shoes look beautiful. They smell beautiful. They shine. I can almost see myself—two of me—reflected in the toes. As the shoemaker slips them onto my feet, puffs of talcum powder rise like silent salutes. He ties the laces. I get up and walk around the room.

"How do they feel, Sir?"

I hesitate to tell him. The shoes are so beautiful I would like to take them home immediately. I stand on my toes, rock back and forth for a moment, wanting to be sure before speaking.

"The lower part of each shoe fits fine, the upper presses on my insteps."

"That can be easily taken care of—a slight adjustment to the last." He takes a piece of chalk from the pocket of his smock, presses here and there, asking where it hurts and then carefully marking the spots. "They'll be ready in a week. We'll send them to you. You shouldn't need another fitting, but if anything bothers you, bring them right back. And when you're ready for the next pair, there should be no difficulty at all. The instep is the most difficult part of the foot to measure. Sorry about this inconvenience."

The shoes arrive. They fit perfectly. I can't wait to show them to Father. To him they should mean even more than the paneling in my office. The sight of them will be a gift, like the recent news that the bank lease is signed.

I wear them the next time we go to my parents. I don't have to show them to Father—he sees them right away.

"WHERE'D YOU GET THEM?"

I tell him.

"THOSE THIEVES!" He stamps his foot. His eyes pop. His face flushes. "HOW MUCH DID THEY CHARGE?"

"$200. For the first pair. Including $50 for the last."

"THE FIRST PAIR! HOW MANY PAIR DO YOU NEED?" He looks as if he will drive his foot through the floor. Mother goes for a glass of water. "THAT UNCLE OF YOURS—"

Father never finishes the sentence. His mouth locks. His body becomes rigid. He falls back in the chair just as Mother returns.

She looks at him, drops the glass, freezes. "Is he—? Is he—?" she screams, unable to say the word, unable to move.

I fumble for his pulse, can't feel it, open his tie and shirt, put my ear to his chest, listen, listen. For a moment all I can hear is Mother saying, "My God, oh my God, oh my God." Her voice is Father's only heartbeat, only breath. Then faintly I hear his own body breathe.

"He's alive. I'll call the doctor."

As soon as I'm off the phone, we half-carry, half-drag Father to his bed. Although he has lost weight, he feels very heavy. Inevitably, I think the phrase *dead weight.*

The maid cleans up the water on the living room carpet. Mother cries. My wife and I take turns hugging her and holding her hand. Now the word *stroke* keeps coming to my mind. I have never seen one but am sure this is what Father has had. I tell Mother, "He'll be all right.... He'll be all right...." not believing what I say.

Finally the doctor arrives. He motions to us to leave the bedroom while he examines Father. We wait in the den, because it is closer than the living room. My wife mentions the children a few times but her words sound forced and Mother barely responds. I continue to say, "He'll be all right."

After perhaps ten or fifteen minutes—it seems much longer—the doctor joins us. He crosses the room to Mother, puts his hands on her shoulders, shakes his head. "It's a stroke. I want him in the hospital."

"How bad is it?" Mother pleads.

"I told you he's had a stroke. I can't say more until we examine him at the hospital. I'll call for a bed."

When he completes the call, I walk to the door with him. "What are his chances?"

"No way to tell. Months. Years. Depends on his progress. I think he's had a few small strokes in the past. At least I've suspected that when I've examined him—some irrationality. Whatever happens, your mother's going to have a difficult time. You'll have to help her. There's really not too much we can do. The brain dies bit by bit."

Father's right side is paralyzed. He must be fed, bathed, shaved, taken to the toilet. His speech is often garbled. His mouth pulls to the left. Sometimes he grunts, snarls, and swears between words as twisted as his mouth. They are understandable but disconnected, seized at random from some warped trough of memory containing conversations with different people in different times and places. One day he recognizes Mother, the next he thinks she's a nurse or a First World War girlfriend. Frequently he mistakes me for his brother and imagines we are at Reade Street.

"DRINK TOO MUCH PISS ORDER MORE PUMPS AAGH DRINK PUMPS."

When Father is more lucid, we encourage him (as the doctor has suggested) to speak slowly, to walk around the apartment with us, to do more things with his left hand, to squeeze a rubber ball with his right. There are small triumphs—days when he shaves or feeds himself, days when he walks to the living room or eats in the dining room—but mostly now, after months, he sits on the couch in the den, propped against pillows, watching television. As I enter, everything about him looks unnatural, mechanical and stiff: his posture, his eyes as glassy as the TV screen, the tight set of his jaw, his right hand squeezing the ball. He turns slowly and stares at me as if I am another television program. He tries to smile, but his expression turns crooked as the muscles of his right cheek refuse to respond.

"WHERE FROM?"

"Work. The day is over. I wanted to see you and Mother."

"DAY OFF. SEE YOU TOO."

He turns back toward the television set. I watch him watching while he squeezes the ball.

"Your hand's better."

"HAND LEG STOMACH MOUTH BETTER. NOTHING WORSE LEFT. NOTHING."

As I work on one building after another, one lease after another, one mortgage after another, the acquisition of one blockfront after another, Father has one *small stroke* after another.

I hate that emphatic but misleading phrase, find it too innocuous and petty, too small to contain crippling and murder. It is obscenely cute. Icy medical terms, the size of glaciers, are more appropriate—

terms like *cerebral hemorrhage* and *apoplectic* or *paralytic seizure*. Even *stroke* itself (singular and unmodified) seems now too incongruously connected with the force, movement, and rhythm of life—this word so often used in games and sports, in writing, painting, and music. Only when I discover that it is a shortening of *the stroke of God's hand* does the word have sufficient meaning, power, and grandeur. But then, no stroke is *small*.

My uncle seldom visits. He relies on my reports, says he can't bear to see what Father's illness is doing to Mother. By now, she has lost weight, her eyes are sunken, her hair is gray. Father no longer tries to do anything for himself. He doesn't even go to the bathroom; he uses a bedpan which Mother cleans. The flickering images on the television screen are still a presence in the room, his most constant company, but the day's news and yesterday's movies are as interchangeable as the people around him. From being fed in the morning to being tucked in at night, put behind rails so he won't fall out of bed, his life is a continuous humiliation—shared always with Mother and, to a lesser extent, with me.

"She should put him in an institution," my uncle says. "They're equipped to deal with his condition. Your mother's not."

"She'll never do it. She doesn't even like to have nurses around. She wants to take care of him herself."

"She'll kill herself taking care of him. No one can run a hospital in an apartment."

But Mother tries. She fills prescriptions. She places bottles of medicine in neat rows on the night table alongside a thermos she keeps filled. She plans three meals a day. She arranges for the laundress to come in every day so that Father, who sometimes wets himself, can always have clean sheets and pajamas. She pays bills—more now than ever before—from doctors, druggists, testing laboratories, medical equipment firms.... The mail, like everything else, has become time-consuming, tiring, overwhelming.

If the weather is good, most Saturdays, Sundays, and holidays I take Father to the park in his wheelchair. I try to talk to him. I tell him about things that are happening in business, good things intended to put his mind at ease, things that mean he, like me, will receive large amounts of money. Usually he remains silent. Sometimes he responds,

"EASY AAGH TAKE IT TAKE IT" or "WHAT YOU KNOW WHO YOU KNOW." Once, he lifts his left hand, makes a fist, and shakes it at the sky. I ask quietly, "What are you doing?" "WAITING."

I let Father get as much sun as he seems to want, then wheel him into the shade. There, I read to him, not knowing what he understands. Without expression, he stares straight ahead at birds, children, young lovers, the movement of leaves, not really watching any of these but perhaps recognizing them as the same flickerings of life he sees on television.

When we return, Mother is sitting at her desk, writing checks. Her profile has become more gaunt. Fatigue and strain show in the deep lines and empty pouches beneath her eyes. "You've got to get a nurse," I tell her once again. "You've got to be able to sleep nights and leave this apartment when you want. You're making yourself sick. The doctor said he wants you to come in for a physical, but you can't even find time."

Finally, Mother gives in and the parade of nurses begins—males, females, homosexuals, asexuals, whites, blacks, Puerto Ricans. Almost every time I visit there's someone else.

"You can't expect perfection," I say, after someone who seemed particularly considerate has been discharged.

"Perfection! He drank."

There's always a reason. One steals liquor. One steals drugs. One eats too much. One sleeps through the night without changing Father's wet bedding. One is so crippled he can't lift Father from bed into the wheelchair. And all these, even the cripple, are nurses Mother has screened. "You should see *some* the agency sends," she tells me. "*They* need nurses."

Finally, Mother settles on two homosexuals, a day nurse in his forties and a night nurse in his fifties. "They steal as much as the others, but at least they're gentle and polite. Your father needs the gentleness—he's all bed sores now. And the politeness means something when we eat together—the relationship's different from that with a cook or a laundress. As to the stealing, after a while you just accept it as part of the salary."

Though Mother sounds resigned, she spends hours searching for missing jewelry, clothing, household accessories, wondering if she has mislaid the particular object or if perhaps, as has happened sometimes, she has hidden it from herself in trying to hide it from them. Maybe the thefts can be dismissed as trivial—her best jewelry is in the vault—but the anxiety is significant, and it is compounded by the payment of almost $500 a week to the nurses who are causing it. Despite more rest and leisure, Mother is as tense as before, and aging as quickly. As I look at her, I wish that Father would die, wish it for his own sake, for Mother's, for mine. I want the God who has stricken him to finish the job, cleanly now and not in more small strokes. But nothing happens. For the moment, there is no finishing stroke, no *coup de grâce.*

As Father's life drags on and my resentment mounts—some of it directed at him, some at God—business and property itself begin to seem less and less important. The organization we have built—at least ten times the size of the one I joined almost fourteen years ago—very nearly runs itself. The buildings *are* machines to make money. They grind out dollars. Our rent roll swells, giving my uncle and his wife, me and my family, and my parents more than we need but still not enough to buy health.

However, my uncle tries to buy that too. By now he spends the entire winter in Palm Beach and most of the summer, except for one or two days a week, on Long Island, devoting more time to golf and bridge than to business. That he takes care of in frequent phone calls to me, sometimes during office hours, just as often early in the morning before teeing off or late at night after a last rubber. There is no longer the need for lengthy discussions between us about, for example, the design of our buildings. We have had those talks and, on that pad of his, my uncle has shown me that good architecture is expensive, that less *costs* more. "Our buildings aren't designed for critics," he has said, "they're designed for a market, a large market. We're not selling Rolls-Royces." After so many years, it is possible, in even the briefest conversations, to make concessions to external architecture by increasing the size of an entrance lobby or the height of a tower (after packing as much rentable space as possible into the cheaper, lower floors), but the emphasis is on how the buildings work inside and the measurement of that is on a statement of projected income and expense.

The numbers speed back and forth between Palm Beach and New York, Long Island and New York—the exact amount it costs, in lost store income, to enlarge that lobby; in additional construction, to add those tower floors; in interest, to refinance an existing building; in land acquisition, to buy out some leases.... We talk in rounded numbers, hundreds of thousands, millions, and yet all those zeros crowd my stomach and feel heavy as stones. They no longer give me any pleasure, no longer dissolve in alcohol and wash away. They simply hurt. Even without the doctor telling me, I know that my innards are ulcerating as Father's did, that that's where the zeros are going and will continue to go as I tear myself apart, doing business, visiting my parents, writing, and spending too little time with my wife and children.

Business demands the most hours now and deserves the least. I've trained assistants to negotiate leases, the most time-consuming part of my job. What I can't train them to do is to communicate with my uncle. Not only is he often remote and sometimes aloof and impatient but, more understandably, covetous of his own time, his own remaining years. He is used to talking to me in terse telegraphic—or, at least, telephonic—language that he knows I understand because he has taught it to me.

Mother appreciates my visits, needs them, whether or not Father recognizes me and knows I'm there.

My wife and the children are patient, accustomed to my spending as much time on the fifth floor as with them. They know that this is something I must do and, in lieu of me, accept my guilt offerings of jewelry, furs, toys, and equipment.

My writing suffers most. This part of my life, this most direct expression of myself, remains as personal, perhaps even eccentric, as ever but becomes increasingly willed and joyless. My first collection of essays has received some serious and sympathetic reviews. A second is about to be published. But still my public identity is confused. I am considered a professional businessman, an amateur writer. My career in real estate is in itself, its extra-literary self, a way of attacking my writing. Years ago my uncle said that perhaps I should consider writing under a pseudonym. I wish now that I could do business under a pseudonym, if at all.

Several times I have told my wife I want to leave business. "I don't need more money. I need more time. For writing. And for you and the children."

She listens. She smiles. And always she asks, "Have you spoken to your uncle?"

I have to answer, "Not yet."

My uncle and I are now having longer conversations than usual, involving even larger numbers than usual. He is thinking about consolidating all the property into one corporation and offering that to the public. "Time to cash in some of our chips," he says. "I'm not getting any younger. I want my estate to be reasonably liquid."

For an underwriter he has spoken to, I begin to assemble the information on our presently separate corporations. Working with the underwriter and its accountants and lawyers as well as our own, we prepare a current consolidated balance sheet. The figures are impressive, even more so when compared with those of past years. Our profits and cash-flow have increased steadily. The underwriter is convinced that our offering will be very successful. We have, as he says, "a unique package—income assured by long leases with strong tenants, expenses protected by escalation clauses, taxes sheltered by depreciation, and the prospect of continuing growth."

These "healthy figures"—healthier than they feel in my stomach— are the substance of the early drafts of our prospectus. But every other aspect of the business is reviewed. As one conference leads to the next, I begin to feel increasingly ambivalent about our "going public." I know that business will never again be done simply and easily, in brief conversations between my uncle and me. I can already see us separated by walls of written reports, surrounded by cumbersome committees, questioned by outside directors and by minority stockholders. On the other hand, I can also see my paper profits of the past fourteen years being transformed into real money—a personal cash-flow, first of negotiable stock, then of salary, stock dividends, and pension checks, running far into a vague future.

The next draft includes a paragraph captioned *Management*. It provides that, barring illness, my uncle and I will remain with the new corporation for not less than five years and that, if forced to resign or retire, neither of us will enter into any real estate activities competitive with the public corporation. I reread the paragraph. The future is no longer vague. I feel as if I have been sentenced to a five-year term.

"Where did this language come from?" I ask one of the underwriter's representatives.

"It's the usual boiler plate. Part of what we're offering is experienced management."

The usual prison bars, I think. "But did anyone agree to it?"

"It may have come up in one of our early conversations with your uncle. Why? You're not thinking of retiring, are you?" He laughs loudly at the ridiculousness of the thought—no one retires at thirty-six, no one leaves a business that is so successful.

"I'd better discuss it with my uncle."

This is not something that can be done on the phone, not something that can be translated into numbers. I wait almost a month until he returns from Palm Beach. Meanwhile my stomach tightens, my anxiety mounts. I make nervous little jokes to my wife, to no one else, about "going private." I tell her, "It will be easy to announce, just as easy as telling my parents we eloped. He'll understand that this time I'm marrying my muse; he won't be able to say I'm being precipitous."

So much for jokes. I know there won't be any with my uncle. I anticipate his carefully reasoned arguments, his recapitulation of the odds against success as a writer, his hurt at my rejection of him and his values, perhaps the accusation of betrayal and apostasy.

The night before his arrival I can't sleep. The next morning I can't eat breakfast. I rush to the office and ask his secretary to let me know when he comes in. The morning mail blurs as I wait for her buzz on the intercom.

"Something important?" he asks as I enter his office. He looks healthy, sun-tanned, relaxed. It is hard to believe he is in his late sixties, almost exactly the same age as Father.

"Yes. Something personal." My voice trembles. I rush on for fear it may fail me. "I want to leave business. I want to devote more time to writing." The color drains from his face. His expression changes from incredulity to intense disappointment. For a moment I think he will cry. I rush on again, wanting now to give him time to compose himself. "You know that when I joined you I was undecided about my career. For fourteen years—until recently—I've remained undecided. I—"

"Fourteen years!" he interrupts. "Is it that long? It seems like only—" He suppresses the cliché, substituting another: "They went so fast."

"For me too. And you were right about the odds. But your success, your happiness is in real estate. Not because you've made so much money but because this business satisfies you. It's the way you express yourself. It's what you have to do. I have to write."

"You've been doing both."

"Yes. By taking time from my family—and myself."

"Why didn't you tell me this sooner?"

"I wasn't sure until now."

"You mean you couldn't *afford* to until now."

"I could have. I didn't know. Maybe not till Father became sick. And then we got into this underwriting, and I didn't want to leave until it was completed. I want to get that done, and the renting of the new building on Third Avenue and the planning of the next job. I can complete what I have to do in a year. I promise, when I leave, everything will be done. You won't need me."

"I'll correct you again: *You* won't need me." My uncle studies me as so many times in the past I have seen him study a balance sheet, looking for hidden numbers, rational explanations for what seems to be a distortion of the figure on the bottom line. "I don't know how your thinking has become so muddled. Is this your wife's idea? Does she want you to leave?"

"No, she's always said that people do what they want. She'll be as surprised as anyone when I tell her I've finally spoken to you."

"Well, you ought to think it over. I suppose you have some talent for writing—" he spits the word out as though it were dirty—"but whatever that talent is, it's amateur. It can't be compared with your proven abilities as an executive. Here's where you have your background, your identity. Here's where you're outstanding, a professional, useful. I could almost understand if you had expressed a desire to go into politics—or some field where your past experience might be valuable. But writing—" The word, as he delivers it, is again surrounded by an aura of filth.

"I've thought it over. I don't want to leave like this. I feel as close to you as to Father. When I graduated from college, I still had some silly generalized ideas about all businessmen being dull, all writers being interesting. I don't anymore. I accept you. I'm asking you to accept me."

"I did. Think that over too."

My wife is delighted by the news. A few days after telling her, we are at my parents for dinner and I tell them. It is one of those days when Father recognizes me, grunts my name, seems to understand what I'm saying. As I summarize the conversation with my uncle, wanting them to know that I intend to fulfill my obligations, Father moves his head up and down and a smile twists across his face, broadening when I finish.

"EASY AAGH LAST LONGER AAGH LONGER."

Mother begins to cry. "Your father doesn't know what he's saying. You don't know what you're saying. Don't you care about anyone? Don't you even care about your own security?" She dabs at her eyes, blows her nose. "I'm glad *my* father isn't alive to hear this. You would have broken his heart."

"I have enough money. I'm not doing anything to anybody. The organization is strong. I helped to build it. It'll get along without me."

She doesn't seem to hear. Snifffling and still using her handkerchief, she turns to my wife. "What do you think?"

"It's a good decision. He'll be much happier."

"Happier! What do you know about happiness? Ask your parents. They'll tell you. Happiness cost money."

Neither my wife nor I have thought about her parents' reaction—it is surely peripheral—but Mother is half right. My mother-in-law talks, too, about security and the children. She can't seem to understand that, although I will be giving up a substantial amount in salary, stock option and pension benefits, there'll be plenty left to live on and still some to help her, if necessary. "Not since the Duke of Windsor!" she says, emphasizing her shock. My father-in-law says less, as usual avoiding controversy, but I have the feeling that he sympathizes with me, that I have acted out a fantasy which may once, long ago, have been his own.

Their separate reactions are typical of those in the business world. At least half of the men I work with are shocked at the thought of my giving up a kingdom. The rest, many with secret lives they'd like to lead full-time, tell me in whispers that I'm doing the right thing.

The *Management* provision of the prospectus is modified so that I am required to remain with the new corporation for only one year. The leasing of our present project and the planning of our next go well. Yet, as the prospectus is completed and as each lease is signed covering space in the nearly finished building and each problem resolved concerning the design of the next, I seem to become more valuable to my uncle and he seems to become more resentful of my leaving.

I say *seem,* because for the next three months or so my departure is not mentioned. I have nothing more to say. My uncle does, but he waits, as distant from me now as, typically, from his other employees. Whenever I see him, whenever I speak to him on the phone, it's as if he is silently reminding me that he asked me to think it over, that the next move is mine. For him, my past fourteen years of thinking it over don't exist. For me, nothing else does. Those years and the twenty-two preceding them, all spent on thinking it over, are my life—and the foundation of a new life in which I'll write in the morning, with morning energy. So I wait too, until finally he calls me to his office.

"I've thought a lot about our talk," he says as if it happened the day before. "I've tried to look at everything from your point of view as well as mine. I think you've made the wrong decision. Objectively, success is measured by the world's opinion. Everyone in real estate respects you. If you continue to develop the way you have, you'll be at the top of this profession. Everything in your life has shaped you for the position you have—and for the still higher one you will have. In writing, what hope of success is there? In five years, or ten, you'll surely regret your decision..."

The words drone. They sound familiar—familiar as three months before, fourteen years before, a lifetime before.

"I didn't make my decision easily. There's a question of values—"

"Exactly. And obligations. I didn't think I'd need to remind you of how I pushed you along, how I gave you more and more responsibility. It's inconceivable that you can be this callous, that you can leave me on a year's notice, like some hired hand. You know there'll be things to clean up on Third Avenue long after the building's rented."

"I'll do what I have to. But I guess there'll never be a convenient time for me to leave. And I'm beginning to think there'll never be a time when you can accept my decision."

"At least call it your *present* decision. I'm disappointed in that, but I would be even more if I thought you had no sense of obligation—and no flexibility. I'd like to think you'll review everything with an open mind."

My stomach tightens. I smoke another cigarette. I tell him once again how slowly I have reached my decision, explain once again the division of my life between art and business.

He cuts in: "That division doesn't need to exist. There's no business in which you could get more aesthetic satisfaction. And none in which the product lasts longer. You've enlarged some lobbies, eliminated some set-backs, put a mural in our last building. Don't you get creative satisfaction out of those things—and the finished buildings themselves?"

"Indirectly. I used to think that in this, of all businesses, there was a chance of combining art and economics. But you taught me there wasn't. You're the architect of our buildings. That's why we use pawns to prepare the plans, why we can't use real architects. Real architects are artists. They don't design buildings as machines to make money. You'll be able to express yourself through our new corporate structure, through committees, through compromises, through everything. I won't."

"Art!"My uncle flushes. "You've been listening to those critics. Maybe you need a rest. Do you think any of that writing you've done has enhanced your reputation?"

"No—not as you measure it, by the world's opinion, the business world's."

"I don't understand what's happened to you. Your mother doesn't either. What does your wife think?"

"She looks forward to my spending more time with her and the children—and writing. I told you she didn't influence my decision, but she accepted it."

"*She* accepted it! Well, I can't. I've made an investment in you, a long-term investment. You think your primary obligation is to yourself; I think it's to society, including me."

"I understand your point of view—maybe better than you do mine."

"There's no point in our discussing who understands who better. Just think over what I've said—with an open mind. Now let's get to work. First, there's this management agreement."

He pushes some papers accross his desk. Before looking at them, I say, "You must understand. I've made my decision. With an open mind. The decision is made. One of the things we should be discussing is how to facilitate it, how best to fill my job, what additional responsibilities should be given to some of the others."

He doesn't reply to that but goes on to the agreement. The better my analysis of each point he raises, the sadder he looks.

During my remaining months in business there are no more direct conversations about my departure. Everything is indirect. My uncle speaks to me through Mother: "You've really hurt my brother." He speaks through a viral infection that keeps me home for a few days: "I remember when you wouldn't have taken a cold this seriously." He speaks through the final revision of the *Stock Option* clause, exercisable now only after twenty years of employment: "I don't want anyone else losing his incentive." He speaks through the visit of a former employee who retired ten years early, at fifty-five: "Did you notice how fat he's become?" He speaks through my lease negotiations, stiffening terms as if to delay my leaving: "This building's a success. We don't need to accept any more ten-year leases. Hold out for twenty-one. Or get another fifty cents a foot." I feel as if I'm back in the navy, after the war has ended—only now I'm more anxious to return home. Rigid politeness protects my uncle and me in our daily contact, but the divorce is becoming final.

At last I begin to clean out my office. Working with my secretary, I throw away fifteen years of Real Estate Board diaries, send various files to the office manager, send others to the men who will assume my responsibilities, get rid of dusty plans and old architecture magazines, supervise the packing of personal correspondence and a few small pictures I want sent home. In between these chores, there are formal resignations to sign, dozens of them, in duplicate. My secretary hands me one sheet after another, on different corporate letterheads, waiting with blotter poised as I scribble my name. Then she delivers them to my uncle's secretary.

I pass her later in the corridor, this woman in her sixties, who has known me since I was in high school. "I hated putting those papers on your uncle's desk," she says. "They probably ruined his day. Aren't you going to reconsider?"

"I have."

Still later, my uncle comes into my office.

"There might be certain advantages in your not resigning. Perhaps we could handle it as a leave of absence."

"No. I wouldn't want to be on call. I want the break to be clean."

He looks sadly at some cartons in a corner of the office and from these to a dark rectangle on the wall where for many years a picture has hung of us and the Mayor at a ground-breaking ceremony. "Then I guess you've reached the end of the line."

The words sound painfully final, as if I'm required to do nothing now but say good-by. I want to say more, but I find it hard to speak, hard to breathe. "I hope it's the beginning." I pause. "This has been a difficult year for us."

"Each successive year's more difficult." He turns away as though speaking in an already empty room. "There are always more obligations. It would be nice if we were given more lives. Then nobody would get hurt, all obligations could be met. As it is we're forced to make choices." He faces me again. "I hope, whatever happens, you won't consider your decision irrevocable. No matter how difficult this last year's been, the next will be more difficult still. You've been in a position of power. People came to you. You could grant favors. Now you'll be going to others for their approval.... Do you think it was an accident you were good at business?"

"No. I have some talent for it. Hereditary maybe." I smile for the first time. "Whatever it is—organizational ability, discipline—won't hurt my writing."

My uncle smiles too. "I'm not one of those who believes that J.P. Morgan could have written *War and Peace*. Anyway, if I can ever help you, don't hesitate to call. I've always felt great affection for you."

"I share that. If I didn't, there would have been no problem in leaving."

"That's one way of putting it. You could say, too, that if you cared enough, you wouldn't leave. But I suppose there's no more to say. The world may or may not appreciate what you're going to write; like it or not, it will always appreciate what you've already done, the money you've made."

"That's the world I want to leave."

I begin to write each morning immediately after breakfast, fully rested, with more time than I need, more blank pages than I can fill. There is no help, as in business, from outside. By lunch I have produced all I can, typically no more than I did in the same number of hours during the years when I wrote nights and weekends.

I eat a sandwich. I walk uptown, stopping at shops and galleries. I spend money on expensive art I no longer want and on dressy clothes I no longer wear. The walk ends usually at my parents'.

Father's eyes brighten when I arrive. If he recognizes me, he smiles crookedly, grunts my name, touches my hand, seems vaguely aware that there has been some change in my life which permits me to visit more often. "TAKE IT," he says once more. "TAKE IT." When he mistakes me for his brother or some old friend, his eyes are just as bright; his spirit, what's left of it, just as lifted. "FORGIVE FORGIVE," he repeats, forgiving "me" for a binge or a debt of long ago. His voice is loud and rasping as he forces out each word, but only once is it as strong as it used to be. That day, glancing from the television set to Mother and me, he points at us and screams, "D'Y' KNOW HOW I'M LIVING?"

"You're not leaving," Mother says. "You're not going anywhere. You're staying right here."

"ALLSHIT."

She turns to me and explains, as if Father is no longer in the room and as if she has understood his question: "He wanders. Just yesterday he left the apartment. The attendant found him outside the front door, ringing the elevator bell. God knows how he does it. Or where he wants to go." Mother changes the subject and asks, as she has often lately: "How does she—" meaning my wife—"like having you home all the time? How does she like planning lunch as well as dinner? How do her lunches compare with those at business?" And then the big question (once more): "How do you like being *retired?*"

I hate the word as much as *stroke.* I try to explain (again, once more) that I have not retired; have not drawn back; have, on the contrary, moved forward. But Mother isn't listening.

"My brother hasn't been looking well since you left business. He says he no longer has anyone to talk to. You should have lunch with him. You can't talk to yourself all day, up there in your ivory tower."

"Just mornings," I reply, not trying to explain what I'm doing, though talking to myself is certainly part of it; and not trying to defend myself against responsibility for my uncle's health, though I am convinced that he—like Father, like Mother herself, like me—is simply becoming old, old and repetitious.

Actually, I'm working on the first sustained piece of writing I've ever attempted, and I'm moving forward. It's a novel, as yet untitled, which begins: "I didn't buy a pair of shoes until I was in my twenties, didn't have a pair made until my thirties." I'd like to think each sentence, paragraph, and page follows logically from that, but I'm not sure. As I improvise and modify—without zoning laws, without blueprints, without budgets, without measurable odds—I'm sure only that I seek no one's approval but my own, and I'm surprised by how difficult that is to obtain.

The pages pile up. After four months, there are about two hundred of them, full of changes and revisions. I'm just chuckling over the words, "All the world's a page," referring to my life both in business and at home, when the phone rings. It's Father's attendant:

"I've got very bad news. Your father died—collapsed after breakfast." His tone is matter-of-fact, experienced, a bit weary. "Your mother's out. I phoned the doctor. He said he'll be here soon, that you should try to get here before she does—to prepare her."

Suddenly, after all these years, preparation is measured in minutes. I haven't shaved, I'm wearing slacks and a turtleneck sweater, but I stop only to put on a jacket and to tell the maid where I'm going. Then I run to the corner for a cab.

On the way uptown, while hoping I get to the apartment before Mother, I scold myself for that silly witticism, "All the world's a page." It doesn't feel like a page now. It has the weight of all legal documents and all literature combined.

Father's doctor and the attendant are there. They have put him on his bed, closed his eyelids, placed his arms at his sides, drawn a sheet up to his chin. His mouth gapes, but he is absolutely silent—a false waxy effigy of himself. The one thing I want is to hear him scream.

"I'm sorry," the doctor says, "but it was expected. I'll take care of the death certificate. You'd better contact the funeral chapel. I'll call later."

He leaves me with the attendant, who also says he's sorry and that it was expected. Like *stroke* and *retired, expected* is a word I begin to hate. The expectation of death doesn't make it easier to deal with. Thanking the attendant for his services, I suggest that he leave.

Mother doesn't arrive for about an hour. I hear her key turn in the door and go to meet her. When she sees me she knows immediately why I'm there. She won't let me take her coat but walks with me directly to the bedroom, to the bed itself, where she begins to sob. I hold her as she bends down and kisses Father. "Good-by, darling," she says to him and then, turning to me, repeats words I heard long ago, "He was the best looking man I ever met."

In the afternoon, my uncle arrives. I've seen him only a few times during recent months, in passing, at the office, where I've had to resolve a few pending details.

He asks, "Is that what you wear these days?"

"I was working. I came right over."

"I suppose at the funeral you plan to wear something more appropriate."

For many weeks after Father's death I'm angry at my uncle. I resent his resentment of me. I avoid him during my few visits to the office. But I can't avoid him in my writing. He sits next to me on one side of my desk, Father on the other. There, while I write, my anger is dissipated. I begin to think that my uncle and I can never again really be friends, never again really talk, that he, as much as Father, can only be part of my history, a ghost sitting beside me. However, as in my writing itself, I yearn for an impossible dialogue in which our two voices will blend, each totally accepting the other.

I'm finishing my novel, still thinking I want to see my uncle, to try once more to have that talk with him, when Mother calls to say he has died in his sleep.

As in everything else, compared with Father, my uncle dies more efficiently. But despite the shock, the lack of expectation and preparation, I don't feel as great a loss. Mother is still alive, and so much about her reminds me of my uncle. It is Father's screams I miss. It is toward his side of the desk I turn.

Away from the desk, I feel his presence even more strongly as sometimes I shout at my wife or the children, as I repeat myself, as my memory weakens. Father lives with me as I die with him. I am no longer watching. I, too, am dying and thinking about joining him. I will tell him I am sorry I was not a better son. He will tell me he is sorry he was not a better father. We will talk in whispers. We will finish unfinished business, having nothing to do with the office or with the public.

I am looking now into a mirror, watching Father die. Behind me my son and daughter stand, also watching Father die.

Drinking Smoke

The two Christians met many people,
men and women, who were going to
their villages, with a firebrand in the
hand and herbs to drink the smoke
thereof, as they are accustomed.

Tuesday, Nov. 6, 1492,
The Journal of Christopher
Columbus

Even as a small boy I want to smoke. Cigars, at first. They are what men smoke: fat, dark brown Havanas.

In the card-table corner of the living room the air becomes dense and dizzying. Beneath this mantle of blue-gray clouds my father, my maternal grandfather, and my uncles play auction bridge. They light and relight their cigars, chewing them short at one end as they burn short at the other. One uncle purses his lips and blows rings; I watch in awe as these move up from the card table, lose their distinct shape, and become lost among the dark clouds.

If I show no expression and make no comment, I am permitted to stand behind Father and peek over his shoulder as he arranges his cards, bids, plays his hand. The tip of his cigar is about a foot from my face or perhaps for a moment it rests, almost as close, in an ashtray at the corner of the table. Either way the smoke drifts into my eyes and nose and mouth, where I feel its sharp masculine bite. However, I remain as expressionless and silent as the pictures on the cards being played.

I am not taught how to play cards or how to smoke. These things happen naturally. They are absorbed.

Sometimes Father says my standing behind him brings luck. This makes me happy. So does his letting me empty ashtrays. The butts and ashes swirl darkly in the toilet bowl.

When the game is over, the women return to the living room. Mother opens the windows, complaining that the odor of tobacco gets into the upholstery, the carpet, the walls themselves. She says this odor is unclean. Intuitively I understand it lurks at the very core of the men's world of games and sports and business. I have seen grand slams go up in smoke. Later I will see athletic championships and big business deals go the same way. I will watch smoke pour from Father's mouth as if his mind is on fire. And I will watch also as cigars die in the crushing embrace of his jaws.

Grandfather sinks into a deep chair, relaxing with his final cigar of the evening. He turns it slowly as he smokes so that it will burn evenly and the ash will not drop. This is another game—seeing how long an ash he can produce without dropping it—a game he could not play while playing cards. Though seventy, his hands are steady. They are the strong hands of a Russian blacksmith, who became an American ornamental iron contractor and then, with the help of a college-educated son, a builder. His hands have supported the family and look as if they still could.

Mother does not smoke until I am almost six, when her mother dies. Then, in grief, she begins. She smokes constantly, as if trying to catch up on all the smoking the men have done. She brings to smoking a new quality—elegance. At first she smokes Marlboros with what is called an ivory tip. Then she switches to a red tip so that her lipstick will not show. Ordinary packs of twenty will not last a day. She buys flat or cylindrical tins of fifty. From these she fills a thin gold case with a sapphire-studded clasp. As her consumption increases she begins to use a cigarette holder. It becomes part of her, alternately part of her hand and part of her face. She smokes nervously, in quick puffs, but gently, without aggression. There is no biting or chewing. As previously I got Father's cigar boxes, I now get Mother's tins to fill with marbles, chestnuts, matchbook covers, the things I collect.

So far I smoke only through my parents' mouths and nostrils, but by the time I finish grade school I try two or three of Mother's cigarettes. I puff them in front of the bathroom mirror, getting the smoke in and out of my mouth as quickly as possible. I attempt to blow it out through my nose as if inhaling, since inhaling itself makes me cough and feel dizzy. I like what I see in the mirror: a little movie star, perhaps a Dead End Kid, tough and with a lot of savvy. Inevitably, I steal one of the expensive cigars from Father's humidor. (Taking Mother's cigarettes did not seem at all like stealing.) I bite off the tip, the way I've seen him do it, and spit the end into the toilet. I try to light the cigar. This is work, not like lighting a cigarette. I use several matches, circling the end of the cigar as he does to get an even light. The smoke is strong as steel. I cough, wondering how he can smoke this powerful thing, he and the others—Grandfather, my uncles, movie gamblers, bankers, cab drivers, businessmen in general. I feel more guilty about wasting the cigar, flushing most of it down the toilet, than I do about stealing it.

Several times at high school I smoke cigarettes given to me by classmates. By now I can more easily blow the smoke out through my nose to give the impression I'm inhaling, but real inhaling still makes me cough and feel dizzy. Finally I buy my first pack of cigarettes. I go to a wedge-shaped tobacco shop at Columbus Circle on the fringe of the first-run movie theater district. The store has cigarettes of all nations. I select Sweet Caporals, which are no longer popular, but which I remember as the brand Studs Lonigan "pasted in his mug." I can hardly wait to get out of the store and smoke one. Walking down Broadway with the cigarette lit, I feel both manly and elegant, as sophisticated as Adolphe Menjou or William Powell. A beggar asks if I can spare a smoke. I give him a cigarette. Nobody has ever asked me for one before.

Weeks later I still have five or six cigarettes left. Mother finds the crumpled pack in the pocket of my reversible. She cries. How could I do this to myself? To my health? To her? To Father? She takes the cigarettes one by one, crushes them, and flushes them down the toilet. I am told to stay in my room until Father gets home from work. I fear the worst—a beating and a cut in my allowance. I cannot concentrate on homework. The geometry problems are blurred through the film of Mother's tears.

Father arrives. Through the bedroom door I hear Mother's voice, then his: "ALL BOYS SMOKE." There is an element of pride as well as annoyance in his voice. The annoyance may be because this is when he usually reads his evening paper.

Father enters my room. In one hand he holds the newspaper, in the other a cigar. He puts the cigar in his mouth so he can slam the door. This he does decisively but not angrily. The noise from the door and then the silence which follows emphasize our isolation: this talk will be man-to-man, Mother might as well be miles away. He puffs on his cigar. I wait.

"YOUR MOTHER TELLS ME YOU'VE BEEN SMOKING?"

"Yes."

"HOW LONG?"

"A few weeks."

"NEVER BEFORE?"

"Once or twice."

Father studies me, looking for the slightest hint of deception, a shift in my eyes, a tremor, or perhaps some symptom already signifying the habitual use of tobacco. My heart pounds. I wonder if he can hear it admitting the terrible thing I have done.

"SMOKING IS A STUPID HABIT—STUPID AND EXPENSIVE AND UNHEALTHY. IT'S LIKE BURNING UP MONEY, BURNING UP YOUR LUNGS. I WISH I'D NEVER BEGUN." He pauses, then says, "I WISH I COULD STOP." This is difficult for him to say, difficult for me to hear. It hasn't occurred to me that there's anything he can't do. "I BEGAN, JUST LIKE YOU, BY HAVING AN OCCA- SIONAL CIGARETTE. PRETTY SOON I WAS SMOKING THEM ALL THE TIME. AND THE CIGAR AFTER DINNER BECAME THE CIGAR AFTER BREAKFAST. I DON'T WANT YOU TO GET INTO THAT. MAKE ME A PROMISE—"

Again he pauses, rests his cigar on my night table, and waits now for the promise. I know, of course, what it must be, but even so I am reluctant, as if with a school friend, to promise in advance. The prom- ise must first be stated.

"What?" I ask.

"THAT YOU WON'T SMOKE UNTIL YOU'RE TWENTY- ONE. BY THEN I HOPE YOU'LL HAVE SENSE ENOUGH NOT TO WANT TO."

It's not a difficult promise. Except for making me feel older, closer to my parents, cigarettes mean nothing to me. *Except*—

"I promise," I say, feeling suddenly that I've done nothing bad and maybe even something good. I certainly don't feel that I've been punished.

As if to confirm this, Father says, "IF YOU KEEP YOUR WORD, I'LL GIVE YOU A CAR WHEN YOU'RE TWENTY-ONE." This he'd intended to use, if necessary, to extract my promise. Now he just gives it to me for being good. He adds, "THE CAR WON'T COST ANYTHING. YOU'LL SAVE THAT MUCH BY NOT SMOKING."

He's smiling as he leaves my room. He has "sold" me and is anxious to tell Mother the good news. In his excitement he leaves the cigar on my night table.

I break my promise soon after enlisting in the navy, just before my eighteenth birthday.

Boot camp is an introduction to smoking. There, between classes and before mustering for meals, we're permitted time for a smoke. Just that and no more. There's no time for anything else. If one doesn't smoke, the time is wasted. I accept a cigarette from one buddy or another. It would be unfriendly not to. The cigarettes are a way of establishing contact. Soon I begin to carry them, if only to reciprocate. After ten weeks of boot camp I find that a pack lasts me easily two days. On leave, before being assigned to a ship, I have no trouble doing without cigarettes. This way there's less chance that Father will ask about smoking. However, I've decided, if he does ask, I'll tell him. I'm certain he'll consider the war an extenuating circumstance and understand how far away the age of twenty-one must seem to me. Like me, he may also wonder if I'll ever reach that age.

Aboard ship, in the Pacific, I really learn to smoke. There's so much time. The navy does what it can to fill it. I chip paint that's almost fresh, hammering away at nonexistent corrosion. I wire-brush. I cover the raw steel with red lead, then gray deck paint. Slowly I work my way from bow to stern. When I finish I start over again. The ship is seemingly endless as an oval track, endless as the Pacific itself, endless as the war. Always now in one hand there's a hammer or a brush (as, years later, there will be a pencil or a pen), in the other a cigarette. Smoking, like chipping paint (perhaps like writing too), is a way of measuring time by waste. In an hourglass the sand is used over and over again; the time returns. But the pieces of tobacco in a cigarette are literally wasted, used up, disposed of; the time is really gone, it will never return.

Four hours on, eight off, I stand watch. Whether in the wheelhouse or at a gun station, I'm allowed ten minutes in each hour for coffee and a cigarette. For fifty minutes I think about that cigarette. Nothing else seems as important. Not the zigzag course we're steering. Not the kamikaze pilots who may be hidden in the sky. Not the full load of ammunition we're carrying for the invasion of Japan. The stars themselves are unimportant, they can't light my cigarette. After fifty minutes I move as quickly as possible from the blacked-out wheelhouse or gun station, down a ladder and across the dark deck, to the hatch leading to the galley. I part the heavy curtains and light up. For the remaining minutes I smoke. Just that. Everything else is details: the coffee, the words spoken.

Cigarettes cost five cents a pack. I smoke through half a dozen brands—all that are available in the ship's store—until I find Camels, my brand, heavier, more Turkish than the others. Soon I don't even have to tell the storekeeper what I want. It's enough to say I want a carton.

I love Camels. Neither with family nor friends have I ever had a relationship such as the one I have now with this cigarette—a relationship so intimate, so steady, so dependable. The Camels are always there, over my heart in the pocket of my denim shirt, asking nothing, ready to give what I want, ready to die for me. I don't yet know that I am ready to die for them, that I would sacrifice myself, my family, my friends, my country for a cigarette. I don't know that the relationship is perfect in its reciprocity.

Not only do I love the Camels themselves, I love their package, more than the American flag, more than any masterpiece of ancient or modern art. No picture means as much to me as this one of a camel placed squarely on the sand in front of pyramids and palms. How calm he is, how unruffleable. How proud, with his nose high in the dry desert air. How timeless: he may give time to others, he is beyond it himself. What a perfect pet he is. Again, it will take years before I know I am his pet too.

Though Camels are loyal to me, I betray them. I try cigars. White Owls, Phillies—these are what the older men aboard ship smoke, the men in their early twenties with stripes on their sleeves and tattoos on their arms, the guys who are making a career of the navy or those who have learned some skill before coming in. Like them, sometimes I smoke a cigar while playing cards. The cigars do not taste or smell like

Father's, but chewing on them is satisfying: I chew time, I attack it from both ends.

Though cigarettes are cheap and we all receive about the same pay, toward the end of the month there are those with money and those without; some are always broke. They have lost their money at poker or spent it all in some port; perhaps having spent everything, they traded their cigarettes for whiskey or sex. Gladly we offer ours as Pop, aged 26, the oldest enlisted man in the crew, delivers his basic lecture on Darwinian capitalism:

"If all the money in the world were divided equally between all the people in the world, it would take about six months for those who had money to have it again and for those who had nothing to have nothing."

"Right."

"You are so right."

"That's the way it is."

Heads nod in agreement. Those who have bummed cigaretts smoke silently.

Little Willy, a heavy smoker who sleeps in the bunk below mine, says nothing. He has no money and no cigarettes, but he neither nods his agreement nor smokes. He will not smoke again until he receives his pay. He sits with his lips pressed tightly together, knowing that he still has six days to go. Like me, he smokes Camels. Several times I offer him mine, and I leave the pack on the table while we play cards. He does not mind borrowing money and returns it on payday, but he is determined to sweat out not smoking till then. By now smoking is, of course, part of my life, perhaps the best part. That Little Willy, this small man with such great pride, can stop, even temporarily, is awesome. I wonder if, when all the money is divided between all the people, Willy won't come out all right. He can exist on nothing but what's in him. He has long sideburns, twenty or more years before they again become fashionable. They, too, come out of him. His is another lecture on capitalism, but it is silent, as silent as smoking or growing hair. Without words he says one can exist on nothing.

The war ends in a cloud of smoke. We dump our load of ammunition outside Yokohama. We pick up troops and take them to Guam.

From there we proceed to Manila for orders. There is constant scuttlebutt that we will go home, but for nine months we drift. We are sent to Mindanao, where thousands of natives wait to be returned to their homes on the other side of the island. It took them two years through jungles and over mountains to escape the Japanese. Our LST makes the trip in a week, one trip after another after another. There seems no end to the natives filing out of the jungle and waiting for us on the beach. Cigarettes are a greater part of our lives than ever. We smoke them constantly; we trade them for bananas, coconuts, souvenirs, women. Cigarettes are time, and time is money.

Finally the job is done. Almost a year after the war has ended, it ends for us. I return home with a Japanese saber, a Mindanaoan kris, and a case of Camels (24 cartons, 4800 cigarettes). My parents are appreciative. Cigarettes are still scarce. We spend my first night home smoking together. I have just become twenty-one, so it's all right.

"WHAT ARE YOU GOING TO DO?"

"Go back to college."

"AND THEN?"

"I don't know."

"YOU CAN'T JUST SIT AROUND SMOKING."

But that's what I do—that and reading. I read about other people in other worlds doing other things besides smoking. And while I read I smoke.

This continues at college. There I also learn to drink. In the navy there wasn't much opportunity, only occasional nights in port. Now I can drink every night, as much as I want, as long as I want. I had not realized how well smoking and drinking go together. Nicotine and alcohol complement each other like two children at the ends of a seesaw. I watch them—aspects of me—go up and down.

By the end of senior year my education seems complete. I've even found a girl—a cousin—who likes smoking and drinking as much as I do. We both smoke Camels. We're meant for each other. Together we climb on the seesaw.

However, my education—ours now—continues. We receive many wedding gifts, most meant to last, but the best is transient, a small jar of Yucatan Purple. We've smoked marijuana a few times at college and at jazz clubs, but not of this quality. Our friend has cleaned it with great care. It is regal in appearance and effect. Up, up we go, past the haze of alcohol, past the highest cloud of tobacco smoke, until we can barely see our bodies down there—laughable little creatures, clutching Camels and cocktails, always wanting something else. Now there's nothing we want, nothing to do, and so much time to do it in.

It will take years in business to understand why this drug, as opposed to nicotine and alcohol, is illegal. Yet the reason is simple. Marijuana is subversive. It bends time, warps it. It makes a mockery of clocks, schedules, programs. Is it any wonder that the political/judicial/economic/technological/etc. system we call The Government is opposed to it? Marijuana itself is opposed to the entire system, incompatible with it.

So in business I use the socially acceptable drugs. I smoke from nine to five, five days a week. A carton of Camels is always in my desk. Seeing to that is one of my secretary's jobs. And I learn to handle first one, then two, martinis at lunch. I learn to smoke more in the afternoon to counteract the martinis. I smile through the day. There is always something good going on inside my lungs and stomach.

Outside me it is much like the navy. Business, too, has its standing watch and chipping paint, its necessary and unnecessary work. But now my real job is to make decisions, something I never had to do in the navy. Each week, for at least two hours out of forty, I make decisions. During the other thirty-eight I chip paint. The trouble is I never know when the two hours will come, what arbitrary pattern of minutes they will fall into. So I must be there all forty hours. I must stand watch. As a civilian I can smoke any time, and I do, all the time. I smoke when I'm reading my mail. I smoke when I'm on the phone. I smoke when I'm dictating. I smoke when I'm negotiating contracts. I smoke when I'm making decisions. The decision to smoke is the first step toward the next decision.

The years burn by. The size of my office grows. The size of my paycheck grows. The size of my family grows. Friends tell me it is remarkable that I haven't gained weight. I give the credit to cigarettes, just as I do when they notice that I'm still smiling when a deal breaks up. I have something to smile about, that carton of Camels in my desk. However, cigarettes aren't a guarantee of good health. The days begin with coughing. My wife and I cough good morning to each other. Often I feel a sharp pain in my chest. Sometimes my hands and feet are cold. My breath is short.

In the early fifties, as evidence appears connecting smoking with lung cancer and other awful diseases, my wife tries several times to stop. She walks around the apartment with a simulated cigarette in her mouth, taking it out only to snap at the children or me. At dinner parties she delivers lectures on the suicidal aspects of smoking. She allows no one to smoke in peace. But soon she herself is smoking again, if unpeacefully. She deserts Camels, tries the new Kents, struggles to get enough smoke into her lungs to satisfy her. Then she switches to a Dunhill holder and takes pride in showing everyone how dark and dirty the crystal filter becomes.

We take a trip to Paris. Her packing is mostly Dunhill filters. Mine is Camels. Mornings, while she prepares her costume, makeup, and smoking equipment, I get in the habit of waiting for her at a small cafe near the hotel. There I read the *Tribune*. One day, as the minutes become hours, I run out of Camels and buy Gauloises. They are a revelation, another step toward Turkey, another step toward Truth. I study the winged helmet on the blue pack, a flying faceless head. The helmet is not as pretty as the camel, but by the time my wife joins me at the cafe table I have switched. Camels no longer give me what I want. Gauloises become my Yucatan Purple. Or they are cigars disguised as cigarettes. In either case, I can see those Turks, even farther in the distance than the Mexicans and Cubans, bending rhythmically to gather their precious crop. I feel the ripple of their muscles. I smoke those muscles, that energy, baked by the sun; and my heart beats to a different drummer.

On the way home we spend a few days in Madrid. In a drugstore there I buy Asthmaticos, intended for asthmatic smokers. These cigarettes are supposed to be made with hemp. I approach them as if they are another leg of my Journey to the East, a Moorish side-trip perhaps. I light one, inhale deeply, feel nothing but a rasping in my throat as the burning cigarette crackles drily. They taste so bad I can't get through a pack, not even with my wife's help. At a restaurant I leave the remaining Asthmaticos along with the waiter's tip. He smiles knowingly.

Like Sweet Caporals, like the brands I tried in the navy before finding Camels, Asthmaticos are a brief affair. Camels I had been married to for some twenty years. Though we are divorced, the relationship lingers, especially when I can't get Gauloises. It takes time to know my new bride. She leaves a different taste in my mouth, a different smell in the room. Gauloises are the most public cigarette. They wear the largest wedding ring. They insist that they have been there, wherever there is.

When I return from Europe, *there* is right in my desk. For a while I might as well be smoking marijuana. Everyone in the office wants to know what I'm doing, what I'm trying to prove. They smell a foreign smell. I offer Gauloises to those who are interested. They smoke, cough, never ask again. Now I'm not only the thin smiling executive but the one with lungs of steel.

The surgeon general's report is published. The number of brands and types of cigarette proliferates. There are new names, new filters, new sizes. My wife tries them all. I remain faithful to Gauloises, *sans filtre.*

My son begins to smoke. I find myself saying some of the same things to him that my father said to me, and I say them with a cigarette in my mouth. For the first time, I wish that, as an example to my son, I could stop smoking. I even do some of the same kind of arithmetic Father did. I figure that for twenty-five years I have smoked about two packs a day, 365,000 cigarettes, at an average cost of 40¢ a pack, or a total of more than $7,000, not counting cigars or more exotic smokes. I have indeed smoked a car, plus optional items.

The arithmetic doesn't impress my son. I notice that in the summer when we take a walk on the beach he, like me, must now tuck cigarettes and matches into the waistband of his bathing suit. I'm envious of the children who run freely, without props.

My son and I used to play a game. We would swim to a point about fifty yards offshore and then see how far back we could swim underwater without coming up. For several years he gained on me, then passed me, but now, after about twenty yards we both come up panting for air.

I must make a four-day business trip. It annoys me, as does having to carry cigarettes on the beach, that for this trip, I must bring a carton of Gauloises, knowing that I probably won't be able to get them where

I'm going and without even being certain that they'll last four days. I decide that I'll try to make it without them and mention this to a friend who has stopped smoking.

"No," he says, "you must take them with you. You must know you have them if you want them. Otherwise you'll be bumming cigarettes from everyone else or buying whatever's available. Whenever you want a cigarette, just tell yourself that you just finished one. I still do that after almost two years."

I'm surprised he still thinks about cigarettes. I believe that if I can stop for four days I can stop forever. Aboard the plane, I find my seat in the non-smoking section: a foreign country with air as clear as Switzerland's. Here, I expect to hear the yodeling of healthy lungs. Yet it's the people in the rows behind the smoking sign—the smokers—who make exuberant noise. Quietly, I drink more than usual. I look at several magazines, hardly able to concentrate on the words. My vocabulary is limited: the only noun I know is *cigarette,* the only verb is *smoke.* I flip past the ads for cigarettes, telling myself that I have just had one. I try not to think about the passengers who are smoking. I try not to think about the carton of Gauloises in my suitcase. I welcome the NO SMOKING sign when it is on. Then I can tell myself that I wouldn't be smoking anyway. I don't like telling myself that I have just had one. I don't believe it. My last cigarette seems long ago.

With the help of many drinks I get through the first day. I fall asleep wondering, if I had to play some silly willful game, it would not have been better to give up alcohol. My liver, vivid in my mind, looks more diseased than my lungs, not vivid at all, dark as an empty theater.

The next morning is the first in many years I haven't started with a cigarette. I reach toward the night table and the Gauloises aren't there. They are still in my suitcase. Will I be able to get out of bed, shave, have breakfast, get to my meeting, get through the day, do all these things without cigarettes? I move sluggishly, as if some switch, usually turned on in the morning, has been left off. Before leaving the hotel room I put a pack of cigarettes in my pocket—just in case.

Just in case what? Just in case the craving continues? Of course it does. It intensifies. At the meeting my mind wanders constantly to my pocket. I touch the lump there, appreciating the relief it contains but resenting it too, this small blue package weighing about an ounce, which grows larger and larger, heavier and heavier. Even before noon

I suggest we recess for lunch, by which I mean a drink.

The drink helps. So does the second and third. So does the food. Everything helps that goes in my mouth. I'm starving. I'm gasping for smoke, for fuel. I'd like to go on eating and drinking forever. Without cigarettes there's no puncuation to the meal, no clear ending; it runs on.

We return to the meeting. I try not to bicker over small matters. There is only one small matter worth bickering about, that pack of cigarettes in my pocket. My body and mind are in constant dialogue. My body says it has become accustomed to nicotine. It pleads. My mind refuses. Other items being discussed at the conference table are unimportant, a background buzz of meaningless words. I wonder if I'm any longer of use to my company. I wonder if it wouldn't be honorable to resign. I feel useless, weak, vulnerable, so vulnerable. I'm like that classic dream-figure who's naked when everyone else wears clothes. I wear nothing, not even a screen of smoke.

After the meeting I have another drink and call home. I think I want to find out how my family is. I discover I want to tell them how I am. I want to tell them about my mouth, my nose, my lungs, my nerves. My wife and children are not particularly interested. They have their own lives, the house, the car, school.

I don't remember having dreamed about smoking the previous night, but tonight that's all I dream about. Cigarettes march through my mind as if in TV commercials. I smoke many of them. I awaken feeling as if all night I have done nothing but smoke. I can hardly believe that the one pack of cigarettes is still unopened in my jacket and that the rest of the carton is in my suitcase. Now I can tell myself I've just had a cigarette, dozens, while I slept.

Each day not smoking becomes a little easier, not much but a little. I smoke only in my sleep. During the day I continue to eat and drink more and more. To avoid alcohol I drink water. I go frequently to the fountain, then to the men's room. I wonder if anyone notices this. I wonder if they notice I'm not smiling as much.

My sense of taste begins to change. It's not that food tastes better, as I've been told it would, but that I have a great desire for sweets. Suddenly I want candy, chewing gum, desserts. Instead of scotch I want only bourbon and martinis.

When I return home, I look differently at my wife. I want to taste her, I want to smoke her, every orifice, beginning with her ears and nostrils and working down. I want to smoke every pore in her body. I want to smoke her toes...I look differently at all women. I have fantasies about blindfold tests. Every woman says TASTE ME.

Perhaps if once (a week ago) cigarettes controlled me, I am now out of control. At the office I try not to show my irritability. At home I let loose. I shout about too much salt or too little, a picture or a piece of furniture being out of place, anything. My son says giving up smoking is not worth this. My daughter says she wishes I would smoke again. No doubt my wife wishes that too, but tactfully she says only that I've changed.

"How?" I demand.

"You're more—more impossible than before."

I go on dreaming about smoking. In one dream I'm, at a store where there are no Gauloises available. I ask for Camels. There are none of those either. Lucky Strikes? Chesterfields? Old Golds? Pall Malls? Picayunes? Sweet Caporals? Nothing. In desperation I ask for Asthmaticos. No, not even those. In this dream I eat candy. In others I get my cigarettes and wake up in the morning with a burning chest.

I gain weight. At first my clothes feel tight. They remind me I should eat and drink less. But now I must have suits let out, I must learn to accept the new pounds which are part of me. Soon no material remains to be let out. I buy new suits, shirts with larger collars. I explain to my wife that I'm doing all this with the money saved by not smoking. In some ways I feel more guilty about not smoking than I ever felt about smoking. Often now I feel the need to explain. I explain to my wife that I don't mind her smoking, that she shouldn't mind my not smoking, that I don't feel superior to her or to others who smoke, that I'm able again to enjoy watching others smoke, that much of this pleasure is visual, etc., etc., etc. My wife says I sound like a broken record. A broken track record, I think. I'm proud of myself. By now I haven't smoked for over a month.

I have a more mysterious dream. In it I go to the Museum of Modern Art and then nearby for a long lunch with several martinis and lots of cigarettes. After lunch I walk along the street looking for the museum, to which I want to return. I see only an excavation. As I look down into the hole a girl says, "I loved your show." I assume she means the excavation. Before I can say anything, she adds, "Especially those big cigarettes." I want to tell her I'm not Oldenburg. But again she speaks: "And now I can't find the museum. It was here just a few hours ago."

"I know, I'm looking for it too. Things happen fast in New York. Maybe the museum was relocated. Maybe they moved it across the street."

We cross Fifty-third, looking for the museum. We rush up and down the block and around the corner. We are still searching when I awaken. Again there is the burning in my lungs from the fires which won't go out, fires begging for fuel ... The dots indicate a continuation, a continuing desire for cigarettes. But what does the dream mean? Anxiously I grind my teeth. Perhaps I need medical help.

It happens I have my quarter-annual appointment with the periodontist. For years he has told me that if I cut down on smoking, my teeth and gums will be in better shape. Now I'm not so sure. The heat and nicotine may be harmful, but so is the acid which builds up from the tension of not smoking. I wonder to what extent one's health is dependent on external factors. Just as the best athletes break the most bones and strain the most muscles (including the heart), and just as the best swimmers drown, the body takes its revenge on our efforts to lead a so-called healthy life.

I look around the waiting room. Everyone is smoking. It's a way to deal with waiting. The smoke moves up sinuously from magazines. It's alive. As in childhood, smoking has begun to *look* attractive. Here and in movies revived on TV and in restaurants and bars, the handsome, high-strung people, those who look as if they have something to smoke *about,* all smoke. It's the most elegant tic. I don't feel elegant. Once again I'm the only naked person in the room. I sit, heavy in my chair, thinking how much the cigarette companies must love to see thirties' movies revived, with all that carefree smoking in the days before talk of a relationship to cancer—or even periodontal problems. Are the stars all dead, they and their particular styles of smoking? Valentino, Stroheim, Bogart, Powell, Menjou—in my mind I am listing them and watching them smoke when the nurse announces that the doctor will see me.

He clucks his tongue, signifying that my mouth is in bad shape. "You'd better see me again in two months rather than three. What have you been doing?"

"I've been *not* smoking."

He smiles, waits. "And?"

"I'm eating more. Especially sweets. And I'm drinking more. Sweet drinks. Bourbon rather than scotch."

"Very common among alcoholics—"

He leaves me with that thought, suspended in the air along with the drill and other dental equipment, as he places the mask over my nose and feeds me nitrous oxide. For a moment I fight the gas, wanting to formulate a reply. I think, dentists aren't really doctors—they're doctors who couldn't get into medical school—and doctors aren't psychiatrists, and psychiatrists don't know much about alcoholism anyway.

The dentist scrapes the roots of my teeth. My thoughts move along with the steady flow of laughing gas. I wonder if tartar formation, tooth decay, gum damage, and the rest couldn't be detected just as they begin and the conditions be corrected before they become serious. Perhaps quarterly, even bi-monthly checkups aren't enough. Perhaps I should see the dentist every month, every week, every day. Yes, every day at some appointed moment my teeth should be checked, cavities nipped in the bud. Yes, yes, yes,...thirty-two times yes. So much for the teeth. The rest of the machinery must be checked too: the eyes, the heart, the mind...I see myself spending a large part of the day—at least the entire morning—preparing for my trips out into the other world, the one outside my own body. My life will be like that of an airplane: checkups, maintenance, refuelings, flights. We deserve the same attention as expensive machines...

The gas is turned off, the mask removed. I rinse. Half an hour has passed. I've forgotten what the dentist said about alcoholics. I don't want a drink. I want more gas. I wish it flowed through me all the time as nicotine once did. I want to feel good.

It's strange that, though I didn't think much about my health when I was smoking, just as I didn't think much about smoking when I was smoking, I think about both so much now. In this I'm not alone. The newspapers are full of stories about health: new drugs, new operations, new statistics. I seek more traditional medical wisdom. I love articles on acupuncture. I love this, from an interview with Alice Roosevelt Longworth: "...nothing to say on that subject [sex] except, if one wishes to talk about bodily functions, fill what's empty, empty what's full, and scratch where it itches."

The embers will not die. They still burn in my lungs, though I try to drown them in alcohol. I've refused marijuana because I don't want to be that directly reminded of smoking. A friend who has given up smoking assures me that they're not the same thing, that there's no risk. I accept the joint passed to me. How good it feels to place this skinny cigarette between my lips, to suck in the smoke, to hold it in my lungs. My friend is right. Marijuana is different from tobacco. It is gentler, less demanding, less insistent. One doesn't always want more. One is content.

Occasionally now I smoke marijuana. It is soothing and as full of chuckles as nitrous oxide. It is the laughing leaf. My wife marvels. She says I'm becoming easier to live with. I'm determined to make her marvel more. To celebrate the first anniversary of not smoking, I produce a cigar and light it after dinner. My lungs catch on fire. My head whirls. Alas, I can't smoke without inhaling. I feel so dizzy I put out the cigar. I also feel stupid. However, a few weeks later, when I'm high on alcohol and marijuana, I smoke a single cigarette, just to show I can do it. This becomes a sort of parlor trick, one cigarette every few weeks. My wife marvels. I marvel. My will seems indestructible, except when I'm high or asleep, and it relaxes.

Yes, I still dream about smoking, but one night I dream that the cigarette doesn't taste good and I crush it out. This is a step forward. A more recent dream:

I am running in some very long race, perhaps the Boston Marathon. There is no limit to my endurance. My wind is endless. While running I think: not smoking has made all the difference. The race ends. My position doesn't matter. What's important is I've finished. There are many women at the finish line. None of them cares about my lungs, none looks at my heaving handsome hairy chest. Without exception they stare at my feet. I follow their eyes to the pools of blood in which I'm standing. The women remove my shoes and socks. My feet are raw. The women bathe the bleeding sores with alcohol and then bandage the cleansed wounds. One whispers, "You should take better care of your feet."

A dream without cigarettes! But in most I smoke, and often when I awaken I wonder which is more real, the dream or the reality. Life without cigarettes is a fantasy. I never really wake up—not the way I did when I used to smoke that first cigarette of the day as if I were biting into an alarm clock.

It's time for my next appointment with the periodontist. He tells me my gums are looking still worse, bleeding too much, healing too slowly. "The condition may come from too much alcohol," he says, "*but*...are cuts anyplace else on your body healing slowly?"

"This morning I picked a scab off my leg. Scraped it several weeks ago."

"That *is* slow. Have you had a thorough physical lately? There's always the chance of diabetes."

Under nitrous oxide it's amusing to think one could get diabetes, via alcohol, from giving up smoking. But when the gas is turned off and I return to my office, I call my doctor, my real doctor, for an appointment. He tests my urine, my blood, the parts of my body. I don't have diabetes. I don't have anything. I am in good shape, except for being a little heavy—always this emphasis on shape, as if I am a piece of sculpture. He probes the shape of my mind, too, this phrenologist. Why am I drinking? What do I want? What do I *really* want?

What do *I* want? What does *he* want? What do *they* want? What, per day, is the minimum requirement of love? Of hatred? Of self-hatred? I want cigarettes to love me, as I love them, even if I have rejected them. If dentists want to be medical doctors, medical doctors want to be psychiatrists and, I suppose, psychiatrists want to be God. I skip out of his office knowing that, no matter how much excess weight I'm carrying, there's no excess sugar in my blood.

On the street a distinguished-looking man passes me, smoking a pipe. An expensive one, I'm sure. How smug he looks, with his moustache bristles standing at attention above the pipe. How contented. It occurs to me that smoking a pipe—all that fuss, all that bother, all that biting—may be his way of dealing with a lack of contentment. He may have diabetes. A lack of contentment? Is that dentist right? Am I an alcoholic? Do I perhaps use not smoking to legitimize drinking?

Another friend gives up smoking. My wife says that now this friend is less agreeable, always yawning into the phone, often drunk. As my wife speaks, I realize that these criticisms are intended also to apply to me. At our age—the friend's and mine—it's as dangerous to stop smoking as to continue. But not at my son's age. I keep telling him to stop *now*.

One night he walks into the living room, what I have called the parlor, I am doing my parlor trick, that one cigarette I occasionally—for no particular occasion—permit myself. He beams. He is so happy to see me smoking. Perhaps now I'll stop bugging him.

A friend, yet another friend, is telling a story about the Depression. It concerns a man who lived for two years in the Camels sign above Times Square, the sign which blew smoke rings onto Broadway. Every evening he would dress up, Homburg and all, as if visiting his office, and go to the top floor, and then, after the elevator left, climb an iron ladder to the sign above the building, and sleep beneath the warm lights, basking there. My son loves this story, as I do, as everyone does. This is an un-smug, un-discontented man dealing with an un-smug, un-discontented sign. Neither man nor sign has ever thought about gums, diabetes, cancer.

Though I tell my wife and son otherwise, not smoking is, at the moment, more expensive than smoking. There are the doctors' bills, the mounting cost of alcohol and food, and now I must go to the tailor again to have the new suits let out. He, too, studies my shape. He says that if he lets the suits out I'll just go on eating too much, that I looked better when I was smoking.

I try a new parlor trick: two cigarettes. I can take them or leave them. Two is no harder than one. Soon I discover that three is no harder than two. But always they are someone else's, the American filters of my wife or a friend, never my beloved Gauloises. Finally, after almost two years of not smoking, except for these tiny lapses and after this recapitulation of other brands, I buy a pack of Gauloises—just to have them around.

How quickly that pack goes. At first I allow myself one cigarette after each meal. Within a week I'm smoking one before breakfast. The experience is dizzying. It's like being on top of a mountain, a mountain which it took two years to climb and which will take perhaps two weeks to descend. I check the speed of my descent. I try to stay high on the mountain. Up there—smoking more, but still only occasionally, still measuring the cigarettes out by half-packs per day—smoking is a new experience. It is a high. Reality—the reality of smoking all the time—still seems far away, far below. I can still taste and smell. As never before, the Gauloises leave their taste in my mouth, their smell in the room.

One weekend I drive my son to college. After lunch I join him in having a cigarette. Suddenly the highway signs become significant, the way they might on marijuana. Each sign contains a message, a nicotine vision, with many levels of meaning: TOURIST INFORMATION. DIVIDED HIGHWAY ENDS. REST AREA. Even the speed limits, changing up and down, are significant, though in an indecipherable psychic code.

In a 60 MPH zone (miles per hour but also minutes per hour—hah!), we're behind a car with a large barrel on its side in the baggage compartment, the cover of which is tied down as far as it can go. We try to guess what's in the barrel. My son thinks beer. I think nails. Whatever it is, we agree it must be very heavy and wonder how it was lifted into position. When the car turns off the highway we can see the top of the barrel. It is open and empty. This, too, seems significant.

Though I'd like to preserve the sense of elation I feel now when I smoke, as imperceptibly as the movement of smoke itself I drift back to a pack a day, then two. My body's confused. It's not yet sure if I've definitely returned to smoking. At times it still becomes dizzy. The dizziness echoes my indecision. The appeal of this dizziness is as much a return to childhood merry-go-rounds and see-saws as is having something in my mouth a return to lollipops, candy bars, and ice-cream cones, even if those weren't fuming and tobacco-flavored. For a day I don't smoke at all, telling myself that I want only to be dizzy the next day. I tell myself other things too on other days when I stop—for example, that I can't be a little bit in prison, have, say, one foot in prison, but must choose between freedom and imprisonment.

An older man says he, too, was addicted to smoking until he had to give it up for his health. For a while, without cigarettes, he couldn't read, write, make a phone call, make love. He talks about a surgeon who, after giving up smoking, forgets the procedure half-way through a complicated lung operation. The surgeon excuses himself from the operating room, smokes a dizzying but exhilarating cigarette, remembers the procedure, and returns. It's a story I understand too well.

But all stories seem to be about smoking. I read Benjamin Constant's *Adolphe,* concerning his ambivalence in breaking off affairs with Mme. de Charrière and later Mme. de Staël. For me now, the names of these lovely ladies might as well be those of cigarettes. "Constant l'inconstant," my anti-hero.

Some days I put my cigarettes, matches, and ashtrays away. On other days I bring them out. As I perform these rituals, I wonder if I must spend the rest of my life under tyrannical rule, either internal or external, a slave to my own will or to that of nicotine. Not to smoke at all and to be free are not the same thing. To be free is to be free to smoke or not and that, I know, is a freedom I no longer have. And yet I like to tell myself that to be free is to be able to make decisions, that each cigarette I smoke is as much a confirmation of my freedom as those I don't smoke.

When I try to stop, I can no longer tell myself I've just finished a cigarette. I know that I didn't smoke for two years, that in smoking I express both a desire for pleasure and a fatalistic acceptance of death. Smoking is as much an ambivalent gesture of sensuality and unconcern as it is physically a mixture of stimulation and disgust. Smoking or not smoking is an inaccurate metaphor for dying or living, unless, as I do, one accepts death as part of life. Not smoking is a habit too.

I take my wife on another trip to Paris. There she insists that a vacation is the time to stop smoking. One is less nervous, she says. I reply that my smoking has nothing to do with nervousness but with pleasure. I tell her how much I enjoy Gauloises at the source, how much I enjoy Cuban cigars here where they can be bought. The vacation goes up in smoke.

When we return we learn that a close friend, a heavy smoker, has inoperable lung cancer. We visit him in the hospital. Forcing a smile, he asks his wife if he should put his sperm in a sperm bank. He presents various arguments. Pro: another baby for her, his posthumous child. Con: the possibility that cancer is genetic. He speaks of cancer as casually as if it were a headache or the "walking pneumonia" that the doctors at first thought he had; of cobalt treatments as casually as asprin. The casualness is desperate, the humor black as tar and nicotine. His laughter is half coughing. When we leave, I say a silent prayer for him, for all of us. And I begin to smoke more than ever.

For several days I smoke incessantly and then, at four packs a day, I stop. An agonizing day creeps by...two...three...a week...two weeks…It's much harder to give up smoking the second time. There's nothing to prove. I think I can do it, I have done it before. I cling to this fantasy of exact duplication and forget that in nature there is only approximate cyclical repetion, that exact repetition is the ally of death—another habit. Even stopping smoking, restopping, which would seem to be an affirmation of life, must be a new living experience.

I'm living it. Now many weeks have passed since my last cigarette. Again I'm thinking about cigarettes all the time, every day, and I'm dreaming about them at night. In one dream I study my teeth, the color of tobacco. And then suddenly I am tobacco, and I am packed into a cigarette, one among many insignificant particles. In a sweat I fight my way out of the paper cage. When I escape I reach once again for a cigarette as if for an electric switch that isn't there, and after meals to wash down the food, and at cocktails to lighten the load of the alcohol. Yes, often in sleep I am a cigarette, and I reach blindly for myself.

That is when I *can* sleep. There are nights when I can't, when all I do is think about cigarettes, count them, play variations on those tired old arithmetic games, seeking new stunning cigarette soporifics. I try now to measure the distance in miles through which I've smoked. Say, very conservatively, that the total number of cigarettes has reached 400,000. (I eliminate everything exotic and hand-rolled as being too sloppy for me in my present role as computer, if not as sucking machine.) Multiply 400,000 by 2½ inches per cigarette. That comes to exactly 1,000,000. Divide same by 12. That's 83,333.33333 etc. feet, an irrational number, an infinite repetition, a habit. I had guessed a distance from here to Virginia, or maybe even as far as Cuba or Mexico or Turkey. But no, I divide 83,333 by 5,280 and get only 15½ miles—the distance from New York to Yonkers or from Wellfleet to Provincetown, a bug's walk, mine! I swing from one extreme of infinity to another. They meet in midbrain/midair, like two puffs of smoke.

Less incessantly now my body howls its pain and deprivation. It gets up in the morning, it absorbs its food and drink, it does what it has to do, it functions without cigarettes. I begin to think that I can no longer enjoy them. They smell bad. They taste bad. By not smoking, I've learned to smell and taste them when my wife and others smoke.

I wonder if cigarettes, like whiskey, are an acquired taste, a taste which one must learn not to taste. But I don't dare test this theory. I'm in a position where I can neither enjoy smoking nor not smoking. I can enjoy only the illusion of absolute freedom to do either.

An almost full carton of Gauloises remains in my desk, a different carton, in a different desk, at home. After so many years I've come to think of smoking as positively useful and productive. With the burning of each cigarette, the crushing of each empty pack, the discarding of each empty carton, there has been a sense of real progress. But now I'm not sure if smoking the remaining cigarettes or discarding them would be the greater waste.

I don't know if I'll ever smoke again. I can imagine being sentenced to death (by some external force rather than by life itself) and being offered a last cigarette. Perhaps my hands are tied. Perhaps I am blindfolded. I can imagine parting my lips, as I have so many times before, and accepting the cigarette. I can also imagine refusing it.

Moving in Place

My wife clutches my arm, digging her fingernails into the biceps, telling me thus forcefully but secretly—she doesn't want the real estate broker to know—that she likes the apartment, loves it (her nails dig deeper), lusts for it (deeper still). It is a grip I know well after twenty-five years of other apartments, vacation homes, the brownstone we have lived in during the last sixteen years. It is a grip that will not let go until the place is hers. It is also a grip I encourage—I don't pull my arm away. Now as in the past, I want to give her not just jewels, flowers, small tokens of affection, but whole environments, one larger than the next, to play with and possess.

Her message is already tattooed on my arm as, for the second time, from room to room we follow the broker, a pudgy but mobile middle-aged lady who seems to know the price, the maintenance, the special qualities of every co-operative apartment in the city. We listen to her describe what we see: "uncounted rooms"—entrance foyer and gallery, both terrazzo. "Banks no longer have the money for floors like these." She catches her breath. "Not to mention," she says mentioning, "the pantry, the laundry, the storage room—amenities no longer provided in your standard twelve-room co-op." She is excited by the bargain she is offering, reaches toward the ceiling. "Eleven feet throughout—double-hanging space in the closets, which would be rooms in the newer buildings. But you know what space is—you've lived in *a house*." She, too, lives in a house; she smiles complicitously.

We know what space *was*. Sixteen years ago. Before we noticed that much of it was wasted by stairs and floor landings. Before we discovered that everything from toilet paper and cigarettes to vacuum cleaners and TV sets had to be duplicated on each floor. Before our son became interested in drumming and hi-fi equipment. Before our second child, a daughter, was born and began surrounding herself with dolls, stuffed animals, minature furniture. Before my wife began collecting Bennington and quilts and other Americana. Before the paintings crowded the walls and spilled out into the stairwells, along with the files from my study. Before the bookshelves were filled and new ones had to be added. Before "finishing" part of the basement. Before having an architect study and negate the feasibility of another room on the roof...Before all this we knew what space was, but we are here now because we no longer know.

Many conversations, most of them started by me, have led to our being here. My wife has at last admitted that the house has become crowded and inefficient. She knows that our elderly live-in maid has difficulty getting up and down the stairs, that she would be hard to replace, that even the men hired to do heavy and high cleaning pant, complain, drift off. She wants the children to have more isolated space. She wants a room of her own. She wants me also to have more privacy and quiet. She is tired of my complaints—and those of my secretary. She is tired of the garden behind the house, tired of watering and weeding. When we entertain, she is tired of the awkward vertical movement from the living room, downstairs to the dining room, and back up again to the library for coffee. It is all steps, with no easy horizontal flow, except on a nice night when she can use the garden. Otherwise her beloved big parties are uncomfortable; the stairs become congested.... And yet, though she admits the disadvantages of the house, it is—in her mind, her heart—everything it contains: her, her family, her things. There is no separating the house from its contents. A move is unthinkable. Whatever is wrong with the house, there are worse things wrong with apartments. Haven't we lived in them before the house? Don't I remember what it is like waiting for an elevator, being in one, having to say good morning, good afternoon, good evening, good night to elevator operators and doormen when the days and nights aren't always good? She knows what she doesn't want: an apartment.

I remind her of one we have seen years befoe, a "maisonette," the ground floor and basement of an apartment house overlooking the East River. No elevator. A better view than that from the brownstone.

All the advantages of an apartment house—the horizontality, the service, the security—with none of the disadvantages. She listens, says what we saw was unique, says she'd consider something like it, gambling on the unlikelihood. To strengthen her bet, she adds that she likes our present neighborhood, reminds me that it is central to everything—just east of Fifth Avenue shops, a few blocks from Third Avenue movies and not too far from Broadway, near office buildings, right at the pulsing heart of the city. "I don't like exclusively residential neighborhoods. I want to see something besides mothers and nurses wheeling baby carriages. I like those models carrying their portfolios, and spastic messengers with fat rolls of blueprints. I like a choice of banks."

Money distorts true odds. Within a few days the broker comes up with the apartment, the maisonette, we are seeing, very similar to the one seen long ago. It is five blocks from our house, a different neighborhood, as five blocks (or even one) can mean in New York, but still close enough.

The broker says, "It hasn't been listed yet—it's in the hands of an estate—but I have entrée to the lawyers. They've given me a price."

It seems much more than we can get for the house, and the estate wants all cash.

The earlier conversations with my wife; the gap in price, plus maybe as much again to fix up the apartment and move into it; my wife's sharp enthusiastic grip—all these are on my mind as we re-enter the living room. Here the broker spreads her arms as if to describe a room that got away: fourty-four feet, eight times her arm spread. Her small red fingernails tremble, lost in this grand optimistic space, a vision of the 'twenties, a product of the boom.

"See the thickness of the walls. They...."

Yes, she is right, they don't build them like this anymore. Yes, two comtemporary co-ops could fit in this one—maybe three, considering the height of the ceilings, the cubic content. Yes....

We don't have to be sold. We are standing now at the bay window of the living room, watching a tanker four hundred feet long, two city blocks, move slowly up the river like a toy put there for our amusement, along with distant prop-like (now pop-like) Pepsi Cola and Paragon Oil signs. Pepsi, Paragon—these and the view itself are liquid and alive. We might be in Venice. How few places, like that, like *this,* are left to show the relationship between sea and land. Here five large rooms look out on the river and the other seven (plus), facing north and south, all have oblique views of it. Yes times twelve (not counting foyer, gallery, pantry, laundry, or storage room). Yes, yes, yes, yes, yes...

"It's overcast today," the broker observes, "and besides these windows haven't been washed in months. Can you imagine what this view would be under the right conditions?"

I look at my wife. She looks at me. We can imagine. Not only brighter days but darker ones, an exciting range of weather, sky, river traffic. This is no little garden to cultivate. This is a world—with sky. We raise our sights.

I make an offer substantially below the asking price—one-third cash, one-third a year from now, the balance in two years.

The broker says, "If you get it for that, it will be the best buy since Stuyvesant bought the island from the Indians. But I doubt if your offer will be acceptable."

Disappointment and anxiety flicker across my wife's face. Her nails are digging into my arm again. I say nothing. As we leave the building, elevator operators sitting in the lobby jump to attention.

"You like it, don't you?" my wife asks when the broker leaves.

"We won't find anything better."

"Then why didn't you give the broker more leeway?"

"She's experienced. She knows we're seriously interested. She'll get back to us. Don't worry."

The broker calls the next day, says that the offer is unacceptable, that the executors are unwilling to drop the asking price, which has gone out to other brokers, suggests a compromise. "There are no guarantees. Another broker may bring in a better offer. And of course everything is subject to your approval by the Owners Committee."

"Of course. We'd better see the apartment again."

The physical space and the view are as beautiful as we remember, but now we look more closely at air-conditioning units, kitchen and laundry equipment, chandeliers and sconces, venetian blinds, valances, draperies—almost all in poor condition. Soot drifts in under some of the windows. The linoleum in the kitchen and laundry is worn through.

"We'll have to strip almost everything," I say to my wife.

"Oh, no, there's a lot that's usable."

"What?"

"I like the gas dryer in the laundry. It's a collector's item. And the old stove. And the glass doors on the kitchen cabinets."

In short, she likes the apartment. As I strip it, she is salvaging things in it to add to those in our house. As I anticipate expenses, she is discovering economies of the sort she finds when buying things on sale that she wouldn't ordinarily buy. She feels that she has a bargain. I know that the move will cost much more than orginally estimated— more in time and effort, as well as money.

We will eliminate the pantry wall and open up the kitchen area. Two of five maids' rooms will make a comfortable study for me, two more will make a nice room for our maid, leaving one, which will have to be carefully planned to accommodate my secretary. To my wife each wall knocked down is a saving, one less room to deal with, the erasure of a line on a plan, but I am beginning to think about the lines within the lines—plumbing and electrical work and patching. There are bookcases and storage walls to be built, a bar, a wine closet.... There's a lot to be done.

As we leave, the elevator operators jump to attention. I would eliminate them too and automate the elevators, or, better still, eliminate the entire building above the ground floor, slice it off clean and watch it float down the river. Yes, as my wife has found assets in old gas dryers and other things that I know must go, I begin to find liabilities in things that must stay.

"Don't you think the terrazzo in the entrance area is pretentious?" I ask.

"No, I like it."

"But it's cold and institutional. Like walking into a bank."

"I like banks."

"But do you think the children or some of our friends will feel comfortable? Maybe the whole place is a little too grand. That Owners Committee. Those jumping-jack elevator operators.... Will you feel comfortable going to the supermarket in jeans?"

"I won't pay any attention to the operators."

Though I know this isn't true, I know also it's a way of saying once again that she likes the apartment, wants it.

It takes only a phone call to close the deal verbally, more than a month to close it on paper. During this period we visit the apartment every few days and spend many evenings studying the plan. On it we knock out more walls, restore one that the previous occupant had removed, build bookshelves, bar, storage walls and other cabinet work, place furniture. My wife is happy. All of our furniture will fit, and there'll be room for more, a need for more, especially in the living room. She has cast her bread upon the waters. Now her possessions will multiply. She pencils in new couches, new chairs, new tables, new surfaces for bric-a-brac. The plan is a dense maze, Celtic in its complexity, primitive in its *horror vacui*. I flinch.

"What's the matter?" she asks.

"I thought this was a chance to get rid of some of the junk, to simplify our life and make it more efficient. You have so many chairs we can't sit in, so many things that don't work."

"They're pretty. What do you want?"

"Less."

Actually, as much as she, I want to add what the new apartment needs, but to do this within the context of subtracting the superfluous and unfunctioning objects that have accumulated in the house over sixteen years: the billiard chair, the cracked green-glass art nouveau pedestal, the warped table inlaid with broken crockery, the mechanical lark lure, the antique cheese press, the peeling store signs, the dozens of zany object which my wife (often with my encouragement) found irrestible and which I now resist. Tears come to her eyes as I reject these fragments of her life, our life, our life together, a quarter of a century of fashions, trends, impulses, path-findings and -followings, moves.

"Some of what you call junk has become valuable," she says. We are still bickering when friends, a couple from out-of-town who haven't seen us in some time, come by for drinks. They can't believe we are going to sell our beautiful house. Suddenly we are both calm, cool, rational—a team. Almost in unison we explain the reasons for the move: the need for more usable and efficient space; my wife's needs, the children's, my own; the better view, the service, the security. Our friends tell us about their move, a few years before we knew them, from a small house to their present large one, his ulcer attack, her migraines, their near-divorce, their children's hostility.

"How have *your* children reacted?" they ask.

We hesitate. We cannot now speak in unison. Our daughter has made it clear that she doesn't want to leave the house, that what we are doing is spiteful—uprooting her, her dolls, her stuffed animals. She has seen her sunny new large room with its bay window hanging over the river. She likes the old room better. And our son? He has refused to visit the apartment, doesn't care what his room is like, likes his old one fine. Thus there are hints of the next generation's dissent but none of our own. Our public stance shows nothing very complicated about a move, nothing worth fighting or getting sick over, no disruption which can't be minimized by proper planning. When our friends leave, we swear that even if our marriage or our bodies fall apart we will never tell. The world will see only our new home, not the bills—economic, physical, psychological.

But already, with the closing still a couple of weeks off, I recognize that we need help. I have so far used a broker to find the apartment, a banker to arrange for the ten percent on contract and the rest of the one-third cash I will need on closing, a lawyer to go over the papers. I am willing to let medical doctors, psychiatrists, marriage counselors, other specialists wait in the wings. What I—we—need now is an architect or a designer or even a decorator, someone to take care of all the details of moving.

My wife says, "We've moved before without help. I don't want anyone to decorate our home. I want it to be ours."

"The situation is different. We moved from a comparatively small apartment to a house. We didn't have two grown children. We didn't have a maid. I didn't always work at home. I didn't have a secretary coming in. We didn't have thousands of books and records and pictures and pieces of china.... Whoever you get isn't going to change what we have, just help you place it. It's one thing to draw a shelf on a plan, another to specify the material, its thickness, the type of support. Every line you've drawn on those plans requires more lines, explanations, supervison of the actual work. I can't give my full time to that during the next six months. Neither can you. And even if we could, we're not qualified to do the job. The mistakes we'd make would cost more than the service of a professional. One of the reasons for moving is to correct the mistakes we made in the house."

"They're not mistakes. You said yourself that our situation has changed."

"That too."

My wife looks hurt. For several minutes she stares at the tangle of lines on the floor plan as if wandering among them, following various dead-end paths, going back, starting again, seeking some central answer.

"Who do you suggest?" she asks.

I mention several architects and designers.

"None of them is right. None knows us well enough to do the job."

They don't have to know us well, maybe the less well the better. Then they can be more objective. All they have to do is find the right solution to our needs, express our wishes. Just like brokers and bankers and lawyers."

"You make it sound so simple. What if your wishes and mine aren't the same?"

"They mediate. Or we separate, move in different directions."

"Not funny."

We decide to call a designer who worked on the apartment of friends who say the man is flexible, thorough, dependable. My wife is wary. She knows that all designers are willful dictators. She remembers that somewhere the architect Richard Neutra said, if he wished, he could break a previously happy marriage by the design of the house in which the family is to live.

"Maybe the converse is true too," I remark.

Again she says, "Not funny."

The designer is in his early fifties, half a dozen years older than we are. His graying beard and moustache are neatly trimmed, tapering to even more closely cropped hair around the ears. The top of his head is bald, scrubbed-looking, possibly polished. His features, too, have a sharp, clean, buffed look. He wears an open shirt with an ascot, a safari jacket, tight twill pants, tan chukkas. His clothes are sharply pressed, immaculately clean. He presents a sense of meticulous measure. From the top of his head to his feet there are no concessions to the excesses of the day's fashion—no wide lapels, no flare to the trousers. He looks right for the job—like us, a trifle dated. And with him is an assistant in his early thirties with much more hair, more collar, more pants bottom, no ascot, no tie—a link, he seems, to the hip present. Together they will understand us—and maybe our children.

They go through our house, asking what works, what doesn't, what stays, what goes. They comment enthusiastically about a few pieces, remain tactfully silent about most. They like the house itself, wonder why we want to leave, ask us to explain. While we talk the designer makes notes and directs his assistant to take various measurements and Polaroid shots. The tapemeasure whirs, the camera clicks.

After about two hours we walk to the apartment building. As we enter our apartment, I say, "I wish I didn't feel as if I were still in the lobby. This is the single space I like least. It's so big and cold and forbidding."

"It won't be," the designer replies, "not with pictures on the walls, good lighting, a rug, plants, maybe some woodwork."

"Yes," my wife says, "I don't mind the entrance, but the whole place is so empty."

"That's what we're here for," the designer replies.

We walk through the apartment, quickly first, so they can get a general sense of it.

"Splendid!" the designer announces in almost every room. "Splendid scale!...Splendid openness!...Splendid view!..."

His assistant is silent the first time through, concentrating, it seems, more on architectural details than on the overall space, perhaps wondering again why we are moving, perhaps hiding some objective judgment.

"What I like," he says the second time through, "is the lack of fussy details. You don't find that in many buildings of this period. We can clean up the window line in the living room and get rid of the mantel there and in the bedroom, and all these chandeliers and sconces and drapes."

As he finishes, he yanks a dessicated, stained, faded drape from the valence. It falls, letting light in through the dusty window.

"But we want some of the warmth and charm of our house," my wife says, looking sadly at the drape on the floor, her eyes emphasizing how much could be done even now by just washing it—perhaps in her own tears.

The designer looks paternally at his assistant and my wife. The assistant has been a bad boy, but a good bad boy. My wife has been a good homemaker, but a bad good homemaker. "No two places have the same character," he says. "We must find the particular warmth and charm that suit this apartment."

They are busy now, taking more notes, measurements, photographs. They check measurements against the plans. They rap walls, discover a hidden niche in my wife's study, two covered bookcases and another window in the living room, and another niche near that.

"We could tuck a little bar in here," the designer says.

"We don't want a litte bar," I reply.

"No," my wife adds, "we want a big bar, a bar bar that you sit at—on stools."

"Oh."

"Oh."

The afternoon goes this way. They make discoveries we have missed on ten visits to the apartment. We reiterate demands that we thought were clear at our house, from the way we've lived, the way we've talked to them about our "program," as they call it.

"We'll have to visit your house again," the designer says. "We'll need the lineal feet of bookshelves, kitchen cabinets, hanging space in closets; phone locations; TV, kitchen and laundry equipment—you know. And we'll have to come back here frequently. When do you take possession?"

"The closing's set for two weeks from now. Next week we appear before the Owners Committee. The lawyer for the seller said that's routine. The committee's already checked our references. The lawyer's given us keys. I'll give you one."

"Well—I thought everything was definite—but until the purchase is completed, we can work on a time basis, the usual $50 an hour. If we go ahead, that will be applied against our straight 25%. I'll send you the standard contract."

"We'd also like an estimate for the cost of the job and the time it will take. We leave for the Cape in early June and want to move into the apartment before then."

"We can't prepare an estimate, even a rough one, until we agree on what's to be done. We'll make sketches. If you approve those, we'll proceed to working drawings and contract bids. If the contractor starts work by early February, you should be in in four months — barring changes, of course, and finishing work that can be done over the summer."

An appointment is set for the assistant to come to our house again in a week, when he'll do the additional necessary mesurements and get detailed information on kitchen and laundry equipment. Meanwhile he and the designer will stay at the apartment for another hour or so and then visit it as necessary. They hope to have preliminary sketches to show us in about two weeks, soon after the closing. No time will be lost; none can be if we're going to move by June.

"They're very professional," I say to my wife as we walk home.

"All right," she snaps, "I'm not. But I don't believe in this whole idea of instant design. It took sixteen years to get our house looking the way it does. It grew organically, not from some master plan. One piece of furniture led to another, one accessory led to another — "

"They can save you all that time."

"I don't want it saved. And I don't want to be saved. I don't want to be dictated to.... They don't like women anyway."

"There was nothing to indicate that."

"Oh, yes, there was. Did you see the way they looked at our furniture. And the first thing they want to do in the apartment is tear out the mantel, the best thing there. And how many times did I tell them that the bar in the house is too small, that I like to sit at a bar and look at the water, the way we do on the Cape?"

"None of that was aimed at you. They have to begin somewhere. They'll do their sketches and we'll criticize them. You'll get what you want."

"Maybe — with a lot of condescension. They don't talk to you the way they do to me. With you, everything's so cozy, so clubby, so man-to-man — all that talk about contracts and estimates and working drawings and schedules. You just have to say yes. No wonder you get along so well. All you care about is how long the job will take, how much it will cost, how everything will function. I care about how everything will look."

"It will look beautiful. Give them a chance. Tell them what you need, without stipulating design. Don't ask them to duplicate the house. If you want that, there's no point in moving. Wait and see their sketches."

"I'll wait."

She meets with the assistant designer. At his urging and mine, she goes through the house, room by room, closet by closet, shelf by shelf, cupboard by cupboard, looking for things that can be discarded, sold, traded for other things we'll need more.

"He's right. You're right. I don't need it all, but these things mean something to me, they're part of my life, memories, three-dimensional souvenirs." She smiles imploringly.

I suggest items: lamps that will be replaced by built-in lighting, furniture that will be replaced by storage walls, the art nouveau pedestal, the warped table, the store signs, some paintings and sculpture that have become more valuable in the market than to us.

Well, maybe one lamp she never really liked that much. Maybe the warped table, maybe one or two works of art that have become *really* valuable. But not the pedestal, not the store signs, not....

"I've been unreasonable," she announces the night before our meeting with the Owners Committee. "They should design the apartment; I'll furnish it." She returns to the floor plans, squeezing pieces in here and there. "The pedestal will look marvelous in that corner. It will be a little surprise."

"To everyone but me," I reply.

There is no stopping her. They will design the apartment, she will furnish it, decorate it, give it its warmth and charm. I glance at the plan she is scribbling on in bed. Penciled lines extend beyond the boundaries of the apartment, like furniture hanging out of the windows.

"You don't think there's any chance we won't be accepted?" she asks.

"No, the lawyer said they've checked everything."

"Wouldn't that be something?"

"What?"

"If we didn't get in."

"Yes, it would be something."

I turn on my side away from the light, wondering just what, more specifically, it would be. During these weeks while my wife's enthusiasm has increased, mine has diminished, turned into souring detachment. I have already spent too many hours discussing the move with her, and with the broker, the lawyer, the designers. Even now I have little time in which to do anything else. And yet I know I have just begun. The detailed planning and paperwork, as well as the physical move, are still to come. And I must still sell the house. Where once a move meant piling a few possessions into a station wagon or a small truck, I realize now it will mean not that day's work but the next four or five months'. Will it be worth that, trading almost half a year of my life (some fairly large fraction of whatever years remain) for a more efficient home, a superior view? And how much more efficient will the new place be if my wife has her way, if she insists on transporting the clutter of the house? I fall asleep counting rooms, those in the house, those in the apartment, twelve of one, a dozen of the other, a baker's dozen, more.... I don't think it would be so bad if the Owners Committee turned us down. Yes, it would be a rejection. That would be something. But it would be a gift of the next several months of my life. And that would be something too.

The chairman of a large chemical company is also chairman of the co-op. My wife and I soar to his tower suite in a new office building on Park Avenue. It is new on the outside anyway. In his suite everything is old. The mahogany dest and chairs, the couch and coffee table (hunt-style), the prints on the walls—all seem to say they have been there longer than the building itself. I can imagine how smoothly his move must have gone—just a memo or a brief call on intercom and then one morning he reports to this replica of what he had in some older building. I am envious. None of his furniture hangs out the windows.

He introduces us to two more directors of the co-op, the president of the real estate firm which manages it and the president of an oil company. They lead us to the couch and sit opposite us, three men in dark suits, white shirts, muted ties, staring hard. I feel like a hippie in my blazer, pink striped shirt, and knit tie, married to another in her suede suit and turtleneck. Perhaps in trying to reassure her and relieve her anxiety, I've overemphasized the casualness of the occasion. I'd said, "Wear what you want. The worst they can do is refuse our money. Ha ha." The joke no longer rings true. They can refuse *us*.

At last the chairman speaks. He welcomes us to the co-op, says that it is one of the finest, best-managed buildings in the city and that he and his co-directors want to keep it that way.... They and their pre-decessors have established rules to maintain the high standards. Deliveries must be made through the service entrance. Servants must use it too. After midnight all entrances are locked. One must ring for an attendant.... Alterations must be approved by the managing agent. So must sub-leases.... All of this is for our own protection as well as the other owners'. We will receive the full list of rules and procedures.... He invites questions. We have none.

"That was easy," my wife whispers when we leave the chairman's office.

In the reception room another couple is waiting. They are fatter than us, better dressed, a little too well dressed.

"Do you think they'll get in?" my wife asks at the elevator landing.

"Yes. Those men would never put themselves in the position of rejecting anyone face-to-face. They have professionals to do that— probably someone in the agent's office, The Man Who Says No."

"Professionals—I'm getting tired of professionals. I bet you weren't so sure of yourself when those three men were studying us."

"For a moment I wasn't sure they'd accept us. But I was sure that if they didn't, they'd be making a mistake."

I laugh. She laughs. We are happy. One hurdle has been crossed, and the closing is just two days off.

It, too, goes easily—professionally, as I later remind my wife. The work has been done in advance by the lawyers—for us, for the estate of the seller, for the co-op corporation. Papers are handed around the conference table—an assignment of shares of stock in the co-op; a proprietary lease; the check, certified by my bank, for one-third of the purchase price; notes covering the balance due, secured by the stock to be held in escrow; the escrow agreement itself; another check, uncertified, for the adjustment of the month's maintenance .... While my wife and I sign what and where we're told, the broker—that active, talkative little lady—is motionless and silent. She waits quietly (professionally, I think again) for the commission check from the seller. When it's given to her, she glances at it once, like a poker player's down card, recognizes the amount she has previously computed, folds the check, puts it in her purse, and pounces on us.

"I've talked confidentially to a few people I thought might be interested in your house, explained that it was nothing definite, just a possibility. I think I've got some real interest."

"At what price?"

"The price of the apartment—or very close to it."

"Bring them around."

My wife's expression changes. Until then, she may have thought that we were simply buying a beautiful apartment overlooking the East River. Now she knows, really knows, that I intend to sell the house. Until then she was crossing hurdles, winning some race; now she is losing another, one she has been running for sixteen years. Signing all those documents and checks has cured my ambivalence, my detachment. I am committed now to the apartment. The house is only something I have to sell.

On the way home she asks, "Do you think we've made a mistake?"

"No, we did the right thing."

That seems enough to say, enough reassurance. When the designers appear two days later with their preliminary sketches, I discover how wrong I am, how much more reassurance she needs.

The senior designer spreads the plans flat on our dining room table. His assistant places an ashtray on each curling end.

"The entrance foyer!" the designer announces.

There, in that cold space, is a warm, wood wall closet, opposite our present living room couch, above which hang three small paintings. On the floor there are a lot of plants, a piece of sculpture, and a rug, which he explains "could be an antique Afghanistan."

My wife starts to complain. "But it isn't..." *my home at all,* I know she wants to say.

The designer raises his finger, stops her. "I want you to get the whole concept," he says, flipping this sketch over to the next sheet.

The gallery walls are covered with bookcases, each shelf filled end-to-end, except for a few carefully placed art objects, with compulsively sketched books. All that's missing is the titles and authors. But I can see them—from J.R. Ackerley to Louis Zukofsky.

"You've allowed enough space?" I ask.

"Oh, yes. Including the cases in the living room and those scattered elsewhere through the apartment, you'll have 25% more than now."

He turns the sheet. We are in the living room. At one end, about five feet from the wall, there is indeed a large bar with stools, not facing the river but looking south at it through the window he has uncovered. The bar nicely breaks the length of the room and establishes its own area, just as at the other end the uncovered recessed bookcases seem to widen and define that area, where he has retained the ornate face of the mantel but enclosed it and open log storage in a continuous shelf running from one side of the room to the other. A small couch, many chairs, tables, and cushions are scattered informally throughout.

"My mantel!" my wife begins. "We like to sit around a fire, look at it and a pretty mantel, listen to music. What you've done doesn't look—comfortable. All those little chairs and tables.... And we want to be able to look at the river. From the bar. Without craning our necks. And—"

"There's a lot to explain about this sketch. It's a beautiful room but difficult to work with. We wanted to cut its length and make it less rigid. We could have kept the mantel and flanked it with couches and we could have run the bar lengthwise, but that would have made the room more linear. The surface above the fireplace is intended to be limestone or rough-hewn wood—we want your preference—but whatever it is, the material should be warmer than the marble of the existing mantel, and you'll have a lot more surface. The same material would be used for the bar. We think of the entire bar area as being raised on a platform. You won't see the drive, you'll look right out onto the river.... The speakers for your hi-fi will be recessed in the bookshelves or in the fireplace enclosure. You mustn't think of these sketches as anything but preliminary. We want you to study them and let us have your comments as soon as possible. Our next meeting should be in the apartment. Maybe tomorrow or the next day?"

We set a date. Then he continues, room by room, presenting the sketches, explaining what materials he has in mind, the reasons for eliminating certain pieces of furniture and adding others.... The dining room, our bedroom, my wife's study, and the children's rooms need hardly to be touched. He has perfectly rearranged our existing furniture, adding only a storage wall in our bedroom and the study. My office furniture, too, is perfectly rearranged. The room is larger and better laid out than my present one. Not only has he knocked out the wall between the two maids' rooms but he has eliminated the corridor running alongside them and given me that extra space. Similarly, my secretary's office has been enlarged and made more efficient.

We come to the kitchen, an area now, with the pantry wall out, about twenty feet square. Like the sketch of the living room, it is open and informal. A ten by four foot butcher block table with stools around it extends from the window wall. The refrigerator is neatly recessed into an irregularity in the opposite wall. The other two walls have butcher-block counters with the existing glass-door cabinets above, which my wife has said she wants to keep. Mottled dishes, bowls, platters, pitchers (all Bennington, I suppose) are visible on the shelves along with unmottled pieces—everything from Ironstone to Sandwich. But this is my wife's department. She studies the sketch, has questions about knife slots, platter storage, a place for cook books, an herb shelf, more electric outlets, more hooks, more....

The designer takes notes. His assistant goes into our kitchen and for the first time takes pictures there of all the walls, all the things hanging on them—bread boards, baskets, rolling pins, sausages, bunches of garlic, scissors, bottle openers, graters, strainers, a pencil sharpener, a match striker, an old-fashioned yard stick on a leather thong, a nest of metal measuring cups, pipkins, dozens and dozens of utensils that don't appear in the sketch.

"There'll be a place for everything," the designer says.

"And everything in its place," his assistant adds a bit sarcastically.

Once again the designer gives his assistant and my wife that paternal look, lofty, perhaps justifiable, from years of experience.

That night, with drinks in hand, my wife and I study the sketches, not room by room now but foot by foot—in scale, one quarter inch to the foot.

"I hate it," she says as she looks at the sketch of the living room. "All those chairs and tables look like a lot of praying mantises, poised on their skinny little legs.... Maybe those guys are right about the mantel. We will have a lot more surface, and it kind of ties the room together. And maybe they're right about running the bar across the room. But they're not right about raising that area on a platform. That's trendy nonsense. It turns the rest of the room into a conversation pit. I don't like conversation pits. D'you know what I'd like? Another drink."

"Me too: another drink. And me too: no platform, no conversation pit. When we're sitting at the bar we'll be high enough. Besides the platform would be a big expense. For nothing. If we see the drive, we see it. Right?"

"Right. I love it. I love the whoosh of the cars going by."

These are the first unqualifiedly positive words she has spoken all evening: we are making progress. After all, except for restudying the living room and adding details in the kitchen and a few other areas, the sketches satisfy our requirements.

She continues to look at the living room sketch. "It's going to be awfully dirty and noisy."

"Where the windows are working well, there's no dirt or noise. The others will be fixed."

"It'll never be as quiet as this garden."

"I thought you liked the activity on the drive and the river."

"I like it here."

"It's late for that decision."

"Too late?"

"No. I'd rather put the apartment back on the market and pay the designers for their time than go through the trouble and expense of the move and have you decide then.... Also, by then this house will be sold—I hope."

"I don't know how you can be so detached. We've lived here sixteen years. Doesn't this house mean anything to you?"

"Yes, I like it very much; I like the apartment better."

"But you were the one who objected to the lobby, the doorman and elevator operators, our own foyer."

"I'm used to them now, and the foyer's not going to look the way it does."

"The children don't want to move."

"Why would they? They've never known any other home, except during the summer and on vacations. If we're happier, they will be too."

"You really think we're doing the right thing?"

"Yes."

At the next meeting with the designers, we spend most of our time in the apartment living room. There they have taken down all the drapes, and they have completely exposed the window behind the future location of the bar and the bookcases on the wall at right angles to the fireplace. Already the room is brighter and more open, the bar location is right.

I say this, and explain—in neutral, practical terms—that we don't, however, want the bar area raised, that we can't justify the expense of the platform which will create a step up at the entrance to the living room and a step down inside it, both possibly hazardous.

The designers resist. They want clear separation and definition of bar and seating areas. "There's another problem," the designer says, "we have to get plumbing to the bar. We were going to run it under the platform, from the powder room."

"What about running it from the master bath below?"

"That's a possibility. We'll look into it."

We concentrate now on the seating. My wife brushes aside all the insect-like little chairs and tables. "What we want," she says, "is a big table in front of the fireplace and some comfortable couches around it—at least two, maybe three."

"We tried to make the room more informal, more flexible. You'll lose that, once you anchor a seating group at the fireplace."

"I like to stretch out on a couch. So does my husband, the children, our friends—"

"Leather? There are some new Italian couches."

"We'd have to see them, sit in them."

"Maybe if we covered them in the same leather, or whatever material, as the bar stools—"

We can see the revised design concept taking shape in his mind. There are showrooms to visit, shopping to be done. My wife is happy. She will be buying conversation pits that look like couches and bar stools.

We visit the showrooms, sometimes together, sometimes separately because one of us must be at the house to show it. Our broker and others who have received the listing call, make appointments, lead couples (mostly younger than us) through the house. Increasingly I resent the intrusion on my time, and my wife the intrusion on her home. I think she and I have agreed on what will be included in the sale—everything that's attached (carpeting, shelving, lighting fixtures); kitchen and laundry equipment; two complete groups of furniture, in the breakfast room and garden, which were designed for those specific areas. But suddenly she decides that maybe, just possibly, she may want the breakfast room bench, the garden tables....

"Where would you put them?"

"I don't know. There'll be a spot."

"But the price I've quoted to the brokers includes these items. I'm not asking you to throw in any of the other furniture we won't need. We can negotiate that later with the buyer."

In the same way as, by compromise, the apartment is gradually being designed and furnished according to our collective taste, the house is being sold. My wife's reluctance communicates itself to prospective buyers and balances my eagerness, based on the realization that, if I don't get the house sold soon, I will have to borrow still more money.

Our best prospect is a young executive and his wife, with one child, another on the way, who live in a house, just a block from ours. He earns a high salary, can afford the interest on a large purchase money mortgage, but cannot put up much cash. He will accept my price, if I will accept his terms. While these discussions go on during several visits, my wife and his wife have theirs. My wife explains why she doesn't want to sell the house, what it means to her, what she has put into it, dozens of hidden conveniences, her time-consuming solutions—a concealed shelf in the library that can be used for coffee and brandy; the built-in tray storage next to the refrigerator; the way the former dumbwaiter shaft has been utilized (on the ground floor for more kitchen counter and cabinets, on the second floor for the bar, in her bathroom for a recessed vanity, in our son's room for an additional closet); what we have done in the basement; security precautions—the bars on the skylights, the alarm system, the time-switch on the outside lights....

With each word, as my wife moves up and down through the house, the executive's wife wants it more. She says that this is what they would be paying for—the things we have done, the things they have not done in their own house, never will do because they just don't have the patience. I could be listening to my own wife, feeling her nails on my arm.

Suddenly my wife asks, "Why don't we rent the house to them?"

I tell her that that's something the executive and I will work out. After the couple leaves, I begin, "Look, dear—" she is forewarned by my icy affection—"I don't want to rent the house. I have to sell it. I have to pay for the apartment. I have to pay for the move. Rental income would be dissipated in taxes. It wouldn't be good for him either—"

"But if we rent the house and don't like the apartment, we could come back."

"We haven't moved yet! And I don't want to move again. Ever."

The executive calls me the next day. "I've been thinking about your wife's suggestion of renting." I suppress any comment. "I've talked to my lawyer. He says it won't work. I need the mortgage as tax shelter. But suppose, through my firm, I can arrange a loan from our bank instead of the mortgage from you. Suppose I paid all cash—well, I don't want to renegotiate or anything, but my lawyer says I'd be entitled to some discount—"

"I'm disappointed," I lie. "I thought we had agreed on price."

"My lawyer says a discount for cash is customary."

"How much off the price does he think would be fair?"

"Twenty thousand."

I would close the deal immediately but say, "Let me think it over."

I wait for two days before calling, tell him I've had to persuade my wife. We review basic terms, go over the items included in the sale. I get his lawyer's name, say I'll have mine forward a contract.

Our meetings with the designers are more pressured now. We must turn over our house by June 15—"barring acts of God"—fifteen days later than our original schedule, but it is already the first week in February and no work has begun. The designers can't have a contractor bid on the job until they have completed working drawings and specifications. I urge them to select a contractor and give him the working drawings for the areas that have been approved.

"Doing it piecemeal can be very expensive, especially if there are any changes. This isn't like a commercial job where we can establish unit costs. Here everything is individual."

"There won't be any changes," I say with pretended confidence.

Sets of plans are printed and sent out for bids, with just a few areas marked HOLD—the kitchen, my wife's study, and the master bathroom.

We have talked a lot about the bathroom. In our house we have small separate baths with straightforward white plumbing fixtures. In the apartment there is a single large bath off the bedroom. The former occupant, a wealthy widow, had decorated it in 'thirties Hollywood style—glossy black paint on the walls; black enamel sink, tub, and toilet; angular chrome lighting fixtures; mirrored vanity and sink enclosure on which the mirroring has darkened with age.

"I love it," my wife said when she first saw it.

"It doesn't have a shower."

"We can put one over the tub and install sliding doors. That's all we need to do. It's perfect."

"Well, maybe if we paint the walls white," I begin.

"White! The black is what makes the room interesting."

"Like a crypt.... When we install a shower, we'll need tile over the tub. Do you want that black too?"

" Maybe the tile could be white, just that pocket of white, an accent."

"To make the black blacker?"

"Right."

"I have a confession: I don't know if I'd be happy washing in a black sink. Of course I've never tried, but somehow black doesn't seem as clean as white."

"Well, if you're going to change the sink, I'd like two sinks. We're used to two. We often wash at the same time."

"On the Cape we only have one."

"The Cape's different. We're never rushing to dinner parties. We're never rushing—maybe two white sinks set in a black counter. And my vanity at the other end of the bathroom could match the counter. And maybe a big shaggy white rug on the floor where I can do my exercises...."

Thus the design of our bathroom begins to emerge, has been emerging now for weeks, months. I have gone along with black accented by white, but my wife doesn't know what the black material should be—marble? glass? formica?—and she isn't sure if she wants drawers in her vanity, or shelves, or a combination of the two. The designers have been called in. They know our intimate needs for electric razor and water-pic outlets, a hook for a douche bag, a rug to exercise on, how many towels we use; but they don't know what black material my wife prefers, how many drawers and/or shelves she wants. For reasons of cost and practicality they recommend formica and submit a sample. No, my wife says, it's too matte, too gray, too slate-like. She wants something as shiny as the walls and plumbing fixtures.

The contractors' bids, excluding the HOLD areas, come in. The lowest is almost double our "budget" figure. We go over it in detail; eliminate items (refinishing floors which will be covered by carpet, canvassing walls, recessing air-conditioning units, matching new doors to existing woodwork). We substitute domestic tile in the kitchen and laundry for imported quarry tile.... Still the figure is large.

"At least we know what it is," I say to my wife. "I've told them to go ahead on what's approved, but we've got to resolve the design for the bathroom, the kitchen, your study."

Under the pressure of the revised but still-high low bid, she finally goes along with matte black formica and decides on a combination of drawers and shelves for her vanity.

"Splendid!"

In the kitchen the designers have given her exactly the equipment, counter and storage space she needs. There are little things she is not so sure about. She will place hanging hooks later. She will teach these designers about delayed, rather than instant, design.

"Splendid!"

In her study, the question is what she wants in the storage wall. At various stages of design it has contained mostly files, then mostly hanging space, then mostly shelves and drawers. Her present desk, which will not fit well in the room, has two files. Since she will be getting a new desk—she has seen a hexagonal Victorian piece that would look beautiful in the bay window—why not have two file drawers built into it? All right, there'll be no file drawers in the storage wall. We re-measure the hanging space she presently has and compare it with what exists in the apartment. There is at least ten percent more in the apartment. All right, no hanging space. She will not have room for her dresser, so what she needs is drawers, right? No, that is what she has been thinking about all these weeks, she does not want drawers, has never really liked them, likes things folded on open shelves. She wants shelves, lots of shelves, adjustable shelves.

"Splendid!"

The designers erase HOLD on their tracings and proceed with the final working drawings, send us and the building's managing agent prints for approval, get a price from the contractor for the additional work, get our approval on that too.

Things are moving now, changing shape. Walls are coming down. Channels are being dug for electrical and plumbing work. Debris in heavy canvas bags is being carried out of the apartment. The place is a mess. Cement and plaster are everywhere. It hardly seems possible that we will be living here in about three months.

Between visits to the apartment, we are shopping again. We need kitchen stools. We need rugs. We need a wall covering for the dining room, just the right rough linen, one that will be "splendid."

The volume of mail increases. It is mostly bills—from the designer, from the contractor, from various showrooms. I am no longer working. I am no longer doing anything but moving. All my wife and I talk about is the move. We make love talking about it. We dream about it. We wake up talking about it. Our daughter says, "I'm bored of it." My wife barely has the energy to correct her grammar. Our son tries a fancy new word on us. He says our behavior is "obsessive." I scold him feebly for his lack of interest in our new home.

When I'm not dreaming about the move, I'm unable to sleep, thinking about it. I place furniture, sculpture, paintings. I pay bills. I decide which paintings and sculpture must be sold to pay the bills. In my mind, I visit art galleries and antique dealers, as I will, in actuality, during the coming weeks. My nights are as full as my days. Sometimes during these hours I move from the specific details of the move to more general problems of moving. Why, I ask myself, am I doing this? Why is it so hard? I don't ask my wife because she has by now accepted the move and made, even if under duress, all these final decisions that will make it possible. Besides, she is asleep.

I count the moves in my life. The little hops from apartment to apartment, made by my parents during the Depression. Their final move, to the East Side, made while I was overseas during World War II. The dormitory room I shared with my wife, before she was my wife. The more furnished apartment in The Village, with its extra room for a child or children, where I used to write in fear of losing that room.

There is always one bare room that I love and never want to relinquish and, over the years, there are the others, more and more furnished, over-furnished, that I love too and share with my wife until they spill over into the empty room and we have to find new emptiness, fill it, and move again. Yes, I have felt the need for both the empty and the cluttered environment — at different times and finally (luxuriously) at the same time.

The moves, measured in blocks, have always been small, though none as small as this one. I was born on the East River, when the Flower Free Surgical Hospital was located at York Avenue and 63rd Street. My paternal grandfather lived in a brownstone far east on 52nd Street. Father and his brother would wave as their father — the grandfather I never knew — went by on the Fall River Line headed to or from Boston on business. In the new apartment our living room cannot be more than a few feet from where Father as a child stood waving. Yes, the East River is my river.

Still trying to fall asleep, I count boats we have seen on our visits to the apartment. Tankers, freighters, tugs, barges, scows float through my mind like so many rooms, some empty, some heavy with cargo, some full of garbage.

The East River is my river, but I know more about the Hudson. I can imagine Henry Hudson standing proudly near the ship's wheel as he approaches New York Harbor. What do I know of East? Was he an Englishman too, a navigator and explorer establishing Dutch claims? What was East's first name? Something less majestic than Henry? John perhaps? Long John East, a gangly but capable sailor in his teens. Lieutenant John East by the time he is twenty. And then quickly Captain John and Sir John, knighted because he will not sell his services to the Dutch or anyone else. His descendants will sell theirs. Alas, there has been a thinning of Sir John's blood. I see these descendants, young and tall as he was, at the wheels of the Circle Line, guiding their boats around Manhattan and explaining the sights to German and Japanese tourists. I count these boats too....

All this is waking thought, conscious counting, anchored in reality. Like a sailor on watch, I refuse to fall asleep, fearing punishment. I know that if I give in, I will drift off into that realm of fantasy in which I am always moving, moving, moving....

Shelves, cabinets, closets begin to grow on the walls. The detailing of the woodwork is elegantly simple, the grain carefully matched, the oil finish protective without being shiny. The bookshelves in my office and in the gallery and living room—all designed and approved early—are ready first. They stand warmly, cordially inviting Ackerley, Acton, Adams.... It will take days, maybe weeks, to fill these shelves, dusting each book and placing it alphabetically, and this is just one part of the move. I must not forget, still thinking alphabetically, art, Bennington, clothes, dishes, equipment, furniture...things....

I call a mover, ask for an estimate of his time, my dollars. He stomps through the house, beginning in the basement. He opens closets, asks if we intend to move this or that. He chews on a cigar as he studies works of art, calculating their size and weight, his esthetic for everything. I calculate his size and weight—just under six feet, probably 260 pounds. I guess he can lift twice what I can. I am no mover. I am a movee. He says that the job should take two packers five days, working eight hours a day, regular time, and that the move itself will require four men and two vans for a least two more days. It seems impossible that all these men, all these hours are needed to move us. Yet the estimate in dollars is small change within the context of the entire move, the big change. I will sell a Tiffany lamp.

"You can't sell that lamp," my wife says, "It's the first one we got."

"When we bought it, it cost a hundred dollars. It's worth three thousand now. To a dealer. But not to me."

"I like it."

"I like it too, but we don't need it."

The mover, the designer, the contractor, and I work out a logistical schedule. In mid-May my secretary's office, my own, and all the books will be packed and moved. For two weeks I will be in the apartment, at compaign headquarters, getting the offices set up, arranging the books, making last-minute decisions. At the beginning of June the second wave will begin, the art and antique china, followed immediately by the third and final wave, furniture, clothing, essentials. As you see, I have begun to think in military terms. I suspect I am suffering from battle fatigue.

The Monday morning the packers arrive I explain just how I want the books taken off the shelves (sequentially), how I want them placed in the cartons (sequentially), how I want the cartons labeled (sequentially). The packers smile. They understand what I want. They also understand that books have a will of their own. Half of the first row — Ackerley et al. — is removed from the shelf and placed vertically in a carton. The space remaining to the side and on top still has to be filled. There the rest of the shelf takes on a new order in the carton, according to thickness and height. If the right size isn't available, in sequence, the packers find it, perhaps on the next shelf, perhaps on the one after that. The awkwardness and irregularity of life enter the carton and are sealed for shipment; I can try only to keep them to a minimum. I hardly dare turn my back to answer the phone or read the morning's mail.

That day, among the bills I initial and hand to my secretary, the solicitations I throw into the basket, the magazines I can no longer keep up with, the notification from the bank of yet another overdraft, there is a letter from close friends, that rarest of communications. The couple is in New Orleans. There, in an obscure antique store, they have found an illuminated turn-or-the-century dentist's sign, of hammered tin, in the shape of a large flattened tooth, roots down, four feet from biting surface to tip of longest root, two feet wide, half a foot thick, with the word DENTIST in green glass on both faces and one edge. $500, plus shipping. A steal. The wife has described it. The husband has drawn a small sketch. They love it. They can't use it. They've thought of us.

"Just what we need," I say, laughing as I hand the letter to my wife.

She studies it carefully. Her eyes brighten. "It might work over the bar."

"We have a fixture there."

"It's ordinary."

"Yes, it gives a lot of light. How much do you think would come through those little green letters?"

"Enough. It would be intimate. We could try it anyway."

"At the same time as we try the apartment while we rent the house. No."

I think the subject is closed. I spend the day running up and down the stairs between the library and my office and my secretary's. Cartons are everywhere — in those rooms and downstairs in the entrance hall and dining room where the packers have begun to pile them for the move. At dinner, surrounded by cartons, my wife resumes:

"You can't lose on Americana. That sign is bound to go up in value. I'll take the risk. I'll take care of the shipping. I'll have the existing fixture taken down and this one put up. If you don't like it, I'll sell it. All at my responsibility...."

I remain silent. My wife goes on at length, explaining that our daughter will want the tooth, that it, like the Bennington, will some-day be hers, in her home, for her delight and that of her family. I shouldn't only think of myself, I should think of her, our little girl.

"She's eleven!" I reply. "You'll spend a thousand dollars before you're through. But maybe that's a bargain. Let me cut through every-thing: I don't like the tooth. I don't want it over the bar. I don't want to store it in a warehouse while it enhances in value. I'm not an antique dealer."

She makes one last try, shows the sketch to the children.

"Oh, gross...Gross..." they agree in the vernacular of the day.

A tooth for a tooth — I am familiar with the concept, expect now to give in to my wife on moving some unneeded pieces to which she has tenaciously clung despite tempting offers from dealers. However, I do not expect to give, precisely, a tooth of my own.

The next morning, my left jaw aches. I can't brush my teeth there, can't even shave comfortably over the spot. My head throbs with psychosomatic theory. *Le corps a ses raisons...* I restate my instruc-tions to the packers ("to the extent possible," I qualify now), review a few items with my secretary, leave her writing change-of-address notices, and rush to the dentist.

The rear upper-left molar is impacted. It must come out. The nurse sets up an immediate appointment with an extractionist and hands me a slip on which a dental diagram is printed. The rear upper-left molar has an x drawn through it.

I have not had a tooth pulled in twenty years or so. I remember then having had to wait several days for an appointment with the busy specialist in his small old-fashioned suite on the ground-floor of a Fifth Avenue apartment house. Now I enter a large new office building, not far from that of the chairman of the co-op. Five dentists have their names on the doors leading to an entire tower floor. Inside there are two receptionists at a long formica counter, behind them a secretary typing bills, off to one side a large waiting room in which more than a dozen men and women are seated in a grid of plastic chairs, tables, and magazine racks.

I give the printed slip to a receptionist. She clips it to a form on which she types my name, address, occupation.

"Medical plan?"

"None."

"No medical insurance!"

I might as well have said I'm a Communist. I feel the need to assert my Americanism: "I'm moving."

"Take a seat. We'll call you as soon as possible."

I sit among the other anonymous toothaches. Like them I flip through the pages of magazines, looking mostly at ads. I want nothing. Just a tooth taken out. Less than nothing. A negative need.

My name is called. I am led down a bright vinyl corridor to one of many narrow recovery cubicles, each containing a built-in cot with a fresh sheet on it, a fresh case on the pillow, a blanket folded at its foot. There are hooks on the back of the door, a dimmer switch on the bullet-shaped lighting fixture over the cot, a volume control for the Muzak, and a removable spittoon, sterilized and waiting on a bracket extending from the wall.

"Make yourself comfortable!" I'm told.

I remove my jacket, hang it up, stretch out on the cot, turn off what my son calls bubble-gum music. I can't chew it.

A nurse enters, asks if I have any history of heart trouble.

"None," I reply, waiting for her to exclaim, "No heart history!"

But she is already taking my pulse.

"Are there any anesthetics you're allergic to?"

"Novocaine makes me jittery. I'd prefer something that makes me feel good. Nitrous oxide—" I suggest tentatively.

"The doctor will have to make that decision."

I am led down another bright corridor, past a young black mopping the floor with disinfectant, to one of the operating rooms. The doctor looks at the form with the slip clipped to it, says my name, waits.

"Yes. And of the five names on the door—?"

I smile. He doesn't. He mutters a name, nods to the nurse, and a needle enters my arm. For a moment, there is the shock, the sting of it, and then, rather than the euphoria I requested, temporary oblivion.

Fragmentedly, I remember returning to the cubicle. My arm is over the nurse's shoulder. The corridor is still being mopped. It is difficult to get past the mopper. I do not know where I am. A hospital? A factory? The new apartment? "Is the move over?" I ask or think I ask. The nurse helps me onto the cot. Her rubber-soled oxfords squeak down the corridor. The room is silent except for the hum of air conditioning...I doze, awaken, use the spittoon, fill it with blood, doze again, awaken again, spit again.... The nurse turns the light on, the music up (a peppy mid-day tune from some musical tragi-comedy). She rinses the bowl. I ask the name of the anesthetic I've been given.

"Sodium pentathol," she replies, "the truth serum."

"Oh. Then you won't mind my saying I hope I don't see you again."

I intend to take a taxi, feel that I must return home quickly to supervise the packers, my secretary, my wife, that without me the move will stop, the world will stop. But outside the controlled environment of the office building—its cold blue light, its constant temperature, its acoustic insulation, its sleek plastic surfaces—the world whirls, sunlight bounces between buildings and sidewalks, spring breezes toss scraps of paper, a man chases his hat down the street, skirts billow, cab drivers shout and honk their horns, a luncheonette exhausts the smell of hamburger.... I decide to walk, enjoying the truth all around me, this sodium pentathol world. Several times on the way home I spit blood into the gutter. *Le sang a ses raisons...*

At home there has been progress. Cartons are piled high. The bookshelves are empty. The packers are now wrapping the smaller works of art. My wife watches with magic marker poised. The house is beginning to look naked.

"How did it go?" she asks.

"Painlessly," I answer, having no choice but to tell the truth. "The nurse said it will hurt later when the sodium pentathol wears off. Just the opposite of the theory that the truth hurts—it doesn't hurt at all."

However, knowing that it will, I take a tablet of codeine with a martini, before eating a soft lunch of scrambled eggs. Then I sign some letters and checks and go to bed, intending to nap for an hour. When I awaken the children are home from school. My secretary, the packers, the cartons of books and small art are all gone. New cartons, not yet set up, are piled in the hall.

It is my first full day in the apartment. Carrying an attaché case filled with dust cloths, I say good morning to the doorman and elevator operators. Like the attaché case, the words are a lie. It is not a good morning. It is unseasonably hot, and my jaw aches. I open the apartment door. There are more false good mornings: half a dozen workmen are drinking coffee on my time.

In the gallery more than a hundred cartons are stacked three-high in double rows. I glance at a couple of the top cartons. One is marked K-L, another, this one in my wife's handwriting, SMALL ART. I flee the bulging cartons, the empty shelves.

By comparison, the office area looks manageable. The furniture is already placed. There are only some twenty cartons. I take off my jacket, roll up my sleeves. By the time my secretary arrives, all the cartons are open and a quarter of them are empty. Reference books are on their shelves. Lamp and clock are on my desk. Beside it, a photograph of Father smiles ambiguously. I am not sure he approves of my new quarters, perhaps finds them still a bit messy.

I spend the rest of the morning helping my secretary place files, stationery, supplies, typewriter, duplicator, calculator, electric pencil sharpener.... I find an electrician to extend the cord on the typewriter, a carpenter to rearrange the shelving in her closet, a painter to do minor touch-ups. By one, she announces, "We're in business."

She may be. I'm not. There are still cartons to empty in my own office and, of course, those dozens in the gallery. I need fuel.

I wash, roll down my sleeves, put on my jacket, say good afternoon to the elevator operators and doorman, cross the street to the shady side, and walk west to a small bar and grill on First Avenue. There I am just finishing my second bloody mary when the designer and his assistant appear. The designer is immaculately dressed in white suit and shirt, black loafers, bright blue ascot. He looks air-conditioned. By comparison his assistant, in an open flowered shirt and bell-bottomed corduroys, looks only primitively ventilated. I ask them to join me for lunch.

"We got to the apartment just after you left," the designer says. "It's really shaping up. I can't wait till the books are on the shelves."

"Me too," I reply.

"And the art," the assistant adds. "That will make so much difference. Very important how it's hung. I see clusters here and there, and large expanses of empty wall."

I see my sandwich, perfectly centered on the plate, with a pile of french fries on one side, cole slaw on the other—all appetizingly old-fashioned.

I have too many books. Too many I've read but barely remember. Too many I never finished. Too many I'll never start. More, surely, than I can ever digest. Each book, as I place it on the shelf, reminds me of my failing memory or my lack of perserverance or my neglect. All, even the books I've loved, are like enemy scalps, wall decorations commemorating past victories, present defeats.

Tearing at filament tape and cardboard, I attack the cartons as they are placed, in no particular order. I want first only to create a space in which to work. Squeezing each book tight so the pages won't be bent, I dust around the edges, place it alphabetically on a shelf above the third level of cartons, knowing that later, when I've cleared enough cartons to get to the lower shelves, it will have to be shifted, that the alphabetical fragment of which it is a part will have to join the rest of the alphabet still waiting in cartons.

I am, arbitrarily, among the P's, chided by an Anthony Powell title: *Books Do Furnish A Room.* Have I criticized my wife for being too possessive and too interested in decor? I am the same. We should be married, live together, move together. We deserve each other. Later, among the C's, I am chided by Céline's *Castle to Castle.* Not only haven't I read this novel, but its title seems, again, to describe my present activity, its "irrelevance," as they say these days. Yes, I feel aggressively irrelevant. I wish Dr. Destouches were here to discuss my problem with.

I have filled a K-L shelf, the one of P's, the one of C's, another of T's. It is slow going. The workmen have left. My secretary has left. I am alone with my six thousand books on my desert island, wondering once again if perhaps I am traveling too heavy. I imagine tossing the books one by one out the window, watching them float down the river to public libraries, universities, hospitals...Is a potlatch still a potlatch if subsidized by government tax-deductions? Slicing off the building above the ground floor is a grander fantasy.

I return home and have three martinis. I listen to my wife's day. She has spent it going through old letters, trying to decide which to pack. She has decided by packing them all. Her day has been like mine. During dinner the children talk about school. They hate it. They, too, have lived a decisionless day.

Before the packing began, I put aside a few books. I try to read one that has been on the shelf for more than ten years: Frank Jenkins' *Architect and Patron*. The words swim in my tired gin- and vermouth-soaked mind.

> ...the architect-client relation does not always follow such an easy course as that between the doctor and his patient. When a man consults his doctor the circumstances are generally not of the happiest, the former is in some sort of danger and is prepared to put himself with complete trust in the hands of his professional adviser. He does not presume to argue with the doctor's advice. When the man engages an architect, the position is normally quite different. He feels justification that he is employing someone to carry out his wishes; he seldom seems to realize that his architect is—or should be—capable of interpreting those wishes more clearly than he can himself.

Ah, yes, the happy, healthy need for an architect. I mark the passage, think of showing it to my wife, put the book aside, look through a pile of accumulated magazines, can't read these either, can barely concentrate on the pictures in them. I wash up, go to bed, try one of the magazines again, fail again, turn out the light, try to sleep, fail once more, think: *A doctor tries to cure the patient's illness, a designer tries to express it.... La maison a ses raisons....*

My wife asks, "Would you like me to read to you?"

"Yes."

This is a sure soporific. She has a reading voice entirely different from her speaking voice. The former was learned in grade school from a teacher who emphasized emphasis. Each word is given great weight. She begins:

"The/ high/ cost/ to/ American/ business/ and/ industry/ of/

alcoholism/ among/ employees/ has/ caused/ a/ growing/ number/ of/ companies/ to/ take/ action...."

I am on my way, smothered as if by the weight of twenty-two blankets.

"The/ Cambridge/ Mass./ consulting/ concern/ of/ Arthur/ D./ Little/ Inc./ estimates/ that/ 4/ ./ 5/ million/ American/ workers/ suffer/ from.... What did I say?"

"workers suffer from"

"...Companies/ lose/ 8/ billion/ dollars/ a/ year.... 32/ million/ dollars/ each/ working/ day...."

Each word is in its carton marked FRAGILE...HANDLE WITH CARE...THIS SIDE UP....

I sleep for about two hours, awaken, ask my wife, "Are you asleep?"

"No."

It is my turn to play soporific. I make exhausted love. Now my wife is asleep. I smoke, thinking about the remaining books, the small art in cartons that I have pushed aside, pictures that will have to be hung, the larger ones yet to come....

On my way to the apartment I meet a neighbor I haven't seen in many weeks. He asks, "What are you doing?"

"Moving."

"I know about that. I mean, what new project, new book, are you working on? You look tired. Have you lost weight?"

"A few pounds," I say, knowing it's close to ten.

"Better take it easy. Why'd you want to move anyway?"

"I don't remember."

That's true. Of course I remember the reasons I had—the better space, the greater efficiency, the better view, the greater security (everything seemed better or greater then)—but I don't remember why I thought these things were important enough to trade for so many days, nights, pounds, a tooth.

As I arrange the books, I wonder if, knowing what I know now, I would have made the move. With each book I put on the shelf, my doubts expand and go far beyond the immediate lost time, lost weight, lost tooth. There is a more general lost confidence. I am no longer sure about my relationship to my wife, my children, my work. All are pulling in different directions. All must be reexamined, rearranged, like the books, the art, the furnishings.

This evening, I decide that if possible, if I have the energy, I will try to write, try to present what a move means in terms of past experience, present irritation, future reorientation. I am full of ideas about moving as a metaphor for life, for writing itself. I see it, like life, like writing, as a re-arrangement of experience. Each carton is packed with three-dimensional experience, ready to be opened, dusted, replaced, reseen.

Moving as a metaphor for life? I wonder. No, moving *is* life, just as a pen moving across paper is life, or the fingers moving over typewriter keys. Though the movement is circumscribed—by the 8½"×11" dimensions of a sheet of paper or by a few city blocks—the possibilities are infinite. Infinity is not a metaphor.

I still have three-quarters of the books to do, but I leave earlier than the previous evening, determined to go home and write. As I walk the few blocks, I smile thinking about how my wife will admire my coming home from a hard day's work and sitting down to write. She has often complimented me on my discipline, my will, my courage. Though I've told her that for me writing is a compulsion, she doesn't believe it, won't understand that I have no choice, that particularly at this moment, after weeks of not writing, I am suffering from something like withdrawal symptoms, that I must write, must confess.

She is in my daughter's bedroom, helping her pack toys and dolls.

"I'm going to write for a couple of hours before dinner," I tell them.

"Good," my wife replies. "You're more agreeable when you're writing."

There are no compliments, no congratulations. She has changed. *She* is more agreeable when I am writing.

I make a martini and drink it slowly while staring at the yellow pad before me, as empty as an unfurnished apartment. I can't decide if I want to begin a story (what's redundantly called autobiographical fiction) or simply a journal entry (what should be called fictionalized autobiography). I make another martini, sip it. If it's going to be a story, the first marks on the sheet are easy: my name and address at the upper lefthand corner. I write these, using for the first time my new address, the address to which a check or a rejection slip will be sent.

Now, if I had a title, I could proceed halfway down the page. *Moving,* I write, thinking of it as a working title. I have completed half a page in half an hour. I have only to decide now where a move begins, and begin it.

My mind is still full of ambitious ideas: an entire aesthetics of moving, of trying (and often failing) to get things right—yes, as in writing, as in business, as in all of life.... I will make the general idea of moving transcend my specific move. I will make materialism transcend my materials, possessiveness transcend my possessions. Big ideas will transcend little ideas. Big things will transcend little things...

I will...not write another word for the next half hour. The word *Moving* sits still on the page. I will...make another martini....

Perhaps I should be working in my journal, collecting notes for the transcendent moving story I will write. I open the notebook, the twenty-sixth fat, typed, single-spaced volume of my life as I wish others to think I've led it. (The first twenty-five volumes are already lined up on a closet shelf in my new office, more than a million words, preserved less for future reference than present need to get them out of the way.) My last journal entry is dated more than two months ago, the longest lapse ever.

I make another martini, take out another legal pad, date the upper righthand corner (it is by this device that my secretary can tell my so-called non-fiction from my so-called fiction) and scribble: *All writers would write alike if they didn't drink different drinks.* I wonder if that will ever fit into the piece I intend to write about moving or if, like that other million words, mostly unused, I want these only packed away. *Le corps a ses raisons...*

There is a knock on the door. "Dinner," my son says. No one from Porlock was ever more welcome. I am being told that it's time to move.

It is a week later. The books are on the shelves. I am hanging the art. I have lost a few more pounds. My fingers are cracked and cut from constant dusting, washing, tearing at filament tape and, even worse now, adjusting picture wire. If Captain John East is a hero, the inventor of picture wire is a villain—a German-American, no doubt, with a mind of steel in many strands, all twisted and knotted. By the light of an oil lamp I can see this bloody-fingered fiend working in his nineteenth-century tool shop. I watch the expression on his glinting bespectacled face, impatience turning to rage, the infamous night he strangles his wife and children....

One day twists into the nest. The small art is up. The large art arrives. I pound picture hooks into the walls, trying to get the art off the floor before the final wave of cartons, furniture, family.... If only I could hammer hooks into the center of wall panels, nowhere else. If only I were that innocent. If only I had never heard of Piet Mondrian. But, like the designers, I have heard of him. His ghost is more real than those of John East and The Inventor of Picture Wire. It is neither heroic nor villainous but here, in my mind, in black and white and primary colors. Too often I struggle for asymmetrical balance, matching small pictures against large ones, measuring the weight of surrounding voids against that of surrounded art. The wall is my canvas, the ruler as much my divining rod as Mondrian's. Like The Immaculate Dutchman, like my own designers, I am cleaning up, moving from one mess to create an environment for the next.

Just before noon, the first van appears and parks on the side street below my office window. The mover says that he and his men will break for lunch, then unload this van, and go back to our house for the last load, mostly furniture.

"Good afternoon...Good afternoon...Good afternoon..." Once again I am on my way, out the door and down the block, to the bar and grill. I must walk quickly, eat quickly to be back in time to receive our possessions.

By now the bartender recognizes me.

"The usual?"

"Yes," I answer emphatically. The unusual has disappeared from my life, my vocabulary. I live only in a world of books, dust, cardboard cartons, pictures, picture wire, picture hooks.

"What's new?" he asks as he slides my drink to me.

I smile as if I have a secret. The bartender understands. He is paid to understand. For a split second we live in the same world, use the same words. But, as his reciprocal smile spreads into a leer, I realize that his vocabulary is as limited as mine, that what's new can only be a woman. What else could account for my lost weight? ...He is discreet.

He doesn't press. He's there to listen, only if I want to talk.

I do. I leave the bar, drop a dime in the phone, and dial the house.

"I'm just having a bite—a swallow. The movers will begin unloading the van in about half an hour. I guess you'll get to the apartment later in the afternoon—"

"Not before evening. You have no idea what it's like here. There are packing materials all over the place. You can have your boozy lunch. I have to clean up. I don't have time to talk."

"Another?" the bartender asks.

"Yes," I reply as emphatically as before.

The moving men begin to bring in the cartons, dozens of them marked KITCHEN, five of these sub-marked BENNINGTON, which are handled with great care—the men have their instructions from my wife—more care than the sixteen of LIQUOR, the two of CANDLESTICKS, the two of ASHTRAYS, the three of MATCH STRIKERS. Three cartons of match strikers! How these small objects sneak into our lives and accumulate. It is easier to resist an antique dentist's sign.

I watch for the large wardrobe cartons, remove the clothes on hangers and transfer them to closets, fish shoes from the bottom of these wardrobes. It seems right that we have more shoes than match strikers. But a hundred and fifty pair for a family of four—that's excessive. Everything is: the number of suits, dresses, coats, hats (also thrown into the wardrobes), belts (looped over hangers).

Cartons are coming in more quickly now, two and three at a time, light ones that can be tossed around: BLANKETS, PILLOWS, CUSHIONS, QUILTS, LINENS, TOYS, DOLLS.

The moving men leave. I finish putting what I can into closets. I line up the empty wardrobes for the men to take away when they come back. I find cartons of my shirts, sweaters, underwear, socks, handkerchiefs and unpack these as I wait for the movers to return.

A little after three the phone rings. It is my wife. She tells me that the movers say they can't possibly finish by four, that they will need at least four hours of overtime or that they can complete the job in the morning on regular time. What's to be done? The beds are there, the bedding is here. The food is there, the dishes are here. She, the children, the maid are there, I am here.

"We've been had," I tell my wife. "But I don't want to go through another day of this. Let me speak to the mover." He gets on. "What are we talking about *in dollars?*" I ask in the kind of tough voice I imagine guys at the Pentagon use.

He computes the difference between regular time and overtime. I agree to a figure. The van rolls, loaded with furniture, plants, a few suitcases, last things.

A taxi follows. In it are my wife, her jewelry, the children, the maid, and two thermopaks of food from the refrigerator. Almost immediately my wife tells me that she forgot some things in the freezer, that she will get them the next day.

"Forgot!" I reply. "You want to go back."

"Don't you?"

"No. Never. It's past."

"The house is part of our lives. You can't just chop it off."

"You can't hang onto it either."

She smiles, too tired to bicker. Her smile is filled with exhaustion and mystery. She will, I know, try not to let go of the house for a little longer.

It takes a week to open all the cartons, unwrap their contents, and put things in place. It is like a Christmas for which we have given ourselves everything we want—and more, much more. There is the surprise of unwrapping things and seeing them as if for the first time. And there is also, hidden inside corrugated paper and jiffy pads, so much duplication, waste, guilt.

Our possessions not only possess us, they move us. These things take over, each demanding its place. The Bennington plates and bowls and pitchers spread out in the glass kitchen cabinets. The match strikers and ashtrays claim tables throughout the apartment. Candlesticks and small art objects fill open shelves. Cusions and pillows find their chairs and couches. The furniture itself asks to be moved six inches this way or that, wanting enough space, wanting to be made comfortable.

Old things begin to look new in their new setting, the new setting itself begins to look old. The apartment starts to "look like home"—

home, placed on its side, given a quarter turn from the vertical to the horizontal. Time warp becomes space warp. The collective magnitude of our possessions shrinks as each piece is distributed, appearing to be only what is needed in a given place.

What my wife and I do and what the children do is different not only in scale. They get settled autonomously and pretty much duplicate the rooms they had in the house. Our son sets up his drums and hi-fi equipment, arranges his records and tapes, puts up his posters. The look, the feel, the sound of his room are all familiar, only the view outside has changed. Our daughter, too, recreates her past environment. The stuffed animals are at the head of her bed, the dolls on the couch and chairs, the miniature furniture grouped as always on shelves. But the children have worked alone, as already they play alone; I have only helped them hang a few pictures and move some heavy pieces of furniture. My wife and I have worked, continue to work, hope to play, *together*. Ours is a collaboration, much more with each other than with the designers. Everywhere we look there is our controlled clutter, our compromise between the functional and decorative. What we have done, what we are continuing to do reminds us of our need for each other. More than with any painting or piece of furniture, we see each other freshly. Why don't we, too, look new in our setting? — our final setting, I think, as I have thought in each of our previous homes.

The closing on the house is substantially a repetition of the closing on the apartment. This time we meet in the mortgage department of a Wall Street bank. There are a few more people present, a few more papers to sign. When everything is done, I turn over the keys to our house.

"That's a lot of money for a bunch of keys," the young executive says, laughing.

I explain how the shunt key on the alarm system works: "Before you open the front door, you turn the shunt lock from a verticle to a horizontal position. Once you're inside, you turn the switch, on the alarm box, from on to off. Then you turn the shunt back to vertical and, if you want the alarm on, you turn the switch on again. In addition, there's a release switch above the inside of the front door—"

"I'll be glad to go back to the house and show you," my wife tells them.

Later, when she returns from the house, their house now, she says, "It's so sad, all those empty rooms, empty shelves, empty picture hooks, empty frames of dirt where the pictures hung—I want to get this place really finished before we go to the Cape."

"But you can't, you know that. There's work that has to be done during the summer—the vanity and sink in our bathroom, the linen on the dining room walls, the hardware for the sliding doors of the storage walls, paint touch-ups, missing electrical fixtures—"

"If we stayed an extra week—"

"You still wouldn't finish. You'd just be in the workmen's way. And besides, the new furniture won't be delivered till late in the summer."

"I don't want to leave. You go ahead with the children. I'll stay here for a week or two."

"I want to leave. I want you to leave. I want to get back to work. I can't do that and open the house on the Cape and take care of the children. I need you."

"To do those jobs?"

"That too. But more. You decorate our life."

"You haven't told me anything like that in a long time."

"I thought it was obvious."

"I thought you thought only I needed you."

On the drive to the Cape she still talks about how sad she is to leave the apartment, how much work still remains to be done. Her mood doesn't change until we cross Buzzards Bay. Then she begins talking about the antique shops in Sandwich...Barnstable...Yarmouth... Dennis...Brewster.... There are so many things she needs—little things, she emphasizes.

Choosing a Name

I begin nameless. I am not even *I*. I am *we*. I am two separate halves of me—one half, a millionth part of Father's ejaculation, a sperm like so many others, fighting its way blindly up a dark tunnel toward the other half, a single egg in a swarming nest.

There is contact in the dark, microscopic penetration within the larger coital penetration, fertilization without so much as an introduction or a handshake. We are an unlikely couple, an aleatory happening, defying huge odds—this anonymous sperm and anonymous egg—as we embrace, exchange genetic information, become one, giving each other everything but a name. *We* is *me* now, determined to survive even if I have to stand on my head.

Father withdraws, rolls onto his back, to Mother's left. This part of the bed is cool. He lies there, enjoying the feel of the sheet, finding it refreshing, exciting. He wonders if Mother would like to make love again, but she is already asleep, breathing heavily, perhaps dreaming. Besides, tomorrow (Wednesday, October 28, 1925) is a working day in this busy pre-Christmas season when retailers begin to discover they haven't ordered enough shoes. He pulls the mussed top sheet and blanket over her shoulders and up to his chin, closes his eyes, is soon snoring. Neither Mother nor Father knows I am in bed with them.

If I'm a boy, Mother wants to name me Robert. "A good, straight, American name. Nothing bad can be done to it. Bob, Bobby, Rob, Robbie—they're all nice."

"BERNARD!—THAT'S THE NAME I WANT. IT WAS GOOD ENOUGH FOR MY FATHER. SHOULD BE GOOD ENOUGH FOR YOU. AND OUR SON. IF YOU DON'T LIKE IT, YOU CAN CALL HIM BOB OR BOBBY."

"I can, and you can, but everyone else will be calling him Bernie. I hate that."

"THEY DIDN'T CALL MY FATHER BERNIE. THEY CALLED HIM BARNEY."

"Not much better. I'm beginning to hope it's a girl."

Mother pats her stomach. I kick to establish contact and assert my maleness. Father speaks for me.

"IT'LL BE A BOY. IT'LL BE BERNARD."

"But just suppose—"

"I'D WANT *HER* TO BE NAMED JOSEPHINE—FOR MY MOTHER."

"Josephine! Can you imagine a daughter named Josephine? The French Revolution's over."

"LOOK. YOUR PARENTS ARE ALIVE. MINE ARE DEAD. I DESERVE CONSIDERATION."

"Yes, but your family has such awful, fancy ideas about names."

"THERE'S NOTHING AWFUL OR FANCY ABOUT BERNARD OR JOSEPHINE."

"And your sisters and brothers? Do you think they have normal names too?"

The reader may judge.

Bernhard Friedmann, born 1859 in a suburb of Budapest, comes to the United States with his mother and two sisters (two older brothers remain in the Old Country) in 1875, soon after the death of his father. An immigration official at Ellis Island suggests they drop the extra *n* in Friedmann. Then he turns to the tall, sharp-featured, gray-eyed son. "I'd get rid of that *h* too. We travel light here. We don't drag our roots around with us." He studies the young man carefully for a moment. "You look like a *goy* anyway," he adds, intending a compliment.

Through a family connection Bernard obtains an apprenticeship in a shoe factory. He works hard, learns the trade, advances. In 1883, after eight years, he starts the B. Friedman Shoe Company, originally a childrens' shoe factory, behind his home on Columbia Street, on the lower West Side.

Now he works harder than ever, sometimes sixteen hours a day, supervising the regular twelve-hour shift and then refusing to pay others for overtime jobs that he believes he can do better himself. With success, he changes, becomes increasingly demanding and short-tempered, loses his hair, grows a cropped beard, buys expensive clothes, struts a bit, begins to remind some of his *landsleit* of hussars left behind in Hungary.

Bernard is respected and feared. Though he is prematurely bald and looks older than his years, he is still a very handsome man, a very eligible bachelor who deserves the best. He is a Jewish *goy*.

Josephine Goodman is Queen of the Hungarian Folk Festival. In her late teens, six years younger than Bernard, she is nevertheless a mature woman—just over five feet, six inches tall, with brunette hair down to her shoulders, ample bosom and hips, lovely legs (what Bernard can see of them beneath native costume), and perfect posture—bearing regal, head high. Bernard understands why Josephine is queen of the festival.

He finds someone who can introduce him to her and her parents. They are from his family's section outside Budapest but wealthier, more cultivated. Mr. Goodman has an established tanning business. Josephine who, like Bernard, came to New York at sixteen, studies English at an American high school.

They dance at the festival, touching only each other's hands. Soon after they become engaged. They marry. They move to 52nd Street, near First Avenue. They breed. They do the naming which, so many years later, provokes Mother's question:

Sadie (born 1888),

Stella (1890),

Bella (1892),

Dina (1894),

Leonard (1896),

Julius (known as "Jimmy"—1897),

Flora (1899), and

Milton (known as "Dick," later legally changed to Richard—1901).

"YES, THEIR NAMES ARE NORMAL, MORE NORMAL THAN THOSE IN YOUR FAMILY."

Again, the reader may judge.

Harris Urias, born about 1867 in Dünaburg, Latvia (later Dvinsk, Russia), leaves Dünaburg for New York at about the age of twenty-one with the intention of bringing his family here as soon as he can save enough money from his work as an ironmonger.

About is a word that belongs to Harris, as if he owns it. He is about five-foot-six but doesn't look short. He weighs about one-sixty but doesn't look fat. His thinning hair is about red but doesn't look red; it blends into the flushed, freckled pigmentation of his scalp, so that he doesn't look bald either. His mustache is scraggly. He doesn't have time for the barber. Nor for the tailor. When he buys a new suit, he uses it until it wears out, then buys another. It is not surprising that he retains neither dates nor documents. He saves only money.

Like my paternal grandfather, Harris loses part of his name during immigration—in this case, the letter *a* in Urias—and, simultaneously, its long *i* becomes short. He is told that Harris Uris sounds better. Whether it does or not, no one any longer calls him Harris. At the iron foundry, owned by an Irishman who employs mostly Irishmen, he's Harry. And he's still Harry about six years later when he has bought the place and puts up his new sign: H. URIS IRON WORKS. Harry or Harris, let them choose, just as long as they buy his manhole covers, fire hydrants, gates and grills, fences and stoop rails.

By now he has brought his family to New York, employs three brothers at the foundry, and supports three sisters (one born here soon after his parents arrive). He can afford to get married. He chooses Sadie Copland (originally Kaplan), the sister of his friend and partial namesake Harris Copland, who has also come to the States from Latvia. Harris and Sadie Uris have four children:

Percy (the *P* for a recently deceased Aunt Pearl, the name itself as close as they can come in English to Pesach—born 1899)

Madeleine (the *M* and the *a* for another recently deceased relative,

Uncle Max; her name itself, fancier than any in Father's family, found in the society pages—1900)

Gertrude (also found there and "close" to Gittel, Harris's mother—1902), and

Harold David (named for Hillel David Hilkowitz, the Uris family doctor—1905).

Madeleine is my mother. In self-conscious, conforming childhood, she drops the middle *e*. During the summer of 1920, she (Madeline now) meets Leonard Friedman through his youngest sister, her friend Flora, at the Takanassee Inn, a boarding house near the ocean in West End, New Jersey. Even before she meets him he is a romantic figure. In photographs which Flora shows to Madeline, he wears a tailor-made chief petty officer's uniform, with storekeeper's insignia of crossed keys on his left arm and, below that, a black mourning band for his father who died in 1917. Flora points to the band which is difficult to see against the blue serge. It provokes as much sympathy as a sling or other evidence of having been wounded in action. Leonard is at once fatherless and the surrogate father of his five sisters and two brothers—Sadie, Stells, Bella et al. Flora tells Madeline how attentive he is to her, to their mother, to their other sisters, to their brothers, how gracefully he carries the weight of the family on his broad young shoulders.

At the Takanassee, Madeline discovers that the photographs don't do justice to Leonard. They flatten his clean sharp features, blurring definition. They transform modulated ruddy flesh tones to a uniform gray. They make him look balder than he is, though his hair is very thin. Even his clothes look better than in the pictures. His linen summer suit has texture, drape, style. The cloth ripples with the sea breeze and with each step of his rolling sailor's walk. "He's gorgeous," Madeline whispers to Flora, "simply gorgeous."

The Urises and the Friedmans meet again, during subsequent summers in Tannersville, New York, at the Fairmont Hotel, another modest family resort, this one far from the sea, in the Catskill Mountains. ("The Jewish Alps" they are called, with the same self-deprecating humor that a Jew who has $100,000 is called "a Jewish millionaire.") At the Fairmont, life centers on the dining room, about half the ground floor of the rambling wooden building; then moves out to the porch filled with rockers, couches suspended from chains, and dozens of small portable caned chairs; and, past croquet wickets, a horseshoe pit, and several hammocks, to a small pool and a weedy tennis court.

Madeline and Leonard are close friends now. In the morning, before the sun becomes too hot, they play games and take walks with other guests in their twenties, and sometimes they drive with her brother Percy in the Uris family Packard to a nearby golf course. Leonard is not as good a golfer as Percy—a student at Columbia, where he's on that team and several others—but Madeline loves the way he tees off, really whacking the ball, even if it isn't always hit accurately. After golf, lunch, and Dr. Hilkowitz's prescribed hour's wait, they swim. Madeline has been taught well at summer camp—she can even dive. There is nothing Leonard likes better than to watch her bounce on the board, gaining altitude before a perfect swan or full twist. Madeline holds her shapely legs close together with feet extended, back arched, hands and arms aligned as she slices through the hazy summer air and then the cool green surface of the pool. The splash is quick and clean, compact as she is. Leonard sees her change direction under water, swim quickly to the surface, emerge smiling, smiling at him. He applauds. So do others around the pool—friends, her family, his: "ALL ONE BIG HAPPPY FAMILY."

Harris studies the diving board, a plank held down by a strap of iron bolted to a concrete block in the ground. "It's sloppy work," he says to his daughter, "I wish you wouldn't jump so high and come down so hard. One day it's going to rip out and land on your head. Bang. Like that. At least promise you'll never dive without someone around, someone to fish you out. Promise?"

Madeline promises.

Saturday night, after the most enormous meal of the week—borscht, pickled fish, boiled chicken, pot roast with vegetables and potato pancakes; a choice of sherbet, cake, and pie, any or all; candied fruits, chocolates, mints—the dining room is cleared for dancing. A small orchestra appears, and soon Leonard is receiving as much attention as Madeline does at the pool. He is the best dancer at the Fairmont. There is nothing he can't do—the waltz, the polka, the new foxtrot, the still newer Charleston. Madeline stands on her toes, stretching to reach him and keep up with him. After a few drinks he breaks loose and tap-dances. A man who has something to do with movies asks if he'd take a screen test. Word goes round: "Lenny was offered a contract.... A thousand a week.... Another Fairbanks.... Or Valentino.... Wonder what he sees in that Uris girl?...I'll tell you, her old man's worth a million."

And after the summer: "Too bad about Lenny—just not photogenic.... Who needs to be, if you've got Maddy Uris?"

They would have been married in the spring of 1923, but his mother died then—at fifty-eight, the same age at which his father died. The mourning band goes back on his arm. He and Madeline wait another year.

More than half a century later I ask Mother, "Do I have the Fairmont right? Is that the way it was?"

"No," she answers immediately, "it's all wrong."

"How?"

"Well, for one thing, there was no diving board." She pauses, her face contracts with concentration. Then she says, "Maybe there was."

I am born at 9:05 A.M., Monday, July 27, 1926—sign of Leo, son of Leonard—a cub, gasping for air, the slightest breeze from the East River.

"Bobby, Bobby," Mother coos in the hospital bed, hugging me for the first time. She supports my head as she hands me to Father.

He holds me for a moment, as if checking my weight (8 lb., 7 oz., the chart says). "BOBBY. A REAL MENSCH. I ONLY WISH MY PARENTS WERE ALIVE TO SEE HIM."

But his sisters and brothers and their spouses are. One by one they come to visit Mother and me at the hospital or, a few days later, at home:

Aunt Sadie and Uncle Sam(uel Berger, brewer),

Aunt Stella and Uncle Maurice (Epstein, realtor),

Aunt Bella and Uncle Martin (Rubin, manufacturer of razor straps),

Aunt Dina and Uncle Phil(ip Sueskind, dentist),

Uncle "Jimmy" (another realtor) and Aunt "Ray" (Riesa Starr, née Starrobinsky, a Russian beauty),

Aunt "Flo" and Uncle Is(idore Landsman, radiologist), and
Uncle "Dick" (bachelor).

Carefully instructed by Mother, each of them calls me "Bobby"
and, against all rules, holds me, hugs me, kisses me. It is the same with
Mother's family:
Grandma and Grandpa,
Uncle Percy (Columbia University School of Business, B.S. '20, with
his father six years, during which he has transformed the ornamental
iron business into a real estate and construction company called The
Harper Organization, an acronym of Harris and Percy or, looking
toward his younger brother's future, Harold and Percy.),
Aunt "Gertie" and Uncle Jules (Kaufman, credit-clothing retailer,
with a buying office in New York and a chain of stores, mostly in the
South, called Dejay for his brother David and himself),
Uncle Harold (Cornell University, Civil Engineering '25, with his
father and older brother for a year).

"Bobby...Bobby...Bobby...Bobby...Bobby...." they greet me. I
grow up—through kindergarten, anyway—thinking Bobby is my
name, scribbling it that way: Bobby Friedman. Acturally I am Bernard
Harper Friedman. My first name pleases Father. Even if unused, I
sense that it confirms my destiny at the B. Friedman Shoe Company.
And my middle name pleases not only Mother but her father and
brothers, each of whom thinks I am named, at least in part, for him.
This name too, even if unused, confirms my destiny in The Harper
Organization. All together mine is a *nom de commerce* from which,
like spilled ink, Bobby trickles.

Just before I'm two, my parents must again choose a name. Mother
is pregnant, absolutely certain this time she is carrying a girl.

"Sandra," she argues. "The name has style. And, shortened to
Sandy, it's cute."

"WHAT'S WRONG WITH JOSEPHINE? NAMING BOBBY
FOR MY FATHER HASN'T HURT HIM."

"Because no one calls him Bernard."

"THEY DON'T NEED TO CALL OUR DAUGHTER
JOSEPHINE EITHER. SANDY *IS* CUTE. THEY CAN CALL HER

THAT. IF SHE HAS THE URIS COLORING, SO MUCH THE BET-
TER."

The discussion is academic. The child is a boy. They name him
Sanford Uris Friedman.

In previous stories, the first-person narrator is an only child. I'm
not, but I experience myself this way, the way of an older brother who
looks up and ahead to Father, rather than down and behind. Besides,
my brother is also a writer. He has told, and continues to tell, his own
story in his own way. They are two very different stories, his and mine,
and yet we share the same parents and the same craft. Even now, as we
move further into our fifties, we still wonder how we happened to
choose — slowly, in both cases — writing as a career.

I say to Sandy, "As children, we had no chance to speak. We were
drowned out, never encouraged to express our opinions. I suppose
we're making up for lost time. And punishing ourselves for not speaking sooner."

Sandy concentrates. His brow furrows in much the same pattern as
mine. "Yes, we couldn't get a word in edge-wise," he replies, wryly
quoting an expression of Father's, used frequently (and inaccurately)
in conversations with Mother. "Yes, there's that, the simple need to
speak. And then there's the more complicated need to speak the
truth — at least *to try.*"

He tries. I try. We are a pair of shoes. Or, more precisely, more
truthfully, we are a *line* of shoes and, still more precisely, more truthfully, a line of "casuals" or "loafers." We are Bobsans, one of many
trade names Father has printed on the boxes which come to him from
factories in Boston and St. Louis. The Bobsan, he tells us, is almost as
successful as the Wright line, with its catchy slogan "The Wright Shoes
on Time." And he suggests that if someday we join him in the shoe
business, we can PUSH Bobsans, give them A REAL IDENTITY like
his own Wright's, and Dr. Leonard's, and (later) Dr. Leonard's Easy
Steppers.

Sometimes when Father makes a reservation at a fancy, exclusive
restaurant, he uses the name Mr. Wright or Dr. Leonard. Sandy and I

question him. "THEY DON'T LIKE OUR PEOPLE," he explains, which may be the truth.

Also, in previous stories, Mother and Father have no sisters and only one brother each. This, again, is my experience, filtered through layers of time.

As a child I admire Percy. As a young man I work closely with him for fifteen years. Without his stimulation I could not remain that long in business. During these years Harold is in the office too, but I never really feel his presence there any more than, before that, as a child at family dinners. Though physically larger than Percy, Harold is diminished by him, ground small by the keen blades of Percy's intelligence.

And Gertie? She is Harold's sister, in the same sense that Mother is Percy's. Like Harold, she is large, as much heavier than Mother as Harold is than Percy. She, too, is a big passive presence.

At one of Gertie's family dinners, Percy sneaks a golf ball into his bowl of chicken soup *mit knaydlach*. Pretending that the ball is one of those matzo meal dumplings, he attempts to cut it with his spoon and watches it scoot around the bowl. Seemingly astonished, he tries again. "Gertie, your *knaydlach* are heavier than usual. Do you have a sharp knife?" By now those nearest to Percy know what's going on. They laugh hard, spraying the dining room with a heavy mist of chicken soup. Gertie blushes, leaves her seat at the end of the table, and carries her spoon to Percy's place. There she tests the offending *knaydl*. Once again the golf ball scoots around the bowl. Gertie squints, seems not to believe what she sees, scoops up the ball with her spoon, holds it out for everyone to see. Then she begins to laugh as hard as anyone. The laugh rolls up her body in wave after wave, across her belly, her bosom, her fleshy chins and cheeks. Tears run down her face. She dissolves in her own laughter, disappears then, as she will, years later, when I watch her grow small, much more terrifyingly diminished than Harold, devoured at the end of her life by cancer.

Though I don't feel very close to Gertie or Harold, I see more of them, more of all the Urises, than of the tall handsome Friedmans who, at a distance, seem almost interchangeable. Two tall Friedman aunts, Stella Epstein and Dina Sueskind, look so much alike (in frontal silouhette, if not in profile or in the close-up details of their features) that I pretend not to be able to distinguish between them unless Stella wears her favorite pendant watch. But this game might be played with any of the Friedman sisters except Bella. She is three or four inches shorter than the others, yet still tall enough to tower over her husband, Uncle Martin, a tiny but powerful man with exaggerated features who Father calls THE WALKING NOSE.

The Friedmans, sisters and brothers alike, are known as "the beautiful Friedmans." They are as proud of their looks as other families, including the Urises, are of talents or accomplishments. In further appreciation of their own beauty, they worship their father, from whom it comes. No one except Dick ever speaks an irreverent word about him. And even Dick does this seldom and only when drinking. Then the word, repeated over and over, is "tyrant."

My aunts pretend not to hear. They move away, making room for Father and Jimmy.

"SHUT UP. YOU'VE BEEN DRINKING TOO MUCH. YOU DON'T REMEMBER HIM. YOU WERE ONLY SIXTEEN WHEN HE DIED."

"Yes," Jimmy adds, "you were a child. Too young to appreciate him. He was a wonderful man."

"I remember. He was a tyrant. That's what he was. And he made tyrants out of both of you."

"IF YOU DON'T KEEP QUIET, I'M GOING TO HIT YOU. NOW BEHAVE."

Dick smiles, pours himself another drink, says, "You're right. Let's all sing."

Sadie sits down at the piano, the others gather around her, and they begin "I want a girl, just like the girl that married dear old Dad," led by Dick whose voice is not as strong as Leonard's but more melodious. As the eyes of his sisters and brothers fill with tears, his own twinkle with ironic mirth. His smile says, "That old dad of yours may have been dear but mine was a tyrannical son of a bitch."

Yes, in earlier stories, I have eliminated my brother, six blood aunts, two aunts-by-marriage, two blood uncles, six uncles-by-marriage, countless cousins and more distant relatives. I have also eliminated—

or, in a few cases, changed—the names of people and places. I have felt free to do these things, because I thought of the earlier stories as "autobiographical fictions," by which I mean abbreviations, concentrates, essences, conveniences, inventions, tools, machines, gadgets, short-cuts, substitutes, efficiencies, labor-saving devices—in short, *words,* a few thousand words intended to suggest my life, if not to represent it.

In the present story, I thought that by simply adding proper names I would be adding truth. However, I am no longer sure of this. I flip through the earlier stories. There I have used some peripheral fictional names like "Charlie," the elevator operator in the building where I grew up (325 West End Avenue) and "Pop," an old sailor (age 26) and "Little Willy," a young one (in his teens, like me) and "Bloom's" (Father's favorite haberdashery, actually called Briggs and intended to be reminiscent of Brooks) and "Sir John East." But what surprises me is the number of actual historical names I have used: Leonardo, Shakespeare, Newton, Mozart, Einstein, Franklin Delano Roosevelt, Shelley, Keats, Byron, Rimbaud, Proust, Vermeer, T.S. Eliot, Mayakovsky, Proudhon, Pound, Stevens, Cummings, Poe, Lincoln, Truman, Culbertson, Plato, Joyce, Woolf, Yeats, Martha Graham, Rockefeller, Buddha, Socrates, Jesus, Gandhi, Svevo, Ives, Thomas E. Dewey, Cartier, the Duke of Windsor, Melville, J.P. Morgan, Columbus, Adolphe Menjou, William Powell, Dunhill, Oldenburg, Valentino, Stroheim, Bogart, Alice Roosevelt Longworth, Constant, Stuyvesant, Neutra, Ackerley, Zukofsky, Hudson, Acton, Adams, Anthony Powell, Céline (Dr. Destouches), Frank Jenkins, Arthur D. Little, Mondrian.... The list is long. Some names appear more than once. Others I'm sure I've missed in my great hurry to make a small point—which is that names in themselves add truth to writing only in the sense that furniture adds truth to a room. Both define function and, in so doing, limit it. What can be the function of a roomful of such furniture as I've just catalogued? It can only be a showroom, cluttered with pieces from every period and for every purpose.

I look at this catalogue again and wonder about the difference in meaning to various readers of such names as Roosevelt, Byron, and Christ. These are names of extraordinarily large men, whose lives are subject to many interpretations. Each is a multi-purpose piece of furniture—a toilet hidden in a wicker chair, a couch which converts into a bed, a side table which opens up to seat twelve for dining (thirteen is crowded). As names, as labels, as furniture, they are more overpowering but vaguer and less specific than, say, Leonard Friedman or Percy Uris, who in turn are vaguer and less specific than anonymous (or pseudonymous) characters based on them.

I am left with a paradox: the identity which exists in anonymity, the spirit which resists the seeming specificity of a name.

During kindergarten years, I spend more time thinking about my relatives' names than my own. I enjoy rattling them off like railroad stops. The Uris line: Aunt Gertie, Uncle Jules, Uncle Percy, Uncle Harold. And the longer Friedman line: Aunt Sadie, Uncle Sam, Aunt Stella, Uncle Maurice, Aunt Bella, Uncle Martin, Aunt Dina, Uncle Phil, Aunt Ray, Uncle Jimmy, Aunt Flo, Uncle Is, Uncle Dick. The names are easy—a child can learn them. The relationships are more difficult. Just as I am taught always to designate Mother's and Father's sisters and brothers and their husbands and wives as *Aunt* or *Uncle,* I am taught to do the same with my parents' friends. For example, Mr. and Mrs. William Brown are Aunt Helen and Uncle Bill, but I have another Aunt Helen, Grandpa's sister, Helen Copland, who is married to the brother of my grandmother, Sadie Copland Uris. And Mr. and Mrs. Alfred Beer are Aunt Fanny and Uncle Al; yet, somewhere in Brooklyn, Father has another Aunt Fanny married to another Uncle Al. Father also has two customers named Friedman, not related to him or each other, who are close friends of his: Max Friedman, my Uncle Max, president of the A.S. Beck women's shoe chain and married to Aunt Sadie (the third Sadie, the second Aunt Sadie, in my life); and William Friedman, my second Uncle Bill, a shoe-buyer for women's specialty shops, married to Aunt Elsie, who must not be confused with Aunt Elsie Goodman, another Brooklyn relative, on Father's side. I could go on, especially with Friedmans, the way the New York telephone directory does. However, it is enough to say that I grow up knowing that Urises are rarer than Friedmans.

In my first year of kindergarten Grandma dies. I no longer remember her. She is her name—Sadie Copland Uris. She is an ornately framed photograph which stands for years on Mother's dresser. And like her younger daughter, my Aunt Gertie, she is a distant memory of whispers about the hospital, about specialists, about new drugs, about—*cancer.* The voices fall further and fade.

What I do remember is the talk, a little later, a lot louder, about Grandpa's remarriage.

"How could he?" Mother screams. "Without waiting a year. Without inviting us. 'Iron King Marries in City Hall.' I have to read about my own father's wedding in the paper. She promised she'd wait. She got him to do it. Running off like a couple of kids."

"SHE'S BEEN AROUND. SHE KNEW WHEN SHE HAD A GOOD THING."

She is Mary Schacht, a short, plump woman in her early forties, about twenty years younger than Grandpa, who Sandy and I are told to call Aunt Mary, never Grandma. Her greatest distinction is her bosom. Just as Father names Uncle Martin THE WALKING NOSE, he might name her THE WALKING BREAST—might, but doesn't— names her instead THE POUTER PIGEON, unless Mother's anger at the way Mary is spending Grandpa's money goads Father. Then, after Grandpa has, say, bought her another piece of jewelry or agreed to take her on another trip abroad, she's "NOTHING, WHAT SHE WAS *BEFORE* SHE MARRIED POP."

"What was she?" I ask.

"Little pitchers have big ears," Mother says, then enthusiastically answers my question. "Her father worked for your grandfather— another *landsman* he took care of. Mary became a secretary. The winter after Mother died Old Man Schacht sent her down to Miami where Pop was; literally sent her on this fortune-hunt, with the advice, 'Better an old rich man's darling than a young poor man's slave.' Well, she did it, landed him that winter, married him that spring. Just eight months after Mother's death! The Schachts never had anything. The only relatives I've ever heard her mention are her brother Larry, who's gone out on his own now, in the steel business; and that baseball player, Al."

My eyes brighten at the thought of a ballplayer in the family.

"HE WAS NOTHING MUCH EITHER. A THREE-SEASON PITCHER WITH WASHINGTON. THEY CALL HIM THE CLOWN PRINCE OF BASEBALL. ANYWAY, HE'S ONLY A COUSIN OF YOUR AUNT'S."

Not only are Sandy and I taught to call her Aunt Mary, but so, in conspiracy with Mother, are Aunt Gertie's children and, later, Uncle Percy's and Uncle Harold's. By then there are eleven of us grandchildren warmly shouting, "Grandpa, Grandpa, Grandpa..." and pulling his mustache and playing with his watch chain, while barely greeting "Aunt Mary, Aunt Mary, Aunt Mary…" as each of us gives her the quickest, most perfunctory kiss we can, breaking away from her grasp before we are smothered in her witch's bosom or robbed by her as we understand our parent have been.

When I greet Aunt Mary, I see sadness in her small brown eyes— only that, no malice—but it takes many years before I realize that all she ever wanted from any of us was to be called Grandma. She was the first victim I knew of a name used as a weapon.

Am I preaching? When Mary dies, I ask my parents if they weren't too hard on her.

"Well, she wasn't your grandmother, was she? Anyway, names are inventions. Look at mine. What a leap from Max!"

"INVENTIONS! BUBKIS! IN YOUR FAMILY MAYBE, NOT IN MINE. NAMES ARE GIVEN, INHERITED. THEY'RE NOT INVENTED."

As to my own name, during kindergarten years it's still mostly Bobby, sometimes Bob, rarely Bernard. Of course I know there's more. Mother, who loves stationery, has given me a box of calling cards from Tiffany, engraved *Bernard Harper Friedman*. Though I make no formal visits, I always carry a card in my wallet, partly as identification (of the other larger me, the me I will perhaps become), partly because I like to run my fingers over the sharp raised print, bumping along from one letter to the next, gliding from one name to the next, taking it all in through my fingertips as a very real and proper name, a name with resounding weight like that of Franklin Delano Roosevelt.

Nevertheless, I like Bobby best. I suppose I would insist on it, if that didn't seem too much like begging for affection.

In grade school a change, another possibility, begins. The teacher calls the roll ("…Arthur Feeley, John Fish, Bernard Friedman…") and soon many of my classmates are calling me "Bernie." I know that they are trying to be friendly, even intimate, and yet I feel compelled to tell them, "My parents call me Bobby." If I don't say this and happen to invite them home, Mother corrects them much more forcefully:

"Don't ever let me hear you call my son Bernie. His name is Bobby. *Bobby.*" Her voice rises. *"Du hörst?"* she adds sometimes or, if not, the interrogatory demand is there anyway, in parentheses.

I feel now even more confused about my own names than those of my many aunts and uncles (actual and so-called). They, these aunts and uncles—like my parents, my brother, my grandfather, my cousins—all call me Bobby. Presumably they do so because they love me and feel close to me. And yet I cannot simply separate the world into those who call me Bobby and those who call me Bernie, those who love me and those who don't. In the Bobby group, there are some I like more than others and some I don't like at all. In the Bernie group, the same; and here, among those I do like, are of course some I like more than some in the given group (i.e., the group given "Bobby"). Besides, I know that, at a word from Mother or me, anyone can shift from the Bernie group to the Bobby group which, at this point, enlarges.

In 1935, there are two more recruits. By then Percy has established Joanne Diotte, a French-Canadian model, in an apartment house just down the block from our own (where he lives too, with Grandpa and Aunt Mary). I have seen Joanne, sometimes with Percy, sometimes alone, sometimes walking her prize cocker spaniel. She is mysterious—someone to whom the family, Grandpa in particular, objects. So she is not quite my aunt, not quite Percy's fiancée either, but "his friend, someone he visits," as Mother puts it. Joanne is studying Hebrew, preparing to convert from Catholicism to Judaism. In the spring she becomes Aunt Joanne.

That summer I'm at Camp Menatoma in Maine, learning such necessary skills as how to carve a totem pole and make beaded mocassins. Mother, Father, Grandpa and Aunt Mary come up for my birthday. They are full of news. Less than two weeks before, Harold, Little Harold (*der kleine,* they call him) eloped from a country club dance with Ruth Chinitz.

"HAD A FEW TOO MANY. SHE'S PRETTY, BUT NOT A KNOCKOUT LIKE JOANNE."

Mother whispers, "She's *very* pretty. And she went to Smith."

"Smith," Aunt Mary repeats. "She's the daughter of a restaurant man." The description sounds worn, much discussed.

"THE DAUGHTER OF IS NOTHING. THE MOTHER OF IS WHAT'S EATING POP. YOU KNOW THAT."

Finally, Grandpa himself sums up "the tragedy" of this spring and summer: "I had two wonderful sons. One married a *shiksa* who brought me a dog. The other married a divorcée who brought another man's child."

Of all my many cousins, two strongly influence my life. The first is Aaron Copland. I do not remember meeting him until April 1937, the spring before starting the first of six forms at the Horace Mann School for Boys. Until then he has been only a rumor, always away somewhere — studying composition with Nadia Boulanger in Paris, lecturing at Harvard, giving concerts all over the world. However, even as a child I remember his parents, my great-aunt Sarah and my great-uncle Harris, reaching into worn wallets to bring out newspaper clippings — reviews, awards, American music groups he has founded.

Both sides of Mother's family, the Coplands and the Urises, share Aunt Sarah's and Uncle Harris' pride in Aaron. Though they admit they don't understand his music, they respect it because the *Times* and other authorities do. Except for Percy, Aaron is the one member of the family whose name appears in the papers. Like him, Aaron is "a success." He may not have the genius to make much money, but he does make music — at least, almost everyone says so.

Father is an exception. "YOUR MOTHER AND I WENT TO A CONCERT OF HIS. I CAN'T IMAGINE WHY ANYONE WOULD PAY TO HEAR SUCH NOISE. I DON'T THINK MANY PEOPLE DO. HE'S LIVED MOSTLY OFF CHARITY — GRANTS, FELLOW-SHIPS. WHEN WE WERE ON OUR HONEYMOON, WE LOOKED HIM UP IN PARIS. UNTIL WE ARRIVED HE WAS STARVING, HADN'T HAD A DECENT MEAL IN MONTHS. HE WAS SO SKINNY IT MADE HIS NOSE LOOK EVEN BIGGER THAN IT IS."

"He took us to a lot of interesting places," Mother says.

"INTERESTING! — IF YOU LIKE CHURCHES AND MUSEUMS. THAT'S THE TROUBLE. THESE ARTISTS DON'T LIVE IN THE REAL WORLD. THEY DON'T HAVE HOMES. THEY DON'T GET MARRIED. IT'S NOT *NORMAL*. I HEAR THAT AARON —"

Mother stops Father with a quick look at me and then back at him. It is her *stiege, der kinder* look.

Now, Aaron has a new project — Opera for High Schools. Early one

Saturday afternoon, Grandpa and Aunt Mary, Aunt Gertie and her eldest daughter Jane, and Mother, Sandy and I all crowd into Grandpa's limousine to go to the Neighborhood Playhouse, on Henry Street, in lower Manhattan. There Aaron's opera, *The Second Hurricane*, based on a libretto by Edwin Denby, is to have its third performance, a matinée. I have never been to an opera before. We have some Caruso records at home and, from photographs and movies, I know what an opera house should look like, inside and out, but here everything is drab—the theater, the exposed stage, the set consisting of two bleachers, the audience, even Aaron himself.

He's the same age as Mother but looks older—thin, tired, slightly stooped. His nose is large, as Father has said, and he wears glasses, something none of the Friedmans do even if they need them. Yet, his homeliness is unimportant. I sense more strongly his gentleness and sweetness. I understand that he is about to give us something he has made.

The house lights dim. A student, playing the principal of a Midwestern high school, enters, sees that everyone is seated, turns to the audience, identifies himself, and says, "We are going to perform a piece for you that is partly spoken and partly sung. There are two choruses," he continues, pointing at the bleachers, "this one is supposed to be students...that one is supposed to be parents." After a brief overture, the students' chorus sings, "Have you ever had an adventure? A real adventure when something really happened..." The story is about six children who volunteer to fly to a flooded area with supplies and equipment. The blunt 'thirties message is that their mission can only succeed if they are communally cooperative rather than individualistically competitive. The music is lovely, not "noisy" at all, except when it's supposed to be, when the wind is blowing. I am torn between watching the singers and Aaron, seated near me. Again and again I think that he has made what I'm hearing, that it has come out of him, this physically unimpressive cousin.

After the children are rescued and the last notes played, there is applause, led by the Coplands. The conductor bows to Aaron who stands and bows, in turn, to him. My eyes tear. This has less to do with *The Second Hurricane* than with Aaron. *He* is being applauded.

Two years later, when I am *bar mitzvah*, Aunt Sarah and Uncle Harris give me a copy of Aaron's first book, *What to Listen for in*

Music. Until now, only people in other families write books. Though, except for jazz, I am not particularly interested in music, I am interested enough in Aaron to read every word of his book. I look at it now, forty years later, and see that I have marked a passage in blue ink.

> One of the first things most people want to hear discussed in relation to composing is the question of inspiration. They find it difficult to believe that composers are not as precoccupied with that question as they had supposed. The layman always finds it hard to realize how natural it is for the composer to compose. He has a tendency to put himself in the position of the composer and to visualize the problems involved, including that of inspiration, from the perspective of the layman. He forgets that composing to a composer is like fulfilling a natural function. It is like eating or sleeping....

In that rather ragged and indecisive blue line, made down the margin so long ago—probably with my Waterman pen, also a *bar mitzvah* present—I see a hint now, no more than that, of growing awareness that Aaron's particular intelligence and sensitivity may be an alternative to Percy's and that so may be his different kind of success.

By the time I gradute from Horace Mann, as many of my friends are calling me Bernie as Bob. Very few are calling me Bobby, mostly family friends. Still fewer are calling me by other names. Jack Olsted, who sits next to me in Latin Class, calls me Barney, which I rather like but which never catches on with other friends. And Joan Erpf, the older sister of a classmate and surrogate older sister (i.e., adviser) of several of us, calls me Harper, which she says is distinguished but which I find affected. It, too, never catches on, except for several dates with an anti-Semitic society girl whose name I forget.

And yet, other than as a first name, I like Harper. It is the most interesting, invented, and anecdotal part of my full name. Right now I am applying to various colleges. I feel cheated by those forms which specify Last Name, First Name, Middle Initial. I would not think of going to one that left me, my *H*, dangling and truncated at the end of a line. The truth is I have seriously considered only two colleges— Columbia (Percy's) and Cornell (Harold's). I choose Cornell because it is farther from home.

At college I am Bernie—98% Bernie, anyway. There are a few old friends who call me Bob and one new one, Robert Fox Brodsky, who calls me Burnhole. But that takes time. At first, like almost everyone else, he calls me Bernie. By now this seems no worse that Bob. I even like it—it has become my name away from home. Brodsky, a bona fide Robert, dislikes both Robert and Bob, finds them too common, prefers Fox. So, for a while, I call him Fox, thinking, like others, that it suits his alertness and cleverness, his upright ears and pointed nose; but gradually, as we become closer friends, I resent the connotation of slyness and begin calling him Foxhole. This sounds more solid and down-to-earth. It is of the moment—winter, 1943—when we are thinking about military service. And, finally, it reminds me of a fictional character I admire, Thomas Wolfe's Foxhall Edwards, based on Wolfe's editor at Scribner's, Maxwell Perkins. When Fox become Foxhole, I become Burnhole. It is the first of a series of contractions leading to B.H.

Foxhole and I enlist in the navy and there—when we're not Brodsky and Friedman, which is most of the time—we're both Bob. It is the most neutral name either of us can come up with; we hoist it like an American flag. In the United States Navy, the names Brodsky and Friedman are freakish enough—foreign, Jewish, New Yorkerish—without adding Foxhole and Burnhole. We use these only when we write to each other, after being assigned to different ships.

After the war I return to college and to being called Bernie. I sign everything Bernard Harper Friedman—not only book reports and term papers but stories I am writing for *The Widow,* Cornell's so-called "humor" magazine. There, the editorial board consists mostly of gloomy war veterans as confused as I am about military past, academic present, and career future, but trying, trying so hard, to make it all funny.

I look now, more than thirty years later, at some of these *Widow* "stories"—the loosely contained salvage of weekend and holiday nights in New York, spent drinking and listening to jazz with Foxhole, George Andrews, Eric Donald Hirsch, Jr. (known as Donald or Don), Martin Lukashok (known as Luke), A(rthur) Lewis Philips (known as Lew—he, too, has a mother who thinks she can control his name: "If I wanted him to be called Louie, I would have spelled it with an *o u*"), Albert Avakian (known as Al, later as Aram).... The names, formed and forming, come back to me. The nights from which they come are dim. I pick among once-bright phrases, tarnished by time:

> ...she replies with a seductive smile, air mail, special delivery, thirty-two teeth, moist gums, and a tongue dripping with honeyed and dar-linged words.

> If Daddy said don't tip too high, he must have been born before the turn of the century. This is 1948, and keep the change.

> Nobody thinking or planning. Everything just happening. Like a big spontaneous he-she joke.

> We can understand, can't we?
> Canned oui.

> We drink. The words season our smoked tongues.

I recognize my voice in these stories, as I recognize my name in that full-blown signature which follows them, and as I recognize my face in photographs of this period. That is, I see a family resemblance to my present self. What a deep breath I must have taken before speaking, before signing that full name, before posing for pictures. I appear full of myself, bloated. I wish now that I had signed Bernard Harper Friedman (20), Bernard Harper Friedman (21), etc. They are different people from B.H. Friedman (55), different but related—body cells replaced, brain cells more or less intact, identity a matter of time. Even 20, 21, 55 are approximations. Months, days, hours, minutes, seconds *count,* especially at 55.

At 20, 21 I must have felt trapped within the nineteenth century penitentiary of my full name, along with such old prisoners as Samuel Taylor Coleridge, James Fenimore Cooper, Percy Bysshe Shelley, William Cullen Bryant, Mary Wollstonecraft Shelley, Ralph Waldo Emerson, John Greenleaf Whittier, Henry Wadsworth Longfellow, Edgar Allan Poe, William Makepeace Thackeray, Harriet Beecher Stowe, Henry David Thoreau (born David Henry), Dante Gabriel Rossetti, Louisa May Alcott, Algernon Charles Swinburne—all of them carrying the heavy burdens of their choice.

I tell George Andrews, the best writer among my classmates, "You're lucky. You're in the great tradition of two names." I'm off again, moving quickly through centuries: "Geoffrey Chaucer,

Edmund Spenser, William Shakespeare, Christopher Marlowe, Ben Jonson, John Donne, John Milton, John Dryden, Jonathan Swift, William Congreve, Alexander Pope, Henry Fielding, Samuel Johnson, Laurence Sterne, Edward Gibbon, James Boswell, William Blake, Jane Austen, John Keats, Nathaniel Hawthorne, Charles Dickens, Anthony Trollope, Charlotte Brontë, Emily Brontë, Herman Melville, Walt Whitman, George Eliot—"

"Pseudonyms don't count," Andrews, who has been patient, finally interrupts. "She's Mary Ann Evans to me. Besides, the other writers you named may have dropped middle names. That's what I did."

"Exactly what I'm talking about—making something else out of what you're given. Maybe pseudonyms count most of all. I admire authors who invent their names, obscuring the facts of their lives while preserving the mystery. Permit me: Molière, Voltaire, Stendhal, Balzac, George Sand, Lewis Carroll, Mark Twain, Anatole France, A. Conan Doyle, Joseph Conrad, O. Henry, Gorki, Saki."

I pause. George smiles. I think he is relieved that I have come to the end of my list. But no. "Permit *me*," he says. "Italo Svevo, Colette, Ford Madox Ford, St.-John Perse, Céline, Silone, George Orwell, Henry Green, Nathanael West, Moravia."

I smile now, then applaud, impressed by his greater knowledge of contemporary literature. I have not yet read any of the authors he has just named.

All of this is undergraduate intellectual ping-pong, a sport that cannot be played for many more years. We both know this, and yet we also know that George has won the last game in a burst of ten straight points.

"Why don't you become Bernard Harper?" he asks. "They're two nice names."

"I never could. Not as a Jew. That's not what I want to drop. Anyway, I like Friedman—the suggestion of peace, of freedom, of being freed, perhaps from some ghetto of other names."

"Do you know what I think? You're going to be a good writer, no matter what name you use. And do you know why?"

There's a long pause while he waits for me to ask, "Why?"

"Because you're obsessive. There's nothing more important in writing than that, to be seized by an idea."

"Obsessive! Me!"

We laugh before beginning a catalogue of actors who have taken stage names. It's much longer than the one of pen names.

The cousin who most affects my life is Abby Grace Noselson. She doesn't like any of her names. She has been called Flabby Abby at school, years ago when she was plump, but even now, at 105 pounds, she still worries about her weight, worries about again becoming Flabby Abby, curses the dormitory dietician who feeds her starch. "And Grace," she says, "is simply impossible—impossible to live up to. Can you imagine being named Hope or Charity?" Yet, Grace is the most appropriate of her names. She seems to move effortlessly. Without excess, without flab, surely without flab, she dances through college, through life. And Noselson, that strange near-palindrome? Classmates have, she tells me, fooled with it too, have called her Nozzlenose. I laugh at the absurdity of this and kiss her small, well-shaped, slightly upturned nose, the tip of which is as firm as an excited nipple.

"Nipplenose. Did anyone ever call you that?"

"No."

"You see how lucky you were."

What I call her mostly is Abigail. I like enlarging her name, adding a syllable to it that belongs only to me. The first two syllables, meaning *father* in Hebrew, belong to her maternal grandfather, Abraham Uris, one of my grandfather's younger brothers—dead the year Abby's parents married. My syllable, Gail, means *joy*.

I play endlessly with her name; roll it, like parts of her body, over my tongue:

Abracadabra: Abigail!
Abloom! Aglow! Afire! Ablaze!
liagibA: arbadacarbA!
moolbA! wolgA! erifA! ezalbA!

Abracadabra Abigail,
the only light in the room.

But what do these false palindromes mean compared with ybbA

noslesoN herself, who arches in bed like a hoop? And what do my new little stories mean—stories about Abby Abbidumio, a brunette princess of unspecified Mediterranean origin? I don't know what any of this means. I know only where it leads: to changing her name permanently.

In the office of the Town Clerk, Ithaca, New York, Abby and I fill out forms. Some of the information we provide is exactly the same. (Place of birth: *New York City*. Hospital: *Flower*.) Some is close. (Mother's maiden name: *Beatrice Uris, Madeline Uris*. Date of birth: *Oct. 27, 1926, Jul. 27, 1926*.) For the first time it occurs to me I was conceived on the same day, a year earlier, as Abby's birth. Perhaps *this* means something.

The clerk studies the forms, making sure all the blanks are filled in. He asks no questions. He is a man who can accept coincidence.

A few days later, by coincidence, Abby Noselson becomes Abby Friedman.

When Abby and I return home to announce our marriage, we face many new names. Each of us must learn those of that branch of the Uris family we know least well, and Abby must learn the Friedmans, and I must learn the Noselsons. Having memorized the names of my aunts and uncles in chronological order, she asks to be tested:

"Sadie and Sam, Stella and Maurice, Bella and Martin, Dina and Phil—"

"Forget Phil. They've been separated for years. But not before he ruined my teeth. Continue!"

"Your parents come next. Then Ray and Jimmy, Flo and Is, Aimee and Dick. Whew!"

(Aimee—née Levy—is my newest aunt and already my favorite. She is wealthier and better educated than the Friedman sisters, as tall and handsome as any of them, fairer in coloring. She is a spot of light in the Friedman darkness. Until her marriage she has led a sheltered life, at private and finishing schools and on trips abroad with her parents. Now she moves out into the open, exposed to the Friedmans and to what has become the most meaningful part of Dick's world, Alcoholics Anonymous. There, among others, Aimee meets enough authors to fill yet another catalogue. "It's an occupational hazard of theirs," she says with eyes twinkling, "and of shoe salesmen. Never go into those businesses. I was brought up to think that anyone who had a second sherry was a lush. Have you any idea how much alcohol flows through the average novel? And the average pair of shoes? Poor ravaged soles.")

I continue testing Abby. "Now, Mother's family."

"They're easy—Joanne and Percy, Gertie and Jules, Ruth and Harold."

"Maiden names."

"Up yours."

Abby's family is easy on both sides. Her father signs his name M.B. Noselson, was born Morris Bernard (one of many links we establish), and is known to everyone as Moe. He has only one living sister, Florence—of average height but enormous weight, at least 250 pounds—married to Herman Rosenstein, the same size. Moe's and Florence's lives are haunted by Pearl, their younger sister, who died in her mid-twenties, soon after her marriage to A(braham) W(ilbert) Zelomak, called Zel, an economist who has never remarried and uses the Noselsons and Rosensteins to protect himself from that possiblility by invidiously comparing all women with Pearl.

Abby's mother, Beatrice, known as Bea, has, like my own mother, one sister and two brothers. Her sister Pearl (not to be confused with Pearl Noselson Zelomak) is married to Frank Sheindelman, who has made "some money" selling novelties to military stores but is "doing less well" now that the war is over. Milton "Mickey" Uris works for Moe in the fur-dyeing business ("indeed, a dying business," he says often) and has just married Elizabeth (Bess), an Englishwoman he met while overseas in the army, when his former wife left him for her gynecologist. (After Bess's premature death, he will marry my old friend Joan Erpf.) And Auren Uris—previously, less distinctively, Aaron—is beginning to lose and find himself in the management research field where he satisfies artistic yearnings expressed earlier in amateur painting, photography, and writing. Like Mickey, Auren too has recently remarried; his second wife is a tall attractive blonde, also named Elizabeth (Bet), who expresses her own yearnings in suburban theatricals.

Bea and Moe have a second child, Abby's younger brother, Kalman, named for Moe's father. Kal is still at college (Syracuse), just as confused as I am about the future but without my options. And living at home with the Noselsons is Bea's mother, Abraham's widow, Lina Zalmanovitch Uris. Though almost seventy, she is very helpful around the house, clearly remembers her childhood in Latvia where she received a diploma in millinery, treasures it and the love letters Abe wrote half a century ago on H. Uris Iron Works stationery, and regularly plays poker to escape from the past. She, Bea, Pearl, Mickey, and Auren all welcome me ambivalently. On the surface I am seen as "a catch." Below the surface, there are currents of envy toward Mother's family and a lingering resentment of Harris' abandonment of the iron works—and of his younger brothers, including Abe—for real estate. They speak of the poetry, the logic, the economic justice in Abby's and my marriage. They say, "Abe would have approved."

Moe is not involved with this. He has his own past—as a pre-medical student at City College, until his father died and he was forced to go into business. His strong stubby hands show the years of working with dyes and strong chemicals in a profession where he cannot express his sensitivity or scholarliness. I hate to think of him day after day preparing the pelts of small rare animals. I much prefer watching him at home as his thick stained fingers flip through the pages of encyclopedias, dictionaries, reference books of all kinds. He is not afraid to say he doesn't know the answer to a question and is indefatigable in seeking it—an attitude I have had little experience with in my own family.

Moe adores Abby, calls her Abbel, and soon, giving me more credit as fisherman than as catch, affectionately begins to call me Bobbel. It is not long before Abby and I are using these names and then exaggerating the second syllable so that she becomes Ab-Bool and I, Bob-Bool. It is another short step to calling each other Bool or Boolie. We enjoy the illusion of being one person with one name. As Kafka wrote in a letter to Felice Bauer, "the separation into two people is unbearable."

Just before I join Uncle Percy in business, he says, "For God's sake, stop calling me *Uncle*. It makes me feel old, Elizabethan. And it makes you sound childish."

So, at twenty-two, I begin calling Percy, Percy and my other uncles and my aunts by their first names. I am also calling Bea, Bea and Moe,

Moe. Everyone but me, it seems, has a first name, one. At the office, I am Bob to the staff; Bobby as often as Bob to Percy and Harold; Bernard Harper Friedman when I sign business letters, legal documents, and checks; Bernie to a few old friends, who begin to shift now to Bob; and Bernie also to strangers. In Abby's and my Village apartment, I am Bob or Bobby, Bool or Boolie, except when I write. Then, again, I am Bernard Harper Friedman. I know that. I sign dozens of stories, articles, and poems Bernard Harper Friedman. I save dozens of rejections from editors, addressed to Bernard Harper Friedman.

As my responsibilities at the office grow, as I have more papers and checks to sign, as the payroll lengthens, I shorten my signature, in a single leap, hurdling Bernard H. Friedman, all the way to B.H. Friedman. Theoretically, no name is more real than that which one writes on a check.

At business, I save time. At home, when I also start to use my initials, saving time is not an issue—I don't sign my name that often—but I have some idea about avoiding confusion, achieving consistency. It is the dream of a child attempting to build permanent order into shifting sand. True, with that B.H. up front, there is seemingly more logic in being Bob. Friendly and familiar Southerners, in particular, assume it is my real name—Bob Henry, or Bobby Hank, or something of the sort. But Northern formalists begin to call me Robert and address my mail that way.

So there is no less confusion, no more consistency. For the moment, B.H. is just another disguise. It lacks authenticity until it is published. Only then do I recognize its power, there on the printed page, beneath the title of an essay called "The New Baroque." The initials protect me, preserve my privacy, establish a certain distance (at least the length of *ernard arper*) between me and my readers.

The essay is about Jackson Pollock (born Paul Jackson Pollock) and other contemporary American artists, variously mislabeled Abstract Expressionists and Action Painters—all of whom, except for Bradley Walker Tomlin, have changed or modified their names. However, it is neither their individual nor group names which interest me now. I barely glance at the printed text. My eye keeps returning to the byline as I try to familiarize myself with it. I can hardly believe that I am B.H. Freidman, author—it's so simple.

When George Andrews reads the article, he says, "So you've done it, changed your name, dived into the alphabet soup. Isn't it cold? Crowded with Englishmen? A.E. Houseman, H.G. Wells, G.K. Chesterton, A.E. Coppard, E.M. Forster, D.H. Lawrence, T.E. Lawrence, T.S. Eliot, W.H. Auden..."

"I can't accept Eliot."

"We've been challenging Eliots since college. He's as English now as the rest of them."

"Okay, but there are plenty of Americans too. H.L. Mencken, e.e. cummings, E.B. White, S.J. Perelman, J.D. Salinger..."

"Peewees, B.H., all peewees. I'll only give you half a point for each. You know, you really made a mistake not considering Bernard Harper. That's a name. Even Bernard Friedman's better than B.H."

"You don't feel its power?" I ask, laughing.

"Financial power, maybe. Like J.P. Morgan or P.T. Barnum. But literary power?"

"Wait until it's attached to enough work."

"Are you sure? It's an important decision."

"As sure as I am of my own name."

It's one thing for me to talk confidently, however flippantly, to George; it's another to create the work to which I will attach my new abbreviated name. The fact is I'm not getting much writing done, not even much reading. Business demands too much time and energy. In the hours left over I read periodicals, novellas, short books of poetry and squeeze out an occasional article or story of my own. However, I find it easier and faster to get aesthetic satisfaction drifting through art galleries, easier and faster also to judge and buy art than to make it. Collecting is a comfortable substitute for creating.

As both critic and collector, I get to know the contemporary art dealers, so many of them former antique and diamond merchants who have come here from Europe with their smuggled caches, prepared to liquidate the past and invest the proceeds in the present and the future. They are smooth, these traders in art currency. They pick up quickly on B.H., more quickly than my friends do, and when they're not calling me that, they're calling me Bob, both appellations in strong Continental accents.

"Bey Ahshe, that was an interesting article you wrote. You have an eye. I'd be interested in knowing what you think of..."

Or:

"Bubp, there's a piece I want you to see, a difficult piece. Not everyone would understand it..."

I am flattered. I feel as if I have been welcomed to a fraternity, a sort of Artists Anonymous, full of artists-as-dealers, artists-as-collectors, artists-as-critics. I express my appreciation mostly by buying, sometimes by writing, and am soon allowed into the inner circle of artists-as-artists. There I meet Jackson, Lee, Barney, Bill, Elaine, Franz, Clyff, Mark, Ad, Alfonso, Fritz, Hans, Jim, Jon, Jody, Sal...in a world where one name, like one image, is identity enough. Bernie has almost disappeared, but still I am B.H./Bob or, alternately, Bey Ahshe/Bubp. I wish at times that, like the titles of many of the works painted by these artists, I carried only a number and a year—e.g., *Composition 1, 1926.*

It is time now for Abby and me to do our own naming. When our first child is born we name him Jackson, for Pollock, who has died the previous summer. But just Jackson. Without a middle name. We don't want him to have a name that everyone can mess around with. Yet, of course, everyone does. As a child, he's Jacks, Jacksie, and Jackso. As he learns to write, he prefers Jax, Jaxie, Jaxo, and finally Jaxon (sometimes mistaken for Jason).

With our second child it is the same. We name her Daisy (again with no middle name), wanting to flee the horde of Lindas and wanting also to recapture other, perhaps happier times—well, *different* times anyway, times encrusted in nostalgia, the times of Henry James's *Daisy Miller,* of Daisy Ashford's *The Young Visiters,* of Edmund Wilson's *I Thought of Daisy,* of Scott Fitzgerald's Daisy Buchanan in *The Great Gatsby.* Daisy—a much more fragile and feminine name than Jackson, a floral decoration which we expect to be preserved, possibly pressed between the pages of a book. She becomes Dais, Daisyo, Daisel, even Bool and Boolie, a slip the first time but a lasting slip, transformed to Little Bool and Little Boolie.

Yes, there is an exchange between our children's names and our own. Jackson's friends, with Daisy's following, call me Mr. Friedman at first, then B.H., then suddenly Beehive, inspired, I would like to think, by their sense of my industriousness, honeyed words, and even papal power, but more likely by some feeble disciplinary threat. Either way, Beehive it is for a while, as Burnhole it was. And then a friend of Daisy's pipes up with B.H.-e-o, and that too lasts for a while, just as I am beginning to think that B.H./Bob is final and sufficient.

I am writing more fiction now and feel as if I am simultaneously a swarm of characters created by me and a me created by a swarm of characters. In short, I don't know whose fiction I am, mine or theirs. My head buzzes. At the office, I am B.H., efficient executive, author of checks, contracts, leases, realities of all kinds; and I am also Bob, genial colleague, and Bobby, promising nephew, defiant defender of nepotism. At home, in my isolated room, I am B.H. again, author of fantasies. In the bedroom, I am Bob or Bobby, Bool or Boolie, some-times vigorous lover, more often tired businessman or, still later at night, exhausted writer. In the living room and dining room, with the children, I am both Beehive, relentless dictator, and B.H.-e-o, benign provider, always good...for a raise in allowance. I am not only a character in search of a name, but a story in search of a title. I am a confusion of sub-titles. At times "Choosing a Name" seems just another way of saying "Watching Father Die" or "Drinking Smoke" or "Moving in Place"—all interchangeable phrases signifying alterna-tive autobiographies. Each comes close. None is more or less true than the others. A title, like a name, is always a kind of lying truth, subject to selection, change, false emphasis.

In the hand, heart, and mind of a more compulsive author this could go on forever—that long!—a steady march of footnotes leading to appendixes, geneological tables, indexes. I can imagine such an author listing the names not only of children but grandchildren and great-grandchildren, stretching the branches of family tree, stretching the alphabet itself, on, on, past Z, into some leafy jungle. I could almost stop at A, that darling with her shapely pair of legs so seductively spread. Yet, B is there, just behind, in the B. Friedman Shoe Company, and H, a little farther back, in the H. Uris Iron Works. I, the product of leather and iron, am surrounded by ancestors, as if by a belt with a heavy forged buckle.

I loosen the belt, prepare myself, have only one more thing to do. As others in the past have chosen shields and weapons, I must choose a name. For now, a *nom de guerre.* For later, once again, *nom de plume* and *nom de commerce,* in reserve. I can no more fight than write and do business without a name. It has become impossible to remember, ages and pages ago, when I was nameless.

FICTION COLLECTIVE
Books in Print

Order from Flatiron Book Distributors Inc., 175 Fifth Avenue NYC 10010